the BREAKUP VACATION

the BREAKUP VACATION

A Beach House Novel

Anna Gracia

New York London Toronto Sydney New Delhi

Atria Books
An Imprint of Simon & Schuster, LLC
1230 Avenue of the Americas
New York, NY 10020

This book is a work of fiction. Any references to historical events, real people, or real places are used fictitiously. Other names, characters, places, and events are products of the author's imagination, and any resemblance to actual events or places or persons, living or dead, is entirely coincidental.

Copyright © 2024 by Viacom International Inc.

MTV Entertainment Studios and all related titles, logos, and characters are trademarks of Viacom International Inc.

All rights reserved, including the right to reproduce this book or portions thereof in any form whatsoever. For information address Atria Books Subsidiary Rights Department, 1230 Avenue of the Americas, New York, NY 10020

First MTV Books/Atria paperback edition March 2024

ATRIA BOOKS and colophon are registered trademarks of Simon & Schuster, LLC

Simon & Schuster: Celebrating 100 Years of Publishing in 2024

For information about special discounts for bulk purchases, please contact Simon & Schuster Special Sales at 1-866-506-1949 or business@simonandschuster.com

The Simon & Schuster Speakers Bureau can bring authors to your live event. For more information or to book an event contact the Simon & Schuster Speakers Bureau at 1-866-248-3049 or visit our website at www.simonspeakers.com.

Interior design by Lexy East

Manufactured in the United States of America

1 3 5 7 9 10 8 6 4 2

Library of Congress Cataloging-in-Publication Data
Names: Gracia, Anna, author.
Title: The break-up vacation : an MTV beach house novel / Anna Gracia.
Description: New York : MTV Books, [2024] | Series: MTV beach house
Identifiers: LCCN 2023024662 (print) | LCCN 2023024663 (ebook) |
ISBN 9781668010969 (paperback) | ISBN 9781668010976 (ebook)
Subjects: LCGFT: Romance fiction. | Novels.
Classification: LCC PS3607.R3274 B74 2024 (print) |
LCC PS3607.R3274 (ebook) | DDC 813/.6—dc23/eng/20230524
LC record available at https://lccn.loc.gov/2023024662
LC ebook record available at https://lccn.loc.gov/2023024663

ISBN 978-1-6680-1096-9
ISBN 978-1-6680-1097-6 (ebook)

For the Spice Girls:
Brooke, Rachel, Robyn, Carmen, and Anthony

the BREAKUP VACATION

CHAPTER ONE

"I'll never let go, Jack. I'll never let go."
—Titanic (1997)

Cutting bangs after a breakup was so cliché. And yet, here Grace was, staggering home with a sweaty homemade version of Wednesday Addams's fringe stuck to her forehead.

"Wednesday Addams," she said aloud, using the same accent as King George III in *Hamilton*, making herself giggle. Her theater teacher *had* said to practice different voices. Not that it mattered now.

She swerved back and forth down the sidewalk in her blue-and-white-checkered Mary Jane pumps, pulling out a mini bottle of vodka from her cleavage and taking a swig. It probably hadn't been the smartest decision to ditch her friends when she was in this state, but Grace needed to be alone. That is, she needed to be alone for where she was headed next.

She stopped to check her reflection in a car window, wiping a smudge of something black off her cheek and tucking the liquor bottle back inside her baby-blue corset, right next to her house keys. (Who needed pockets when they had boobs?) She looked a little disheveled, but still hot enough to tempt Josh. Grace could pull him away from just about anything with the promise of boobs.

She turned left at the next street, heading for the weathered yellow house she'd spent the majority of the past six months sleeping in. Josh hadn't specifically invited her over that night, but they still slept together on occasion, so it wasn't like she was a stalker ex-girlfriend who didn't understand boundaries. She could stop by, and it wouldn't be weird or desperate because she was just checking in. As a friend.

Her heels sank into the soft, wet grass, and Grace could feel moisture seeping through the sides of her shoes as she made her way across the lawn toward his bottom-floor window. Usually, she'd be much more concerned about her shoes, but they'd already been ruined when some frat guy spilled an entire cup of beer on them at the end-of-year party. Never before had she so longed for one of her cozy nights in with Josh, curled up on the couch watching old movies together. Preferably barefoot and dry, but she could stay in these a little longer if it meant getting invited inside.

Josh's window was open a crack, the warm night air of late spring ruffling the curtains inside. Grace had been the one to choose them, the tiny film-reel pattern because of Josh's ambitions as a filmmaker. Goddamn, she was a thoughtful girlfriend—between that and the boobs, how had he been able to break up with her?

Grace tapped lightly on the glass three times before struggling to slide the old wooden window up. They'd decided this method was easier since she often came over late at night, so Grace wouldn't have to stand in the cold, waiting for Josh to open the front door. And anyway, Tiff had made Grace leave her phone at home to keep her from texting Josh. Oh, the irony.

"Josh," she stage-whispered, her arms still battling the window casing. It was sort of inconsiderate of him not to leave the window open at least wide enough for her to crawl through, but she was an industrious girl. Her theater teacher always said that persistence was the key to success in acting. Well, that, and nepotism.

"Josh," she rasped again, having gotten one knee up onto the sill to give herself more leverage as she futilely shoved at the window. The scraping sound of wood on wood was truly heinous, but she'd already come too far to give up now. Josh *would* see her tonight, whether he liked it or not.

Of course, she preferred that he'd like it.

Grace heard footsteps hurrying into the room. A moment later the curtains were shoved aside, and Josh's magnificent face appeared.

"Gracie, baby, what are you doing here?"

"Just . . . trying . . . to . . . oof." Grace fell back, her butt landing hard on the wet ground. The window hadn't budged a single inch. "I think your window's broken."

Josh seamlessly opened the window (okay, fine, maybe the alcohol *had* impaired her motor skills) and leaned his head out, his eyes brimming with concern. "Are you okay? What happened?" He looked so worried about her, she nearly teared up on the spot.

Of course she wasn't okay. She was crumpled in a tiny heap outside the window of her ex-boyfriend's, who was looking at her with pity instead of joy. But being the actress she was (or wanted to be, anyway), she pasted on a smile and gave a little laugh as though this were a minor mishap and not moderately to significantly humiliating with a side of literal pain in her ass.

"I was just . . . walking by . . ." she huffed, trying to sort her limbs into a position where she could reasonably stand again, but the ground had inexplicably become rather wobbly. Maybe Northern California was finally getting the big earthquake that was long overdue. She could claim omniscience and say she'd come to warn him, the two of them huddled together under a table or something to stay safe. Proximity was always his weakness around her.

Josh raised his eyebrows but wisely said nothing. It would have been rude to point out that his house was not remotely on the route back to her own house, and Josh was nothing if not unfailingly polite. He'd even been polite when he'd broken up with her.

"Do you need me to call Tiffany for you?" he offered.

"No!" Grace nearly shouted, her arm outstretched as though she could stop him from her position on the ground. Tiff would not be happy to find Grace here, especially since she'd discovered Grace's habit of casually cruising by his house since the breakup. It wouldn't be long until Tiff and Camille realized Grace had ducked out of the party early, so if she could just get inside Josh's, she'd be in the clear. Tiff would never deign to step inside his place.

"I thought you might miss me," she said, smoothing her skirt as she tried to ignore the wetness now seeping into her underwear, ratcheting up her discomfort to a new level. It would probably be off soon enough. "And I know how much you like this outfit, so . . ."

Josh looked pained. "God, you look good. You went out all night in that?"

Grace could practically see his hazel eyes growing greener at the thought.

"Mm-hm," she murmured, trying to sweep the bangs off her forehead in a way that seemed demure. Ew. Her hands were wet from the grass. No matter.

Josh worried his lower lip, as though he *did* want to invite her in, but shook his head instead. "Sorry, Gracie, tonight's not good for me. You know I would have texted otherwise. I thought we agreed to give each other a little bit of space? To make it easier on the both of us?"

"No, *you* decided on space," she spat, angrily remembering his post-sex speech about how he needed to focus more on his filmmaking and didn't have time to devote to the kind of relationship they'd (already) been having.

Josh's look turned pitying again, and Grace chided herself for not keeping her feelings more hidden. It wasn't exactly a secret that she was against the breakup, but it wouldn't do for him to know just how much it had hurt her. Especially when he seemed like he reconsidered that decision every time he saw her. It was only a matter of time before he realized what he'd lost. She just needed to keep herself in proximity.

"I thought you might be lonely," Grace purred, switching back into the innocent voice she knew Josh couldn't resist.

"And now that finals are over, you might have time to *relax* a little."

Josh regularly said that sex was his favorite form of stress relief. Whenever he was upset or anxious, he always turned to Grace, who was more than happy to help, as it were. Him *needing* her proved they'd gone beyond surface-level stuff. He couldn't function without her. But he wanted to.

Josh groaned, a tightly clenched fist in his teeth. "Don't make this harder on me, Gracie," he begged, running a hand through his shaggy hair. "I've been so good the past few days."

She felt somewhat guilty for exploiting his weakness for sex, but not guilty enough to actually leave him alone. This was just as hard on her.

"Josh? Who are you talking to?"

The high, breathy voice floated into the room, quickly followed by a body and head Grace recognized. A face (and personality) Grace loathed.

Villainous music played in her head as Caity "I speak all the languages of my ancestors" Ruiz marched across Josh's bedroom. Grace knew it was childish to have a nemesis in her twenties, but hating Caity Ruiz was what fueled her. Hating her stupid fucking pretend-shocked face when she'd been cast as *yet another* lead this past spring, even though half the class insisted Grace had had a better audition. Hating her stupid fucking balayage hair that wasn't even in fashion anymore, but Santa Cruz was far-flung enough that somehow people still thought it was fresh. Even hating her stupid fucking name. What kind of Asian parent named their kid Caity?

She was probably one of those girls who constantly changed the spelling of it in middle school to seem edgy. Kaytee. Caytie. KT.

Josh had said Caity was dull. Safe. Didn't take chances with her acting. He'd watched Grace ugly cry after she'd lost the role to Caity and reassured her that Professor Tester just had a different vision for the part than she could offer. And now he had *her* in his bedroom like he'd never meant a single word of it.

"Oh, hi, Grace," Caity cooed. She tossed her hair over her shoulder as if she were in a low-budget Pantene commercial. "What are you doing here?"

Even in her inebriated state, Grace could swear Caity emphasized the *you*. Like it was such a shock that Josh's very recent ex might still be in contact with him.

"I could ask you the same thing," Grace slurred, struggling to stand once more before giving up again. "I hope you're not planning to crash our trip to LA next weekend." She slowly pronounced the word "our" to make sure Caity understood that Josh already had one unofficial relationship and wasn't on the market for her brand of know-it-all-ness.

Josh cleared his throat, his hand agitating his hair as he shot Grace a preemptive look of apology that made it very clear that LA was no longer happening. "Shit."

Her brief spark of joy from seeing Josh died. "It's fine," she said dully.

Sure, why not? She already had to trash her outfit and her one summer trip—what was one more loss? What had she been expecting? For her ex to follow through on a promise made long before they'd broken up? It was her fault for not confirming earlier.

Josh looked conflicted, as if he wanted to say something to her but not in front of Caity "I'm always so jet-lagged when I fly back from the Philippines" Ruiz.

He said nothing.

Grace decided now would be an excellent time for a drink. She fished out the tiny vodka bottle from her cleavage and promptly downed the remainder of it. With any luck, it would help her forget that her sworn enemy had just witnessed her, ass-on-the-ground-drunk, in front of her ex's window as he gently rejected her once again.

"Are you drinking straight vodka?" Caity gasped, a hand to her chest as though they lived in the Prohibition era and Grace had been caught slinging moonshine.

God, she *was* a boring actor.

"It's made from potatoes, you know," Grace replied, dimly aware that her words were beginning to merge with one another. "I'm basically carbo-loading. Like an athlete. Team USA!" Grace raised the empty bottle in a mock toast and was rewarded with a chorus of cheers and hoots from a group of similarly drunk students walking down the street. "See?"

Josh cleared his throat again, and Grace felt like a child about to be scolded. But she'd come this far. If Josh was going to make a (bigger) fool of her, he might as well get it over with. Even if it had to happen in front of Caity "I couldn't watch *Mary Poppins* as a kid because Dick Van Dyke's accent was so bad" Ruiz.

Grace was in the final battle scene of *Gladiator*, waiting on Josh's thumbs-up or -down to decide her fate. She didn't mean to be overdramatic, but the rest of her life hinged on this LA trip. Josh had promised to introduce her to his dad, who was a producer with a small indie studio in the Valley. Grace didn't have any connections of her own in Hollywood, and she'd been relying on Josh to help her navigate it all.

"I'll still talk to my dad for you, " Josh said, reassuring her even as he was breaking her heart. But then he shot an anxious look at Caity, and Grace knew more bad news was coming.

"Caity got me a job on her dad's film set down in Cancún. It has that Black French singer girl you listen to in it. Caity and I are flying out in the morning. They've been filming for a few weeks already, but her dad said I could shadow him and help out wherever I am needed until they wrap. It's not much, but this could be huge for my career. I meant to tell you . . . " He trailed off, knowing there was really no good way to end that sentence.

He was leaving her. Literally ditching her to go on vacation with Caity. Her nemesis. Grace was trapped in a fucking horror movie, frozen in place as the killer inched toward her.

"I'm *so* sorry," he apologized. "I'm an asshole for not telling you sooner. Do you hate me?"

"Of course I don't hate you," Grace replied reflexively, even as her heart shriveled to the size of the Grinch's at Christmas. She couldn't be mad at him for taking the opportunity. It *was* a big deal to land a job on a movie set, even if that opportunity came from Caity "Have I mentioned my dad is a director?" Ruiz. If Grace had some kind of lure like that, she wouldn't have hesitated to use it either.

Score one for the bad guys.

Where it left *her*, however, was another question. It was taking all of Grace's energy just to sit upright, let alone do something about the tears pooling in her eyes. All she could do was keep blinking like a haunted doll, her false eyelashes sliding ever closer to the edge of her lids.

She couldn't cry in front of Caity "I only drink water with electrolytes to keep my skin healthy" Ruiz. Crying would mean conceding. Josh would see it, Caity would leap onto the windowsill—Grace's windowsill—like a victorious Spartan, and Grace would be buried looking like a mangled doll come to life, only seven of her ten toes painted because she'd gotten distracted at the time and never finished.

Some enterprising film student next year would probably write a screenplay about it. Maybe even Josh himself. The sad story of the unwanted girl, beloved by everyone except those she really wanted to love her. It would be a tragedy, of course. But with excellent costumes. And a soundtrack of pop songs sung in slow tempo to give it a dramatic indie vibe.

"Grace! There you are! We've been looking everywhere for you!"

Tiff was a blur of hair and tiny legs as she and their much, much taller roommate, Camille, rushed toward Grace. Pulling her up, Tiff brushed the wet clumps of grass from Grace's backside with what could only be described as excessive enthusiasm.

"I should have known," Tiff muttered as she smacked at the few remaining bits of grass clinging to Grace's ass.

"What does that— Ow! Not so hard!—mean?"

Instead of answering her, Tiff turned to Josh. Her eyes were slitted, her smile bordering on feral. "Joshua," she clipped, each syllable ending in its own punctuation.

The side of his mouth curled up as he nodded his head in acknowledgment. "Tiffany. Camille." He said it like "Kimmy."

"Caity," Caity chimed in, pointing at herself as though everyone was just calling out names.

Camille looked amused as she corrected Josh's pronunciation the way she did every time. "Camille." Her French accent made it sound like *Ka-ME.*

Caity's eyes lit up. "Tu es française?"

Oh, absolutely the fuck not. Grace might well be on the verge of puking and unable to fully stand on her own, but she was not sharing another person in her life with Caity "I pronounce it ONvelope" Ruiz. Especially not as Josh told her silently with his eyes that he was so, *so* sorry for breaking up with her but still wouldn't take it back.

Scooping up her chunky heels in one hand and tugging on Tiff's with the other, Grace marched toward the street with the precision of a soldier performing a changing of the guard. She would salvage her dignity in this moment by walking away. She was an *actor*, goddamn it.

If only she'd noticed the edge of the curb.

With bare feet and only a fleeting sense of balance, Grace misjudged the distance and promptly fell into the street, crumpling like a paper bag getting stepped on.

"Oh fuck, ow, ow, ow," Grace cried, clutching her foot as she rolled around on the gritty asphalt. "I think I rolled my ankle." She groaned. "And my back. And my wrist."

"Are you okay?" Josh and Caity called out at the same time. They gave each other a surprised look, and Grace mentally flashed forward to it becoming one of those cute little *things* a couple did all the time.

She was supposed to be the one on the same wavelength as Josh. *She* deserved those little things.

"Hold on tight, we'll help you walk." Tiff pushed her mane of curly black hair out of the way as she reached for Grace's arm for the second time that night. "Camille and I will each prop up a side of you."

"Please, just let me die." Grace moaned. Her last attempt to save face had somehow made the rest of the night seem pleasant. If Josh came outside to check on her—or, God forbid, *Caity*—Grace would have to transfer colleges. Or hire a hitman.

There was no coming back from this.

"I'll give you more alcohol if you get up right now," Tiff coaxed.

That got Grace to her feet. "What kind of alcohol? Something good? Or that terrible wine thing Camille made me drink last time that tasted like potpourri?" Grace turned the word over in her mouth like one of her diction exercises. "Potepurreeeeee. Pot-poory."

"Please stop," Camille begged, using her free hand to cover one ear. "French people are already depressed."

"Oh, Camille," Grace warbled, her drunken brain unable to stay focused on any one topic for long. "I was just kidding around. I do a mean French accent. I've been studying."

Camille made a noncommittal sound, and Grace sucked in a gust of air. "You dare doubt me?" she demanded in a French accent.

"Ah. I see. French accent in *English*," Camille clarified.

Grace laughed. "Of course in English, what else would I be speaking?"

"Uh, French," Tiff supplied.

That sent Grace into a fit of giggles.

"Are you sure she's okay?" Josh called out.

Grace whipped her head around, and even from a distance, she saw the hesitation in his face. Like maybe he *did* want to come after her. Because he cared about her.

"We don't need any help from you, that's for fucking sure," Tiff shouted back, much louder than necessary. "You and your new girlfriend can go back to whatever boring-ass missionary-style sex you were having before we got here."

Grace's eyes went wide, and she sent a sharp elbow into Tiff's ribs. "Why would you say that?" she hissed.

Tiff shrugged. "He looks like a missionary-only kind of guy."

He was, mostly, but that wasn't Grace's point.

"I mean that you're *encouraging* him to have sex with her!"

Tiff mockingly replied with an equal measure of outrage. "Yes! I am! Because then maybe you'll see he's moving on and you should too."

Tears sprang into Grace's eyes again, and Tiff immediately apologized.

"Okay, okay, I'm sorry. He's not moving on. *You're* the one leaving *him* right now."

Grace drew her eyebrows together. "I am?"

"Yeah! Look at you!" Tiff tried to stand a little taller, which was hard since Grace was putting almost all of her weight on her. "You're walking away, and all he can do is watch you go."

"He's still watching me?" Grace asked.

"Do not read into this," Tiff warned, heaving Grace into a more upright position.

"How close is he standing to Caity?" Grace asked, employing the last crumbs of her willpower to keep from looking back at the window.

"This girl?" Camille scoffed. "She has nothing to compare to you. I am sure they are just friends."

"Friends with benefits," Tiff muttered. "Just kidding!" she added when she saw Grace's face. "Camille's right. Nothing is happening, and you are walking away from this so we can bring you home and get you so drunk you'll never even think of him again."

Grace stared into Tiff's face, wishing her best friend was even half as convincing as Josh. But she played along, grateful her friends were trying so hard to cheer her up. "How much do I need to drink so I never think of Caity again?"

CHAPTER TWO

"I'm going to make him an offer he can't refuse."
—The Godfather (1972)

The next morning, Grace awoke face down, sprawled across her bed like a corpse in water. The crinoline skirt she'd fallen asleep in had left imprints on her thighs, and mascara was smudged across her pillows. Her mouth tasted the way it had after Camille insisted they try snails one night.

For being half Asian, Grace wasn't the world's most adventurous eater. And growing up on the peninsula, where pretty much everyone came from backgrounds that regularly pushed the boundaries of what was edible, only highlighted that. Grace just didn't feel the need to eat anything she personally had to scrape out of a shell.

She rolled over and checked her phone, a message with Josh's sad face grabbing her attention.

Josh: You get home ok? You never texted

And with that, the events of the previous night came rushing back into her throbbing head. Josh, denying her entry to his house. Josh, standing there next to Caity. Josh, flying off to Cancún *with* Caity.

Grace flung herself back into the pillows, muffling screams she'd been holding in since Josh had scaled back their relationship to a lower tier like it was a Netflix subscription. Crying was a regular occurrence, but living in a house with other people severely limited her ability to primal scream every time she needed to.

Was the universe punishing her? She'd been so good until then; patiently waiting for him to initiate contact so she didn't seem pushy or needy. But one tiny slipup and *bam!* He was off to Mexico with another girl. Work or no work, it was still bullshit. And if he was so excited about going to Cancún with Caity, why was he still texting Grace? Exes didn't text the other person their literal face first thing in the morning unless one was really evil and trying to torture the other. If he truly wanted to be free of Grace, he wouldn't bother telling her he was worried about her.

You should *be worried, Josh*, she thought.

Grace didn't brush her teeth or wipe the raccoon smudges around her eyes before dragging herself downstairs and into the kitchen that was far too bright and cheerful for her liking. She attempted to shield her eyes as she stumbled toward the table. "Whose stupid idea was it to install a skylight anyway?"

Tiff and Camille quickly coalesced around Grace like she was a sickly patient. They ushered her into a padded chair and

Tiff cracked open a window, careful not to admit she likely did so because of Grace's slight vinegar smell. It wasn't Grace's fault vodka stopped being odorless once it was ingested.

"You want me to put some toast in for you?" Tiff offered in as soft a voice as she could manage. She held up a loaf of multigrain bread with oats and nuts across the top crust. "I'll even put butter on it. Real butter this time."

Grace declined without hesitation. Tiff's latest obsession had something to do with "eco-friendly wellness," which meant all the groceries she bought were varying shades of brown and tasted like cardboard. The last time Grace had been tricked into trying Tiff's toast, Tiff had waited until Grace spit it out before she admitted that the "butter" was, in fact, pureed coconut. And no, it did not "taste just like the real thing," thank you very much.

Grace turned her sad but hopeful eyes on Camille. "Do you think you could make me a mocha?" she whimpered pitifully.

Camille had an excruciating method of making mochas, which involved gently warming milk (the fancy kind that came in a glass jug) in a saucepan and melting shards of expensive French (always French!) chocolate, which was then added to espresso in a double boiler before being briskly whisked into the milk. It took forever and seemed unnecessarily complicated, but it was also the kind of mocha that made Grace feel like a millionaire. If she was going to be pathetic, she could at least get something out of it.

"Of course," Camille agreed, hurrying to the stove like the mother hen she was. "I will put in biscuits for you too."

Grace was grateful for all the attention. It was silly, she knew, to let her friends pamper her like this, but she needed the reassurance that *someone* still loved her.

As Camille stood at the stove, Grace explained what had happened the night before. She skipped the part about trying to climb into Josh's window, instead making it seem like more of a coincidence than a planned excursion gone horribly, horribly wrong. After all, her friends were being so understanding and doting. She didn't want to spoil that with an argument over why she was still seeing Josh in the first place.

"And then fucking Caity 'Oh, I'm just a perfect small little Asian girl' Ruiz showed up," Grace recounted, venom seeping into her voice.

Camille frowned. "She is Asian? I think maybe she is *hispanique*?"

"She's mixed," Grace replied sullenly. "Which she reminds us all of every day. *It's so hard being ethnically ambiguous*," Grace mocked in her fake Caity voice, really nailing the nasally sound that came through her *m*'s and *n*'s. "But, like, pick a lane. You can't take the Asian roles *and* the Latinx roles. Some of us don't get the chance to play *either* because we don't fit some stupid prototype and we're not complete suck-ups with rich dads who probably donated to the school to let us in." Grace sank farther back into her chair, drawing a deep breath after that rant.

She hated that she had been nice to Caity at first. Grace had seen her and immediately thought, *Fellow mixed kid!* But it quickly became clear that Caity "I'm not biracial, I'm 100 percent of two different races" Ruiz was less interested in biracial solidarity and more interested in claiming the title of Best Mixed Girl in class. And there was always only ever room for one.

Apparently even in Josh's life.

"I think we're getting off track," Tiff interjected, having

safely tucked her loaf of sawdust back into the cupboard. "Of course Caity sucks, but the asshole here is Josh. *He's* the one who broke up with you."

"I'd barely call it a breakup," Grace protested for what felt like the hundredth time. "He just can't commit to a full-time relationship right now. It's not like we hate each other or anything."

Camille set down a steaming mug in front of Grace, who wasted no time shoving her face into it. In a horror movie, the steam would be poison and she'd already be dead. It wasn't a terrible idea. At least Josh would come to her funeral. He'd probably be wrecked, thinking about the way he sent her away the last time he saw her alive.

Fuck, that was dark. Grace didn't want to have to die just so Josh would start appreciating her.

"Biscuits will take two more minutes," Camille apologized, as though Grace had ordered them from a restaurant and was paying for her services.

Grace took a sip of her mocha and moaned. "Is this why French people never seem heartbroken? You just go to a café with your scarves and your trench coats, and all your problems magically disappear with chocolate and pastries?" Honestly, it sounded pretty amazing.

Camille laughed, her voice as thin and light as her figure. "This is the France everyone thinks they know. We have . . . what do you call it?—fuckboys there too."

Tiff snorted, and even Grace had to stifle a laugh at that. Camille had been sent to University of California, Santa Cruz, by her parents to improve her English, but most of what she'd picked up probably wouldn't help her job prospects. White collar jobs, anyway.

"That feels like a story," Grace commented, looking pointedly at Camille over the edge of her cup as she risked a sip. It was like molten lava.

"No story," Camille said. "Fuckboys are everywhere, no?"

"Yeah, but at least yours have amazing accents." Tiff sighed. "Try consoling yourself after getting ghosted by some guy who says 'bruh.'"

Camille's flat brows pulled together. "What does this mean, 'bruh'?"

"It's 'bro' for douchey guys," Grace volunteered.

Camille frowned harder. "Douche like"—she gestured to her nether regions—"ah. Never mind. Right now, we focus on you and your problem. This breakup. It's easy to repair, no?"

"If you mean throwing away my dignity and begging him to take me back, I've already tried it," Grace muttered. Remembering how Josh had held her as she cried during their farewell sex after he'd broken up with her was painful enough. She refused to disclose the part where she had to wipe her nose on his shirt (a for sure sign he cared about her), or how she listed reasons to stay together like she could debate him into it.

Tiff's eyes widened into saucers. "You did *what*?"

"Just kidding," Grace lied, immediately chucking that humiliating memory into the closet where she kept the others. "After seeing him with Caity 'I got into USC but chose to come to Santa Cruz for the authentic theater program' Ruiz? Please. I'm so over it."

So what if Caity got Grace's roles and Grace's future and Grace's boyfriend? Her mortal enemy was taking over Grace's life because, apparently, she was better at it. Grace choked down a sob.

Camille wrinkled her pert little nose, even the unpleasant

facial expression seeming almost dainty on her face. "I am not, what do you call? Catty. But this Caity? She sounds terrible."

"She is," Grace confirmed, happily noting that Camille pronounced "Caity" and "catty" almost exactly the same.

"Then she's exactly who Josh deserves." Tiff beamed, her smile brighter than her sparkling gold septum piercing.

Grace tried to fake a smile and laugh in agreement, even though the comment drove a stake through her heart. She wasn't ready to let go of Josh, and despite how the previous night might have appeared to her friends, she didn't think Josh was ready to let go of her either. After all, he hadn't *said* he and Caity were dating. Or sleeping together. Just that they were working together.

Why would someone who'd moved on still offer to introduce their ex to their father? Most of the time, people didn't even exchange last names, let alone bring someone home with them. Grace, of course, knew all of Josh's names: Joshua Patrick Hart. First name from his paternal grandfather, middle name from his maternal grandfather. The only things Caity probably knew about Josh were that he was hot and that Grace liked him. Catty Caity.

Camille stretched past Grace and set a tray of hot biscuits in the middle of the table, quickly followed by a little dish of butter and another of what appeared to be strawberry jelly. "They are from the freezer, but they are okay with enough jam." Camille sounded resigned about it, as if she was offering them cafeteria food just because the biscuits hadn't been crafted with her own two hands from scratch.

This was Tiff and Grace's cue to insist everything was delicious and perfect. Criticism was not appreciated by the chef, no matter what she said. Tiff had learned that the hard way when she once mentioned a cake Camille had baked was a little dry.

Camille dismissed the praise, but her smile confirmed they'd said all the right things. "I am happy to distract you. Maybe this is what you need."

Tiff's brown eyes sparkled with that new-idea look—the same one she got right before throwing herself headfirst into a new hobby. Except in this case, Grace's love life was the hobby. "Of course! A distraction! You need a rebound hookup!"

Grace choked down her bite to cut in before Tiff gained steam. "No way. Besides, every other guy I've met here is trash. Or if they're not trash, they're super crunchy and want to do things like go on bike rides and volunteer at recycling centers and only drink craft beers." Talking about craft beer, as far as Grace was concerned, was an instant red flag. Right up there with anyone who named a superhero movie as their favorite. Fun? Sure. Entertaining? Yes. *Favorite?* Really?

"Remember Calvin?" Grace continued. "Who I dated for, like, a month freshman year, and then had his *mother* call to break up with me?"

"No!" Camille gasped.

"Yes," Grace said, helping herself to another biscuit. "Don't let Tiff convince you that Josh is the devil. He's *by far* the best guy I've met here in three years."

Camille gave a noncommittal head bob. "It's true, I have not met many interesting boys. But the girls are not so bad, no?"

"Not exactly helpful for me," Grace reminded her. "God, what I would give to be bi right now."

Anyone who thought sexual orientation was a choice had clearly never spent a lifetime pursuing heterosexual men.

"Ah, yes, our life is so easy," Camille said wryly. "No violence just to live."

"Ugh, sorry," Grace grumbled. "I didn't mean it like that."

Of course queer people had their own host of problems (which Grace was very sensitive to!), but no one seemed to get spooked like a horse near fire by the idea of exclusivity quite like a straight guy.

I can't commit to being in a serious relationship right now was Josh's official explanation, as if Grace were trying to tie him down for life or something. She hadn't even put pressure on him not to date other people after they'd broken up! All she wanted was a chance to prove herself, and now that chance was in Mexico with Caity "Self-driving cars are the future" Ruiz. Too bad Caity's wildly overpriced EV seemed to be the only one of that brand that hadn't exploded or crashed yet.

"Why don't we travel somewhere?" Tiff suggested. "Camille is going back to France in a few weeks. What better way to send her off than a fabulous vacation?"

Her friends wanted to travel? Holy shit. The universe was finally paying her back for the things she'd been suffering through. Grace could not have dreamed of a better setup.

"What about Cancún?" she blurted out.

Tiff made a face at her. "Mexico? In June? With how much you sweat?"

This was the problem with having a best friend who knew everything about you. Grace needed an excuse, and fast. She downed the rest of her mocha, hoping the caffeine would work its magic and spark an idea that would convince her friends that Cancún was, in fact, the perfect destination.

Josh was powerless to resist her in person. At least, he was when Caity wasn't around. But if Grace could somehow get herself there too, she'd get him to forget all about Caity. And Grace wouldn't need to use her daddy to do it.

"I have not been to Miami," Camille volunteered, slathering jam across her biscuit as she tried not to show how bothered she was by the crumb apocalypse around Grace's plate. "That city has many parties, no?"

Tiff didn't hesitate before answering. "Absolutely not. If you must leave the US, which I still say you should not, your last impression of it will not be *Florida*." It was more pledge than prediction.

"Agreed," Grace said, though her brain was still thinking of ways to sell her friends on Cancún. Grace just needed to convince them that the upsides outweighed the only downside (the heat). Once they were there, Tiff and Camille would get swept up in shopping or drinking or whatever at some point, and Grace could disappear for a couple of hours without raising suspicion. They'd never suspect Josh because they didn't know he was there.

"Los Angeles?" Camille offered.

Another disgusted face from Tiff. "LA isn't a place you vacation. It's the place where you sit in traffic on your way to San Diego."

"Chicago?"

Tiff's rings clattered in succession as she drummed her fingers on the table. "Grace, please help before Claude Monet here suggests we fly to Phoenix or some other godforsaken town because she doesn't understand American geography."

Finally! "I still think Cancún would be perfect," Grace insisted. "Think about it: beaches, clubs, amazing food?"

When Tiff didn't immediately shoot it down, Grace elaborated.

"A favorable exchange rate? Hot beachy guys who don't sunburn in the first five minutes?"

"Is this because of your obsession with *Y Tu Mamá También*? Because you can have threesomes here too."

Grace's face flushed in embarrassment that Tiff remembered how often Grace used to talk about it because, *good God*, that movie had brought on a huge sexual awakening. She didn't care how old Diego Luna was now—he was welcome to use that accent on her anytime.

"That is *not* why I suggested it. I just thought, what's more American than going to Mexico to party?"

Tiff nodded slowly, the wrinkle between her eyes deepening as she thought it over. "Okay, points have been made. I think I could get on board with this. I see surf lessons, yoga on the beach, maybe sailing?"

A wave of panic rose inside Grace. Tiff loved taking charge, and Grace was usually happy to let her—Tiff's parents were bankrolling their trips, anyway. But Tiff also wanted to be doing something at all times, and Grace wasn't going all the way to Mexico only to miss out on seeing Josh because she was too busy doing *yoga*.

"I'll plan it," she volunteered, hoping they couldn't hear her desperation.

Tiff frowned. "Babes, we both know you're not the planner in this relationship."

Or any other, Grace thought. She'd let Josh make plans without her, and now she was stuck, waiting to see where he'd cast her in his life. She needed to make sure she got the lead this time. No way Grace would accept second billing behind a girl who repeatedly went out of her way to mention she'd never had braces. Like Caity beat everyone else by having good dental genetics.

Grace *had* to get to Cancún.

Her shoulders drooped like they had earlier, so her friends would remember why they wanted to travel in the first place. "Maybe it'll help me keep my mind off everything?" she suggested.

Tiff sighed, retrieving her credit card but holding it out of reach. "Are you sure you're even sober enough to be handling money?"

Grace held her hand out, palm up. "Do you want me to start talking about Josh again?"

Tiff clamped a hand over an ear, the other handing Grace the card. "I surrender, okay? Just take it."

A surge of triumph shot through Grace. Operation Get Josh Back was underway.

CHAPTER THREE

"This is how I win."
—Uncut Gems (2019)

Grace's stalking skills landed them in Cancún less than two days later.

She had rented them a sprawling beach house, which Google Street View had said was not too far from Josh's hotel. It had only taken a deep dive into his social media, press coverage of the film, the social media of every identifiable crew member, some light map reading, and a couple long-distance phone calls to figure it all out.

"I feel like I'm on a reality show right now," Tiff yelled as the three of them tore through the massive beach house Grace had rented. "My bathroom shower could easily fit four people."

Grace poked her head in and saw Tiff stretching her little arms and legs across the space as a form of measuring it. It was too funny not to laugh. "Planning a lot of group orgies?" she asked.

"Aren't all orgies group orgies?" Tiff stepped out of the shower and ran her hands over the marble countertops. "You did well, I'll give you that. This place is even nicer than the one we stayed at in Cabo."

Grace swallowed guiltily. The rental price had been outrageous this close to downtown, but she justified it by reminding herself that Tiff complained about any accommodations with less than five stars. Surely she didn't want Grace to skimp on comfort for their girls' trip.

"This place is incredible," Camille marveled as Grace passed her in the hallway. "Did you see the kitchen? I can make a whole feast in there."

Tiff's voice rang out from an unidentified part of the house. "We're here to eat tacos, Camille!"

Camille shook her head with a tsk. "Americans. No appreciation for food."

"Hey now, tacos *are* food," Grace argued. "Though I'm not going to say no to your offer of making breakfast every morning."

Camille's one request for the trip was a grocery delivery, which Grace was more than happy to help find because it meant she could sleep in just a little later. Also because she wasn't paying for it.

She used to feel guilty letting Tiff and her moms pay for everything, but after so many years, Grace was basically part of their family. Tiff was an only child, so paying for Grace to join her ensured she was never alone. So, instead of a regular middle-class upbringing befitting a child of two teachers, Grace had spent her summers taking horseback riding lessons and learning manicure techniques and whatever else had caught Tiff's fleeting interest for the moment.

"I'm taking this bedroom," Grace declared, throwing open the sliding doors to the balcony and letting the warm breeze hit her skin. "Holy shit, look at this view."

Between the vibrant turquoise water, reflective white sand, and the perfectly round sun in the perfectly blue sky, it looked just like a picture in a brochure. It was so perfect that if she'd seen it in a movie, she might have believed it was CGI. Her heart clenched, thinking of how much she wished she could share that very thought with Josh. He always understood the beauty of a perfect location.

She could already imagine him excitedly brainstorming the kinds of shots that would work with this amount of light, and the implications of sand-covered bodies that didn't require unnecessary nudity. That was one thing she always appreciated—he was one of the only college guys she'd met who *didn't* have posters of half-naked women tacked up in his room.

"Who's ready for shots?" Tiff bellowed, walking in holding a silver tray loaded with a tall bottle of tequila and three shot glasses, already filled to the rim.

That pulled Grace out of her thoughts. "Where did you even find those? And what time is it?" she asked, fumbling for her phone. She'd been hoping to take a "walk" while her friends unpacked, maybe casually running into Josh so he'd know she was also in Cancún.

"Any time is shot time, bitches," Tiff yelled out, her other hand cupped around her mouth like a megaphone.

"That seemed a bit much."

Tiff pursed her lips. "Fair. It felt right in the moment, so I went for it."

"I appreciate the effort."

Camille wandered in, having shed her lightweight cardigan, and grabbed a shot off the tray. "*Salut*," she toasted before gulping it down.

Tiff stared at her. "We were supposed to toast *together*. You know, to kick off this trip?"

Camille set her glass down guiltily. "Sorry. I see a shot, I take it. I am like Stephen Curry, no?" She pretended to shoot an imaginary basketball, then paused for effect, clearly waiting for Grace and Tiff to appreciate her joke.

Tiff just blinked at her. "Seriously, Camille, you have got to stop talking about sports around us. Neither of us has any idea what you're talking about."

Camille sighed as she poured herself another shot. "France is crazy about basketball. My father takes me to games all the time when I was young. He wanted me to play."

"You've got the height for it," Grace remarked.

As tall as Grace was herself, Camille positively towered over most everyone else she met. Maybe that's why she could always get away with not wearing heels. Grace, on the other hand, slumped over like a gargoyle unless tiny matchsticks on her feet forced her to stand up straight to keep balanced. Also, they made her legs look amazing.

"Yes. Unfortunately, I am not coordinated." Camille laughed with a shrug as she downed her second shot.

"Hey!" Tiff exclaimed.

"Oops." Camille pretended to seem contrite while she poured herself yet another, this time at least waiting for Grace and Tiff to grab theirs before toasting. "*Salut*," she said.

"To Grace's rebound," Tiff offered.

"To redemption," Grace revised.

Tiff shot her a sobering look. "Babes. You don't need redemption. You did nothing wrong. Remember that."

For the second time in ten minutes, Grace swallowed the ever-expanding lump in her throat. Here her friends were, being incredibly kind and supportive—toasting her!—without knowing it was all just a front for her illicit operations. Josh, of course, was the drug she hoped to be trafficking.

Grace pressed her lips together and flashed her best actress smile.

The show must go on.

"To moving on," she lied, raising her glass in a toast.

"Here, here," her friends echoed, clinking the shot glasses together in celebration.

After an appropriate (but not excessive) number of shots, Grace had loosened up and was anxious to find Josh. "Did you both unpack already? I was thinking of exploring the area."

"If you want to get your hair braided, just say so," Tiff teased.

"That was you," Grace said. "Just like it was you who insisted we get those necklaces with our names painted on a grain of rice."

Tiff pursed her lips. "Hm, that might be true. Do you remember how mad I was when I let Henry Chang try it on and he broke it?"

Grace scoffed. "Are you kidding? That was the first time I seriously thought you might murder someone. There have been plenty of those after that," she added.

Tiff pointed a finger in Grace's face and gave her most menacing growl. "And don't you forget it."

"It would be a lot scarier if you did that with a bunch of puka shells clacking around your face," Grace sang. "Add in a huge, tacky henna tattoo? Maybe in kanji?" She kissed her fingers and released them like a chef.

"Okay, but I'm not white. I'm allowed to get that."

Grace rolled her eyes. "Fine. Sanskrit, then."

"Everyone has bad taste when they are young," Camille chimed in. "Me? I like the hip-hop with the baggy pants and the flat baseball hat." She mimicked a pose, her hand swiping across an imaginary brim in front of her face.

Tiff and Grace stood slack-jawed, trying to imagine the incredibly polished French waif standing in front of them as a lost member of some nineties hip-hop group. It was, in a word, incomprehensible.

Tiff was the first to find her tongue again, clasping her hands in front of herself as some form of protection from that imagery. "Well. That was . . . deeply weird, and I will never forget that as long as I live."

"Literally. Burned into my eyeballs." Grace gaped, her hands cupped around the sides of her face in shock.

Camille clucked her tongue at the both of them. "And you say my English is bad. I know this word, 'literally,' and you are not using it correctly."

Grace threw her hands up. "That's it. I am officially giving up on life. The foreign exchange student is correcting my English. Now I've lost everything."

"Stop being so dramatic," Tiff scolded. "So your English sucks. And you got dumped. And your ex may have moved on to your nemesis. And you have a huge zit coming in on your chin. And didn't your period come early last week? Look on the bright side: at least you're with us!"

"Thanks. That's super helpful. I'm cured."

Tiff grinned. "That's what I'm here for."

"I unpack already," Camille announced. "Maybe we go to the beach?"

"Did you pack SPF one thousand?" Grace asked, and Camille casually flipped her off. "Just kidding, I packed some for you just in case."

As much as Grace would love for her skin to have more of a brownish glow like Tiff's, she couldn't risk the aging effects of the sun. In another five years, Hollywood would probably ask her to audition for roles as a parent to some thirty-year-old guy playing a teenager.

Tiff rubbed the (almost nonexistent) bridge of her nose—her sign that a migraine might be coming on. Grace jumped on the opportunity.

"Maybe you should lie down for a while," she suggested.

"That sounds nice." Camille sighed. "I think I have a little too much to drink. I will lie down."

"It was your idea to go to the beach!" Tiff exclaimed.

Camille gave a casual shrug. "I change my mind."

As she excused herself from the room, Tiff turned toward Grace with a *Can you believe this girl?* look. Grace, for her part, fluttered with excitement. If she could just shake off Tiff now . . .

Grace had already begun to imagine Josh's face when he first saw her. Shock? But good shock?

Tiff heaved a sigh and gave her nose one final rub. "Okay, I'll go to the beach with you."

"I thought you were getting a headache."

"I am. But we just got here. I don't want to leave you here alone."

Ah fuck. How was Grace supposed to sneak out after that? Still, she decided to give it one more try.

"I don't want you to be in bad shape for tonight," Grace said. She'd planned for them to go to a very loud, very crowded club where it would be easy to disappear for a bit. If they ended up having to stay in, it was going to be much harder for her to sneak out.

God, it was like being in high school all over again.

Tiff poured herself a shot and quickly downed it. "It'll be fine. If I just keep drinking, then I won't feel the headache."

"I don't think that's how it works."

Tiff took another shot. "Hey now. I'm doing this for *you*."

The last ember of hope Grace had for escaping that afternoon snuffed out. Day one, and she was already behind schedule. Well, she might as well have another shot too.

"To the most generous of friends," she said. The irony wasn't lost on her; Tiff would be furious if she knew just *how* generous she was being right now.

She is *getting a vacation too*, Grace reminded herself. It helped keep the guilt at bay.

They toasted one last time before drinking, the tequila sliding down her throat easier with each shot. Tequila wasn't Grace's drink of choice, but Tiff had already decided she wanted them to try to drink their way through as many different (high-end) types as possible. This one, Don Julio Ultima Reserva, supposedly had notes of caramel, sweet tea, and lemon cake. Oh, and coconut. Sure. Why not. It had cost only six hundred dollars.

She tamped down a bubble of laughter. This whole thing

was so absurd, stressing out over a few thousand dollars for airfare and the house when they would drink practically the same amount over the course of the trip. And it wasn't like they were really going to sip and savor them. Tiff had just wanted to spend the money for its prestige.

"How long do you need to get ready?" Tiff asked, carrying the tray of shot glasses and much-depleted bottle with her as she exited.

"Thirty minutes?"

"You get fifteen," Tiff called from the hallway.

Grace squawked. "Tyrant!"

"Diva!" Tiff yelled back.

Grace picked through her bathing suits, trying to find the one that was most flattering. She'd long ago mastered the art of the selfie, but this one had to be special because it was going to Josh.

She hadn't yet replied to his "you get home ok" message, and every hour she went without texting him seemed podium worthy. Since the moment their plane touched down, Grace had been counting the minutes to when she could finally let Josh know she was in Cancún.

This was the perfect opportunity to surprise him. She just needed to quickly try on six different swimsuits and then choose the one that was going to make Josh want to leave Caity and come find Grace. No pressure.

She finally decided on the one that showed the most boob. Slathering on shimmering lotion, Grace checked the hallway. Silence. She hurriedly shot a bunch of pictures, half of her face and all of her boobs. She picked the most flattering one and sent it.

Grace: i did make it home, thx for asking

Grace: didn't stay there for long

Grace: girls vacation

The panic hit almost immediately. What if her boobs didn't hold the same summoning power through a phone? What if he thought she was acting *too* interested? One desperate text could potentially undo all the impossible weeks of pretending to cope with the breakup.

Thankfully, Josh replied promptly and appropriately.

Josh: Holy shit

Grace heaved a sigh of relief, collapsing onto the bed.

Josh: But also, you're on vacation right now???

Josh: Where??

Grace: you'll never guess

Josh: I hope nowhere in that swimsuit

Josh: you look way too hot

Grace: that's not a guess

Josh: Pleeeeeaseeee tell me

Grace: how badly do you want to know

Josh: Give me a hint

Josh: Send another pic with some background

Grace: not enough in the foreground for you huh

Josh: I surrender

Josh: Just send me another shot of your boobs

It was now or never. Grace gathered up all her courage and typed.

Grace: we're in cancun

Josh: ??????

Josh: What

Grace: last hurrah for camille before she goes back to france

Josh: Tiff's idea?

Grace: sure

Josh: Too bad

Josh: I thought you were going to say your idea

Grace stared at the screen. Was Josh *hoping* she'd followed him? And how could she get him to invite her to meet up?

Josh: You look amazing btw

Josh: In case I didn't tell you yet

Grace nervously twisted her ear, deciding how to respond. Josh definitely didn't seem *unhappy* that she was in the same city as him again.

Grace: i might have some free time later

Josh: Say more

Grace: you expressed interest in the swimsuit

Grace: i thought you might want to see it in person

Josh: You're trying to kill me

Grace: is that a yes

Suddenly, Tiff popped her head in, and Grace stifled a scream at the interruption.

"Do you think we'll get out the door before the sun sets, or are you still doing your makeup just so it can wash off in the water?" Tiff asked, her hair (mostly) contained in a messy bun that showed off the piercings that went all the way up the sides of her ears. There was a very good chance her entire person was made up of nothing but hair and jewelry.

"Some of us actually need a minute to pull ourselves together," Grace replied, safely stowing away her phone. She didn't need questions about who she was texting. "I'm not trying to get ignored by some casting agent or talent director because they walk by and I'm not looking my best."

Tiff rolled her eyes. "Yes, I know, if it could happen to Charlize Theron, it could happen to you."

"And Jennifer Lawrence, who's now one of the richest actresses in Hollywood. And they both have Oscars," Grace added triumphantly.

"They're also both white. And blond."

Grace deflated. There was that.

But Grace attracted attention everywhere she went. Probably because of her style, with all the loud colors and frills everywhere, but she liked to think there was more to it than that. Her clothes encapsulated who she was (or at least strived to be): fun, confident, hot. Hotness was never a bad thing, especially in Hollywood.

She pulled herself up to full height. "That's exactly why I need to break in."

Tiff shot her a smile. "Hell yeah, you do. Now let's go impress whatever secret drone out there is spying on you."

"I knew you'd understand."

As she followed Tiff out of her room, Grace could hear the muffled chirp of her phone inside her bag.

Josh.

She was dying to know what he'd responded to her invitation, but there was no way to find out now. Either way, her response to whatever *he* responded would have to wait.

Which meant *she* left the conversation first.

A smile curled her lips, thinking about him waiting for her to reply again.

Good. He could be the one pining for once.

CHAPTER FOUR

"Jessica, only child, Illinois, Chicago."
—Parasite (2019)

As soon as they'd come in from the water, Grace had raced to her phone.

Josh: What if I text you the address of where I'm staying?

Josh: Just in case I get off work early

Then, sometime later, another one.

Josh: Are you still there?

Without anyone to tell, Grace had run quiet circles around her room to try to control how much she was freaking out. It felt like she and Josh had gone back in time—to before they started getting more serious, when every text sent her into a frenzy. Grace was relieved she hadn't been there to get them originally or she might have been tempted to go to him right then.

Grace: send it

Grace: just in case

Grace waited for the telltale dots to appear. After staring at her phone for an embarrassing amount of time, she begrudgingly started to get ready for the night, unsure of whether she'd actually get to see Josh or not.

"You cannot possibly be still getting dressed," Tiff exclaimed, coming into Grace's room later that evening with what was quickly becoming the familiar silver tray bearing alcohol, this time a bottle of Tears of Llorona (a mere $250!). In a banana-yellow dress made entirely of elastic straps and sky-high spiked black heels, Tiff looked like the human version of a shiny race car . . . in Matchbox size.

"Wowee," Grace marveled, noting the decided non-frizziness of Tiff's hair and the disappearance of the usual collection of rings that clacked against absolutely everything. "Someone's looking for love tonight."

Tiff snorted. "That's me. Can't wait to settle down with my soulmate."

"Tiffany is looking for a soulmate?" Camille wandered in, wearing black cigarette pants and a leopard-print silk tank.

Tiff's eyes narrowed, zeroing in on the bold print. "Are you *sure* you're not Asian? We're *very* into the animal prints."

Camille shrugged casually, her wide, bony shoulders covered by mere wisps of fabric. "Maybe this is why we are friends."

Grace still had her eyes on Tiff's hands. "Seriously, what happened to all your rings?"

Tiff gave a dramatic little gasp. "I took them off."

"Why?"

Tiff never took off her rings. It was probably why her attempt to take up tennis had been so short-lived. "If Serena Williams can play with jewelry, so can I," she'd insisted. As it turned out, Tiff was not Serena Williams.

Tiff shrugged casually. "Just in case I need to give someone a quick handy in the bathroom. I don't need *those* kinds of screams, if you know what I mean."

"Jesus Christ," Grace muttered, covering her face with her hands. "I did not need that image in my head."

"In all seriousness though, maybe you should consider it," Tiff said.

"Giving someone a hand job in a disgusting bar bathroom? I'll pass."

Grace hadn't given up on the idea she might be giving a certain someone a hand job that evening. Unfortunately, that someone was in a different location, and definitely not someone her friends would encourage her to consider.

"I mean hooking up with someone tonight. When's the last time you so much as kissed anyone other than . . . ?" Rather than say Josh's name, Tiff made a puke face.

Grace's brain drew a blank. Had it really been so long she literally couldn't remember life before Josh? They'd only been seeing each other for six months.

Camille and Tiff exchanged knowing looks.

"We have a saying in France," Camille began. "*Reculer pour mieux sauter*, which means to . . . *euh*, take a break before moving forward. I think maybe this vacation can be a break for you. To meet others, have some fun, nothing serious. After, you will be ready to move on."

"What if I'm not ready to move on?"

Grace hadn't meant to blurt that out. But there must have been a reason she couldn't remember anyone before Josh. Even without closing her eyes, she could imagine the exact feel, taste, and pressure of his mouth. She knew exactly where his lips hit when they kissed. Where his hands would go.

The idea of kissing someone new was . . . impossible. A new mouth could erase the memory of Josh and then she wouldn't be able to remember how he felt, tasted, and pressed. She sank down onto the bed, not knowing if she should say anything more.

"I just . . . I still love him," she admitted. She was still *in love* with him. "Josh was—"

"Aughhhhhhhhhh!"

Grace was cut off by the sound of Tiff making some sound previously unknown. When Grace went to talk, Tiff screamed out again.

"Aughhhhhhhhhh!"

Grace and Camille exchanged a *What in the fuckery is happening?* look.

"*Euh*, Tiffany, are you okay?" Camille asked hesitantly.

Tiff shook her head like a dog shaking off water. "Whew. Sorry about that. I was just trying to block out the name of this absolutely useless excuse of a person I have the misfortune of knowing."

Okay, so changing countries hadn't softened Tiff's stance on Josh.

Grace repeated it like a taunt in her head. *Josh, Josh, Josh, Josh*. "You're not going to do that the entire trip, are you?" she asked aloud.

"Try me."

"Jo—"

"Aughhhhhhhh!"

Grace clamped her hands over her ears. "Sheesh, okay, I get the message."

Tiff could be so fucking dramatic.

Tiff shook her head. "No longer good enough. As a penalty, you'll be taking two additional shots."

"Are you kidd—"

"And you'll spend the night as Carmen."

Now it was Grace's turn to shriek. "What? No! Not happening."

Camille's forehead scrunched in confusion as she scratched at her short hair. "Who is Carmen?"

"No one," Grace lied.

"Grace's slutty persona," Tiff explained. "A long time ago, Grace and I made these alter egos for each other."

At Camille's confused look, Tiff added, "An alter ego is like, an alternate personality. A different you. Carmen is this, like, sexy vixen bombshell who makes guys feel like she's always waiting for someone better to come along, so they're desperate to keep her attention. Carmen's mission is to find the best guy of the night and have sex with him."

"I'm not having sex with someone I just met!" Grace yelped.

Tiff rolled her eyes, adjusting herself in front of Grace's mirror. "How can you possibly still think only PIV counts as sex? What do you think lesbians do? Camille, tell her."

Camille still looked confused. "What is PIV?"

Tiff made the middle school motion of poking a finger in and out of a circle she made with the thumb and forefinger of her other hand.

"Yeah, okay, *I'm* the immature one here," Grace said. "You just want me to turn into you."

"Excuse me, I gave you a way better name than you gave me. Brooke? Really? Like a fucking stream? Pure, sweet, innocent Brooke." Tiff held her hands up like little paws in front of her, eyes mooning at Grace like the cartoon Puss in Boots (Antonio Banderas—another excellent accent!). "You know how they describe actual brooks in real life? Babbling. A babbling Brooke. Babbling!"

Camille looked mildly terrified. "Yes. Okay. I understand."

The chances of Camille knowing the word "babbling" seemed low, but Grace didn't want to dwell on it. The less that was said about those alter egos, the better. She'd mentioned it to Josh once but quickly reversed course, not wanting to start a conversation about each other's sexual history. Since Grace hadn't met Josh until this year, she didn't *have* to know who else he might have slept with at their school. Sometimes, ignorance really was bliss.

"And for *that*," Tiff announced, expertly pouring the tequila with one hand while balancing the silver tray of shot glasses with the other. "She'll be doing an extra shot."

"You already assigned me two extra!" Grace exclaimed.

"Three, then. Plus the three Camille and I are going to have. So six."

At the rate Tiff was assigning shots, Grace was more worried about getting alcohol poisoning than finessing her way to Josh's hotel. She needed to get her friends out of the house and into the club as soon as possible, where both Tiff and Camille could happily drink their way to oblivion.

Grace sighed. "Line 'em up."

Tiff peered at the label before pouring. "It should have notes of caramel and custard."

"Got it."

Grace drank her way down the line, one after the other in a steady beat. She was a fucking *soldier*. Josh had better appreciate all the shit she was going through just for him.

Grace's face was still screwed tight as the liquor burned a path down her throat when Tiff prompted a response. "Well?"

The experts weren't kidding. Tequila really *was* meant to be sipped slowly.

"Caramelly. Custardy," she choked out.

Tiff patted her on the shoulder. "Good job. Proud of you for fully committing tonight."

"This ego alter. I get one too, yes?" Camille asked.

"Camille, no," Grace warned. "You want nothing to do with this. Stay neutral."

Camille nodded somberly, pointing to her pants. "Neutral. Like black."

Grace laughed. It was so very Camille to think in terms of fashion.

"So we're doing this?" Tiff shrieked. "We're really doing it?" Every word out of Tiff's mouth always came with full intensity—it just rotated between passionate but angry, sarcasm that bordered on being real, and full-on wild 'n' out. Right now she was in wild 'n' out.

"Okay, okay," Grace conceded. "But we have to come up with a persona for her."

They inspected Camille as though she were an unwitting guest on a makeover show.

"Milf?" Grace suggested. "We could say she's our sugar mama or something."

Camille looked affronted. "You think people believe I am old enough to be your mother?"

"You *are* wearing leopard print," Grace sang under her breath.

"What about some kind of socialite?" Tiff offered. "You could just be mean to everyone, and they would accept it because you're French."

"How is that different from every other day?" Grace asked.

"My God," Camille muttered. "This is what you think of me? Old-looking and mean? Such good friends, thank you very much."

Grace playfully hit Camille on the arm. "Oh, stop. You know we're teasing. We're just trying to find something that's fun for you."

"I don't think it is fun to be old," Camille replied bitterly.

"What if we just pretend she's American?" Tiff suggested.

Grace shoved a shot into Camille's hand, determined to make her friends catch up to her. "What do you mean?"

"I mean, she just talks in an American accent all night and see if anyone notices anything weird."

Grace waited until Tiff finished speaking before thrusting a shot on her too.

Camille's hand paused on the neck of the soda-shaped bottle, ready to pour herself another. "American accent?" she asked, paling. "Like, *howdy, y'all.*"

"Oh my God, it's perfect," Grace squealed. "Camille, the Southern belle."

"Obviously, she needs a new name," Tiff said, downing her shot and pouring herself another one as the watermark on the bottle slowly sank farther and farther down.

Camille meekly raised her hand. "Do I get to vote? Because this seems difficult."

"No," they both answered her.

Tiff rolled her head around, stretching out her neck as she thought. "How about . . . Tilly?"

Grace squinted, rolling the name around in her head to try to get a feel for it. "Try saying it," she commanded Camille.

"Tilly?" Camille said, putting the emphasis on the second syllable like her own name. *Til-LEE.*

Grace turned back to Tiff. "Nope. What about something classic? Like Annabelle or Annabeth or any kind of double name? I feel like people from the South love that shit. Remember that girl Mary Elizabeth who moved from one of the Carolinas? She insisted everyone call her Mary Elizabeth because both of those were her first name?"

"I think if she's going to pull it off for the whole night, we should keep it simple," Tiff said. "Camille's not going to make it through the whole night repeating something like Clarabelle."

"Fuck it, let's just call her Georgia," Grace said, the alcohol beginning to work its magic in her body. "Then she can tell everyone she's from there."

Camille's eyes widened. "Where is Georgia? Not the country?"

Tiff brushed aside Camille's concern. "You don't need to know; half the people from *our* country don't. And they *definitely* don't know the country Georgia."

"There's a country called Georgia?" Grace asked.

Tiff looked at Camille like, *See?*

Grace shook it off. "Plus side: the silk blouse easily transfers!"

"Related: You know what *doesn't* transfer?" Tiff said. "Everything *you* packed."

Tiff rifled through the options in Grace's unpacked suitcase on the ground, pulling out one of Grace's favorite ruffled skirts—a two-tiered pale blue edged with lace. "I mean, really? The only way this could be slutty enough for Carmen is if you didn't wear underwear with it."

Grace hastily snatched the skirt out of Tiff's hands. "First of all, slutty is the *persona*—I don't actually have to *be* slutty."

"You're saying 'slutty' like it's a bad thing," Tiff said.

Camille frowned. "Is this word okay to use here? I thought slutty means—"

"We're reclaiming it," Tiff cut in.

Lovely. Just as Tiff had tried to do with "cunt," "whore," and for some reason, "floozy."

"Anyway," Grace said, before the entire conversation derailed into an English grammar lesson, "this skirt happens to get me a *lot* of attention in Santa Cruz. And I wear it *with* underwear, thank you very much."

Tiff looked unimpressed. "Only because everyone else on campus dresses like they're in a Nature Valley commercial."

"Says the girl who wears a hoodie and jeans to every single class."

"Why would I waste my good outfits just to sit at a desk for hours?"

Camille cleared her throat, and both Grace and Tiff turned to her. "This is not something Brooke wears?" It was a suggestion, not a question.

A slow smile stretched across Grace's face. If Tiff had to wear her clothes, that meant . . . "Hand over the banana dress," Grace said.

"This is the first time I'm even wearing it," Tiff whined.

She looked to Camille for support. "It cost eight hundred dollars!"

Camille looked unimpressed.

"Traitor," Tiff muttered, turning around so she could be unzipped out of it.

"You two remind me so much of my sister and me growing up." Camille laughed, pouring more shots as Tiff and Grace swapped outfits.

"You have a sister?" Grace's voice shot up like Camille had just confessed to a scandalous crime.

"Of course. Manon. I talk about her."

"You've literally never once mentioned her," Tiff said.

"Yeah, why are you so secretive?" Grace asked. "Are you like a spy or something?"

"Wasn't Mata Hari French?" Tiff wondered aloud.

When both Camille and Grace shot Tiff blank looks, she expanded. "Mata Hari? The spy who was executed for being a traitor during World War One? Or was she just *killed* by the French?"

"Why do you not major in history?" Camille asked.

"Seriously, you're too smart for your own good," Grace added. "Who remembers stuff like that?"

Tiff sighed as she pulled on the blue frilly skirt. "I'm cursed with this brain. But hey, at least I've never had to study for a test!"

"Maybe this is why you get migraines," Grace mused. "Your brain is too big."

"Unlike the rest of me," Tiff griped. She pulled on the chest part of Grace's blouse for effect. "How the hell do you expect my tiny boobs to fit in this? I look like a doll that would sit on some white grandma's shelf somewhere."

Camille covered her mouth to stifle a laugh, which didn't go unnoticed by Tiff. "Hey, Georgia, you're not showing very good Southern manners over there."

"How do people from Georgia say sorry but don't mean it?" she asked.

"They say 'bless your heart.'"

"Ah. Then, bless your heart." Camille made the sign of the cross in the air.

Grace fell down laughing, nearly knocking over the tequila tray. "You're not a priest!"

Tiff glared at her own reflection in the mirror, presenting different angles and disliking them all. "I can't go out like this," she complained. "I have a reputation to uphold!"

"You think you will see someone you know here? In Mexico?" Camille asked, still amused by Tiff's frustrations at getting dressed.

"Tiff knows *everyone*," Grace said with a roll of her eyes. "Or if she doesn't, she will by the end of this trip. You think she's bad about stopping to talk to everyone in Santa Cruz? She's so much worse on vacation."

Camille grinned. "But she cannot if she is in character, no?"

Grace shot Camille a look of appreciation as she attempted to stuff her curves into Tiff's teeny, tiny bondage dress. "You might be better at this than we are."

"*À ta santé*," Camille replied, toasting her with a shot.

"Roll tide," Grace replied, yanking down the hem and hoping for the best. With any luck, she wouldn't have to be in it for long.

"How the fuck do you look so hot in that and I look like—?" Tiff swept her hands down her body.

Grace looked in the mirror. Damn. She *did* look hot. Josh was going to lose his mind.

Camille gave Grace a thumbs-up before turning her attention back to Tiff, who was frowning at the ruffles as though they'd personally wronged her.

"I can fix this," Tiff declared confidently. "Did either of you pack safety pins?"

CHAPTER FIVE

*"Fact is, the law says you cannot touch.
But I think I see a lotta lawbreakers
up in this house tonight."*
—*Magic Mike* (2012)

On the way to the club, Grace began to doubt she could even make it through the entire night. The shots they'd taken back at the house had fully kicked in but had done nothing to help with her anxiety. Josh still hadn't texted her his address or whether he'd be home soon, and Grace wasn't sure how long she could survive in character as Carmen. Just the *idea* of flirting with someone other than Josh made Grace feel like she was cheating, even though she logically knew she wasn't.

"You know, we don't *have* to go out," Grace blurted as they approached the club, dragging her feet forward as slowly as possible. "Or play these parts."

Camille patted her gently, like Grace was a pet pig the farmer knew his family would one day turn into bacon. "You are nervous."

Grace nodded, her fingers vigorously rubbing her earlobe.

Tiff eyed Grace's hand's movements. "You have nothing to feel guilty about, babes. You're single."

Leave it to Tiff to understand what was bothering Grace.

"I know," Grace agreed wearily.

"And while *I* would obviously prefer you stick your tongue down some guy's throat tonight, I'm not going to force it on you, okay?"

"I know."

"Besides, you look straight fire right now. You deserve to be seen tonight."

"I *know*."

Tiff gave one hell of a pep talk, but sometimes Grace wished she'd just sympathize with her. But considering Tiff had never had an actual romantic relationship, that probably wasn't going to happen any time soon. Hell, the person Grace complained to the most about the breakup was . . . Josh. And weirdly, he *was* able to sympathize about it. He never made her feel guilty about feeling sad, or ignored her over the occasional "I miss you" text. He was supportive. Like she was entitled to her emotions, even if he couldn't help change them.

But this night wasn't about being sad. It was about taking back what was hers—reminding Josh that she was hot and amazing and that he missed her. It was about making him *want* to make time for her—realizing he never should have left her. Especially for Caity "I just prefer the taste of Perrier to regular water" Ruiz.

Grace straightened her shoulders, turning her back to the mass of neon lights from the clusters of nightclubs, and thrust her phone into Tiff's hands. "Take a picture of me. And make sure to get the background."

"Why do you never ask me?" Camille asked. "You always choose Tiffany, but she has short arms."

Grace shrugged an apology. "Sorry, but you always have to go with the Asian. I don't make the rules."

"It's true," Tiff chimed in from below, her legs already in a low squat to best capture the length of Grace's legs *and* a full background. "The best vacation photo you'll ever have is from some random old Asian guy with a camera around his neck. We're just willing to do what it takes to get the shot."

Tiff stood and handed the phone back to Grace, who immediately swiped through her choices. They were all good.

"Your legs look almost two meters long," Camille marveled.

Tiff shot her a smug look, daring Camille to question her photo-taking abilities again. When none came, she linked arms with each of her friends, pulling them back toward the entrance of one of the clubs.

Inside, Grace had expected pandemonium. She'd banked on it. But stepping into the club and seeing the sunken dance floor covered in foam, clusters of it floating through the air as partygoers flung their arms around, was a *lot.* It was less music and dancing than just . . . screaming drunk people rubbing up against each other in a pit of foam that was only sort of white. The entire place smelled like stale alcohol, sweat, and . . . an undefinable grossness.

On the plus side, it would be *very* easy to disappear.

"Get us some drinks," Tiff shouted over the music. "I need to go to the bathroom and adjust my cup. I think I put it in wrong." She shifted her body back and forth, as if the movement would get it into its proper place.

Grace briefly closed her eyes, never ceasing to be amazed by Tiff's bluntness. "You know, you could skip periods all together if you just got on the pill like a normal person. Think of how eco-friendly that is!"

"And pump my body full of who knows what kind of hormones for years on end, risking blood clots and death? Thanks for the offer, but I'll pass," Tiff replied, still awkwardly gyrating her lower body.

"What is she doing?" Camille asked with a jerk of her thumb.

"Tiff put her menstrual cup in wrong *again*," Grace said sweetly.

"I'm trying a new brand and still getting used to it, okay?" Tiff shot back.

Camille frowned. "You have your period? Right now?"

Tiff shrugged as if to say *And?*

"But you bring condoms," Camille said.

"Oh, Tiff just lets it bleed during sex." Grace was damn near gleeful at having something to poke fun at Tiff over, especially after having to weather all the Josh comments lately. "Even with strangers," she added.

Camille's eyes widened in shock.

Tiff wagged a finger in Camille's direction. "Don't you judge me, René Descartes. It's simple math: if I have to eliminate five days out of every month, on top of the days I feel like shit because of cramps and bloating, that's severely limiting my hookup window. Just put a towel down and get on with it."

"Literally," Camille managed to reply. Then she paused to add, "Or is it get it on?"

"You didn't need the correction, the joke was good as is," Grace reassured her.

Tiff rolled her eyes. "Who knew the French were such prudes?"

"We are not prudes. Some things are just disgusting."

"I love how even the way she pronounces 'disgusting' makes it sound so dainty." Grace laughed.

"Sorry. Dis-gust-*tang*," Camille tried again, this time using her "Southern" accent.

Tiff wasn't used to being ganged up on by Grace and Camille, and she huffed in frustration. "Whatever. Just get me something strong enough to knock out my cramps before this turns into a full-blown migraine." She stormed off toward the bathroom, elbowing her way through the crowd.

Camille scrunched her nose, taking in the rows and rows of liquor shelved behind the bartender's head. "What should we get? More tequila?"

Grace shook her head. If she drank any more shots, she'd never make it out of the club. She was already a bit wobbly as it was.

She pulled out her phone for a quick check. Nothing. Where was he? Suppressing a frustrated sigh, she refocused on Camille. "No way you're paying for your own drinks tonight. Come on, Miss Georgia, let's go try out that accent of yours."

Camille wasted no time choosing a target: a middle-aged man with light brown skin and graying hairs at his temples. He stood at the fringes of the dance floor, as though he wanted to join but was intimidated by the foam. Understandable. Grace *was* the target age for that, and she wanted nothing to do with it.

"Hiya there," Camille said loudly in her "Southern" accent as she and Grace approached.

The man gave a not-so-subtle look around, as if to make sure Camille wasn't speaking to anyone else.

Camille pasted on a smile so large it bordered on maniacal and repeated her greeting. "Hiya there. I'm Georgia, and this is Carmen. What's your name?" Camille pronounced each word so slowly, it was almost believable she could be from the South. Well, almost believable in this loud space where it was difficult to hear much of anything, anyway.

If the man suspected anything about Camille's odd accent, he didn't show it. "I'm Asa," he said, leaning in close. "Can I get you ladies a drink?"

Grace instinctively took a step back, not wanting him in her personal space. Maybe she was supposed to play the part of a vixen, but she certainly wasn't going to do it with this old man.

Camille beamed as though he'd just won the lottery and his prize was the honor of paying for them. "My friend and I will have . . ." She looked to Grace for help.

Grace waved her off. "Nothing for me, thanks."

Camille shot her a puzzled look before turning back to Asa. "Three boulevardiers," Camille said, remembering to flash a big smile at the end.

The look on Asa's face told Grace he didn't know what the hell it was either.

"Boulevardier," Camille repeated slowly, her fake accent disappearing in her French pronunciation. *Bou-le-var-dee-eh.* She made him repeat each syllable back to her like a small child, waiting until he got the right sound on "dier."

"The bartender will know," Camille said confidently.

Asa looked doubtful, but held up his fingers. "Three?"

"We have one friend in the bathroom," Camille said casually, which seemed to satisfy him as he set off toward the bar.

Once he was out of earshot, Camille sagged with relief. "My tongue is like wood, I cannot do this all night."

"It's so loud in here, I'm not sure that guy even noticed you had an accent," Grace said.

"Or he does not care because we are young and you are wearing very little," Camille replied, raising her eyebrows suggestively at the ample cleavage Grace was currently displaying.

Grace hadn't swapped clothes with Tiff in years, and right then she was remembering why. It was a miracle the dress even zipped up on her. God bless elastic.

"Why did you get me a drink?" she asked as Camille surveilled the foam pit. "I said I didn't want one."

Camille dismissed the complaint with a wave of her hand, not bothering to look back at Grace. "You will love this. Trust me."

Grace discreetly checked her phone again. Nothing.

What the hell was going on with Josh? She knew they hadn't necessarily agreed on meeting up, but he'd seemed pretty eager about the idea earlier. Had he changed his mind? Or had someone changed it *for* him?

Grace wrapped her arms around herself, trying very hard not to think about what Josh and Caity might be doing at that moment. Even the thought of him flirting with her made Grace want to puke.

Camille looked over her shoulder and bumped Grace with her hip. "Don't be sad. We are here to have fun; forget the past. This dress is very sexy," she said with a little shimmy, a sign that Camille was also feeling the shots they'd taken earlier. "You will be so good as Carmen in this."

Grace grimaced. She couldn't explain to Camille that she didn't want to be Carmen at all and it had nothing to do with the dress.

Okay, it had a little to do with the dress.

It wasn't just that she felt self-conscious about being so exposed around guys who weren't Josh, but that she wouldn't want to go flirt with anyone even if she were wearing her usual clothes. It just felt emotionally . . . uncomfortable.

Camille must have taken Grace's silence as sadness because she leaned closer and dropped the "rah rah" attitude. "I understand your heartbreak. Me? I am like this one whole year after my boyfriend breaks up with me. My parents send me to the doctor, they are so worried. A therapist."

It was nice of Camille to be confiding in Grace. But the only reason there was any sadness between Josh and Grace was because he was too stubborn to believe he could be a good boyfriend. He still loved her—it wasn't like she'd *really* lost him.

Still, she didn't want to seem rude. And she was partly curious.

"What did they say?"

Camille paused. "She say the same thing Tiffany and I tell you. It's okay to be sad for a little bit, but you must move forward. You cannot stop life for one person."

Couldn't she though? It was the basis of basically every romantic movie ever. And a tiny part of Grace acknowledged that it was *exactly* what she was hoping for with Josh. She would never want him to give up on his dreams of filmmaking, but shouldn't it at least be a consideration for him? If he truly had to choose?

Of course, he didn't actually have to choose, which is what made his decision all the more frustrating. He'd been managing school and Grace perfectly fine, and she was doing everything in her power to show him just that—that she *could* fit neatly into his life without making it more work. Lovable idiot boy.

Camille gave Grace's shoulders a squeeze. "You are doing your best."

Thankfully, Asa returned and Grace downed her drink to squelch her guilt. Camille was pouring her heart out to console her, and all the while, Grace was planning to get her friends drunk enough to ditch them.

She grabbed Tiff's drink and downed that too. If she couldn't think, she couldn't torture herself.

Camille tried to remain polite, sipping her drink while skewering Grace with a *What the fuck?* look. Asa, on the other hand, didn't hide his disturbed expression.

Camille smiled at Asa and lifted her cup in a toast.

"*Salud*," he said, clinking his glass against hers.

"Roll tide," she replied.

Grace made a noise somewhere between a snort and a cough, which escalated into a full choking fit. Camille shot her a face that made it clear she had no idea what the expression meant.

Tiff appeared out of nowhere from behind a normal-sized person, and Grace thought for a split second that it had been magic. Though that might have also had something to do with the fact that she no longer found the music too loud or the smell too overpowering. She wasn't even sure she could feel her face anymore.

"Where the hell is my drink?" Tiff demanded.

"This is Brooke. Our shy friend," Grace said sweetly to Asa, her fingers prodding her own cheeks for proof of life.

Tiff had the decency to look at least a little ashamed for stepping so far out of character.

"Howdy, friend," Camille drawled, at which point Tiff was unable to school her features from showing exactly what she thought of Camille's "Southern" accent. Grace had to pull her away before she burst out laughing.

"Going to dance, BRB," she called, dragging Tiff behind her. Grace felt bad about leaving Camille to fend for herself with Asa, but he hadn't given off any major red flags. Camille was a big girl; she'd be fine.

"What the fuck is that accent?" Tiff gasped as she tripped down the stairs into the foam pit, dragging Grace with her.

Great. Now Grace would have to leave in a *wet* dress.

"How is that man listening to her and acting like nothing is wrong?" Tiff cackled. "And is he here *alone*?"

The good news was that Tiff was also pretty drunk. She'd fought valiantly against it, but alcohol tolerance couldn't make up for her size.

"I think Camille is just trying to get another round of drinks before she ditches," Grace said, careful to brush away the bits of foam that were too close to her face. Tiff, on the other hand, already looked like she'd walked through a bubble bath tornado.

Next to them, a guy leaned in, his voice sarcastic. "Surprise, surprise, dressed-up girls plotting to use men for free drinks."

Tiff shot him a look of death. "You fucking *wish* someone would use you."

"Easy, *Brooke*," Grace warned, trying to keep Tiff from flying off the handle. She would not let one asshole ruin all her carefully constructed plans.

"Yeah, *Brooke*, my feelings are hurt. But I know how you

can make it up to me." His smirk made it obvious he hadn't been told no enough in his life because suddenly Tiff slapped at something in the foam.

"What the fuck?" she bellowed.

"It's a foam party. That's why you wore a skirt here, isn't it?"

"You're a pig," Tiff spat, dragging Grace deeper into the middle of the pit and glaring at every passing guy like suspects in a lineup. "This place is a fucking nightmare."

Of course that guy had been a disgusting asshole, but Grace couldn't afford to have Tiff sour on the place. She needed her happy and distracted.

"He had a point about the foam," Grace started.

Tiff's eyes were belligerent. "That I deserve to be *assaulted* by wearing a skirt?"

"Jesus Christ, no. What the fuck?"

Tiff wasn't just drunk—she'd tipped over into aggro-land. Grace needed to redirect Tiff's intensity elsewhere if she was going to have any hope of escaping.

"I'm saying you *did* come here to hook up." Grace lifted a foam-covered hand and wiggled her fingers. "Remember? No rings?"

Tiff rolled her shoulders, her bad mood visibly shedding like a snake wiggling out of its molted skin. "Okay, yeah. You're right," she said, shifting back into determined flirt mode. "I just need to find someone who's not a total creep."

"Exactly. That's the spirit!"

Tiff scanned the crowd, her eyes settling on a tall guy a few feet away. "There." She pointed. "I'm going to go climb that guy like a tree."

Tiff waded away toward her new target, leaving Grace in the middle of a foam pit, alone, with no one watching her.

CHAPTER SIX

"Our lives are defined by opportunities,
even the ones we miss."
—The Curious Case of Benjamin Button (2008)

Grace staggered out of the club, the sounds of music from the early 2000s following her outside. Fishing out her phone, she excitedly turned it over in her hands.

No messages.

She stuffed it back into her cleavage with a huff.

She immediately pulled it back out, just to check that it was getting a signal. When it was clear that, yes, it was working fine, she sadly tucked it away again and sank down onto the edge of the curb. All that planning, all those drinks, and she'd escaped for nothing. There was nowhere to go.

She burped once, the alcohol burning its way back up her esophagus. Just another reminder of how she hadn't been drinking as often this past semester because she'd been with Josh.

"Shit, that hurts." Grace ground the heel of her hand into her breastbone. Well, tried to, anyway. Instead, her hand hit the rigid outline of her phone.

An idea sparked. Quickly scrolling through the pictures Tiff had taken of her earlier, Grace chose the best one and sent it off to Josh.

Grace: not feeling like myself tonight

Grace: as you can see

Grace: anyway, lmk if you get off work early

Maybe the alcohol had made her overconfident, but if that didn't get Josh texting her back, nothing would. Even though this dress was very much *not* her style, she looked amazing. Especially in a more conventional, societally acceptable way—not a single curve was hidden in this thing.

"If he wants to see you that badly, he should be here in person," a voice behind her rumbled.

Grace peeked up to find a *very* attractive face looking at her phone, his dark brows raised with a cocky smile and a dimple. Fuck. That dimple really did things to her insides.

Grace tipped the phone toward her chest to shield the screen, noting the way his eyes followed it. A flush of embarrassment crept up her décolletage (but seriously, what else was it called?). "Didn't your mom ever teach you it was rude to read other people's messages?"

"My mom loves being up in everyone's business. But my dad would probably be against it."

He was in a tight black T-shirt, with hints of a tattoo peeking out and a gold chain around his thick neck. From the look of his features, he was definitely some kind of Asian mix, but his dark complexion and wavy black hair made it clear he was not *her* combination of Taiwanese and white.

"So, which one's the Asian one? The nosy one?" Grace asked.

The guy chuckled. "Mixed kids can always spot other mixed kids, huh? Taiwanese mom, Mexican dad," he declared, dropping himself down to sit beside her on the curb.

"No way! I'm Taiwanese too."

His eyebrows shot up at the coincidence, and Grace knew he must not encounter a lot of Taiwanese people either. It *was* only an island, after all.

"We could start a club," he said.

Grace laughed. "I should warn you, I don't drink boba."

"Me neither," he admitted.

"And I've never been to Taiwan."

"Me neither."

Grace couldn't stop a small smile from forming. "Looks like our club is off to a rough start. Might need to put in a call to my mom for some ideas."

"Only child, huh?"

Grace was surprised. "How did you know?"

"It's a gift," he said with a smirk. He leaned back on his hands, his shirt magnificently highlighting the broad chest beneath it. Grace immediately decided that plain black T-shirts were now her new favorite item of clothing.

"I take it you're not?" she asked.

"Ha! I have four older sisters and zero brothers. Just straight estrogen all the time." He pretended to be upset about it, but it was clear he enjoyed talking about his family. He pointed somewhere to the right. "There's an island called Isla Mujeres over there, which means 'island of the women.' That's how my house is—just an island of women."

"That sounds devastating for you," Grace murmured with mock sympathy. "You probably have no idea what to do with so many women around."

"Hm. I think it's the exact opposite. I have so much experience, I *always* know what to do." The guy flicked his eyes down her body a second before shooting her another one of his devastating smirks, and Grace was fairly certain her vagina straight up fainted.

This guy wasn't just hot—he was *movie star* hot. *People would buy posters of him and print his face on T-shirts* hot.

Grace knew she looked good, but *this* good? He could be aiming that dimple anywhere he wanted, yet here he was. Was it the dress? Or the novelty of a mixed Asian girl, especially one with the same background? Was it still considered a fetish if the guy was also mixed?

Either way, Grace pretended his comment hadn't sent very NSFW thoughts through her brain. She mirrored his pose, leaning back on her arms and slowly stretching out her legs as she dropped her head back as if she were in a perfume ad. She watched as his eyes traveled the length of her, pausing only to observe the elastic hemline of her dress creeping up her thighs, before making their way up and over her chest to the curve of her neck.

A tiny rush went through her and for a moment, she wanted to play the part of Carmen. She wanted to flirt for real—to see where else she could get his eyes to follow. Would he be the kind of guy to make the first move, or would he wait for a more obvious invitation? His eyes said he was definitely interested.

Just staring at him, Grace could already imagine herself making out with him. He was the kind of guy she wouldn't even care about being seen making out with. He was the gold coin in a video game—open to being claimed, or wasted if she didn't.

An opportunity.

Her phone buzzed, yanking aside the heavy curtain of drunkenness and pulling her back to reality. She was stretched out across a dirty sidewalk, contemplating kissing some guy she'd met five minutes before. Grace scrambled to her feet and checked her phone. Josh had finally texted her his address. She tugged down the hemline of her dress, causing her to stumble a little over her heels, and adjusted her bangs as an excuse to avoid making direct eye contact.

"It's been real, but I need to go."

He raised an eyebrow. "'It's been real'?"

Okay. She could have been smoother. More proof she hadn't really been flirting—it had just been the alcohol talking. And pheromones. (That was a thing, right? Samuel L. Jackson and his snakes wouldn't lie.)

"It's been fake?" she suggested.

He took a step toward her, and Grace found herself swaying toward him like a magnet. "Has it?" he asked, his voice seemingly deeper than it was a moment ago. "Been fake?"

"Um. I don't know?"

That was the truth, at least. She didn't seem to know much of anything right now.

He took another step closer, slowly gaining on her like a large cat ready to pounce. "I could buy you a drink and find out."

Jaguar. Panther. Leopard.

Grace rattled through as many big cats as she could think of, trying desperately to keep her composure in the face of someone who looked like he could easily devour her.

"I thought American Asians were cheap. It's the international ones that have all the money," she replied faintly, half in a daze from his proximity. He smelled like . . . guy sweat. But the sexy kind of sweat, like the kind you'd lick off. She stared at the base of his neck, a patch of smooth brown skin beneath his necklace. Grace had the impulsive desire to tuck her hands under his shirt and run her palms down his chest, just to see if it was as soft as his T-shirt looked. This was a boy who moisturized.

"Lucky for you I was born here," he replied, now standing so close she could feel the body heat coming off him.

She shivered, imagining that heat wrapped around her as she inhaled more of his scent.

"I think that counts as international, don't you?" His mouth curved up into a half smile, his dimple barely starting to form.

His voice was mesmerizing, like a hypnotist's. Her eyes were locked on his lips, wondering how they would taste. They were good lips. She hadn't spent a whole lot of time inspecting guys' lips before, but these . . . these were good. Full. A dark pink. And currently parted just a fraction, as if inviting her in.

She should step away. She should definitely step away.

She just . . . couldn't.

Her breath was shallow, chest heaving up and down as though she'd been running. Her breath had to be hideous after all that spiced whiskey (and burping), but she seemed unable to give herself any kind of distance.

Had it been like this when she'd first kissed Josh? Had she

felt this kind of electricity crackling through her veins? Right now, Grace was vibrating with anticipation (though a tiny part of her brain reminded her that she was, in fact, wet, and could simply be shivering). Either way, she hadn't felt it until he'd gotten this close to her. He was so close now that their lungs seemed to expand in tandem, not enough space for them to both inhale or exhale at the same time. A game of limbo where she'd either scrape under the bar or knock the whole damn thing off.

"Carrrmennn!" Tiff's voice screeched like a parrot in a jungle, cutting through the music still pouring out of the club and the noise of the cars driving by.

That broke the spell.

Grace quickly stepped away from the black hole she'd nearly been sucked into, a momentary twinge of regret at the interruption. Her body visibly shivered from the loss of his body heat, but it served as a reminder that she'd come to Cancún for Josh. Not mystery hot guys who seemed to have their own orbit.

Fuck. Josh. Now she'd never be able to get away.

"Oh shit, was I interrupting something?" Tiff clapped one hand over her mouth, her other hand clutching Camille's arm for balance. Tiff still had foam in her hair, and Camille's legs were covered with it. They looked like they'd just climbed out of a bubble bath together.

"I think they were about to kiss," Camille loudly chimed in, her terrible "Southern" accent fading into her natural French one to make an intolerable mashup of sounds.

"You guys are smashed," Grace remarked, now fully recovered and a safe distance from the hot guy. She may have been a bit drunk herself, but from the looks of it, nowhere near the level of her friends.

"We had shots," Tiff admitted. "Lots of shots. And a *tiny* bit of fingering." She pressed her thumb and forefinger over one eye, squinting through it like it was a magnifying glass.

Grace smirked, happy to note that she wasn't the only one who hadn't played to character tonight. "So much for the good-girl routine, huh?"

"I wasn't cut out for this life," Tiff declared, flinging an arm out and hitting Camille across the chest.

"Ow! Heaven to Betty, you need to go home before you knock over another table."

Grace ignored Camille's attempt to inject more Southern jargon into her speech (as well as asking where the hell she'd learned that phrase). "*Another* table?"

"They ask us to leave," Camille admitted with a sleepy nod, finally dropping the accent all together.

Grace covered her face. "Jesus Christ."

"—is king!" Tiff shouted, making a giant sign of the cross in the air. "He knows what I'm talking about." She gestured to the guy Grace was still standing next to. "I can spot a fellow Catholic from a mile away."

"Please ignore her, she's beyond help," Grace told him.

"But somehow, Jesus loves her all the same." He grinned, fishing his necklace out from beneath his shirt to reveal a small gold cross hanging from it.

Tiff crowed her victory. "I knew it! Your face has 'confession' written all over it."

Grace groaned, dropping her head down in defeat. "Just my luck. A good ol' Christian boy. I am reliving freshman year all over again."

"What happened freshman year?" he asked, clearly entertained by the show Grace and her friends were putting on.

He'd relaxed his stance and folded his arms across his chest, which only highlighted the size of them.

"She fell in love with a boy who only wanted to save her soul," Tiff called out, not seeming to care that she was involving the entire crowd outside the club in their conversation. "He brought her to church on a date!"

"Oh my God," Camille muttered. "No wonder you think Josh is a good boyfriend."

"We should go," Grace said quickly, tearing her eyes away from the hot guy's biceps and moving toward the street to hail a taxi. Once Tiff got started spilling secrets, there was no stopping her. Grace might not have played the part of Carmen that night, but she still wanted to end the whole thing with at least a little bit of her dignity intact.

"In a hurry to get back to your boyfriend? Show him the dress he's missing?" He shot a glance at the phone still clutched in her hand and raised his eyebrows, challenging her to deny it.

"It's a long story," she said hesitantly. *And one that doesn't need to be explained to a stranger*, she reminded herself.

Grace shoved Tiff, then Camille, into the taxi. Each collapsed in a fit of giggles as Tiff continued to call out details about Grace's life she'd rather not share.

"Ask her about putting her legs behind her head!" Tiff yelled, her body splayed out across the seat (and Camille) to inch her way toward the open taxi door.

Grace squeezed her eyes shut, quickly thanking the universe that she'd never have to see this guy again. "Well. It's been real." (Why was that her go-to phrase?) "Again."

He held his hand out for a handshake, which seemed odd, but she took it anyway. He pulled, and her body crashed squarely into his. Without a moment of hesitation, his lips descended onto hers, their hands pressed together between their bodies like the last line of defense. He tasted warm and delicious and better than she'd imagined. She opened her lips, and his kiss deepened, his free hand pulling her even closer as he skated his fingers up the nape of her neck and into the base of her hair.

Then, in the blink of an eye, she'd been twirled back to where she started. No warmth, no lips, no hands to hold up her head, which now felt impossibly heavy.

"I'm Daniel, by the way."

Grace could only blink, staring in awe at the guy who'd just broken her Josh drought. No, *obliterated* her drought. An entire water tower's worth flooding the area, drowning the mere memory of her drought.

After a moment of hesitation, she said, "Carmen," then got into the taxi and drove away.

CHAPTER SEVEN

"All right, Mr. DeMille, I'm ready for my close-up."
—Sunset Boulevard (1950)

Grace was forced to wait until they'd gotten back home and into bed before she could text Josh and let him know she wouldn't be coming over. He'd been disappointed, of course, which, on one hand, his wanting to see her meant that her sending him pictures was working. On the other hand, she didn't like the idea of getting him worked up and then *not* being available. What if those hormones got directed elsewhere? She hadn't seen cozy pictures of him with Caity on his social media, but that guaranteed nothing.

The other problem was Daniel, whose lips she'd gone to sleep imagining.

Just a random guy, in a random moment, but that kiss had erased Grace's memory of Josh's kisses, and now, the next morning, she was panicked, wondering if she was cursed to remember one insignificant (but fucking incredible) kiss forever. She needed to see Josh.

She shot off a text, asking for the next time he was free, then headed downstairs to assess the situation. Grace was the first one awake—which shouldn't have been a surprise considering the state her friends were in the previous night—but not for long.

"Where's my mocha?" Grace joked as Camille dragged herself into the kitchen, her short hair standing on end and pillow creases still lining her face. She looked even paler than usual, the hangover leeching any semblance of color from her skin.

"My head is like a brick," she moaned. "Why do they love tequila so much here?"

"I think that was all the whiskey in your fancy drink, babes," Tiff croaked, dumping a handful of rings onto the table with a loud clatter and a wince. "Either that or the shots of mezcal."

Grace set out plates of reheated leftovers for each of them, trying not to gag at the thought of actually eating. "What shots of mezcal?"

"Oh, right. You were outside with that hottie. I forgot to ask, what happened there? Everything got a little blurry at the end."

A faint blush stole across Grace's cheeks as the memory of his kiss replayed in her brain. "Nothing, just talked for a minute."

Tiff eyed Grace as she put each ring back on its rightful finger. "*Just* talked? Couldn't be me. I would've climbed that boy like a tree."

"So you've mentioned," Grace replied. "Several times."

"Really? Hm. I don't remember that."

"I think I am better with no breakfast." Camille groaned, covering her mouth and pushing a plate of reheated rice and beans away from her as she rushed out of the kitchen.

Grace frowned. "Should we be worried about her?"

Tiff put on the last of her rings. "I don't have the energy to take care of anyone but myself right now. She'll be fine—she started drinking when she was twelve. The French know how to handle it."

"Yeah, but usually she just sticks to wine. I don't think they binge drink like this in Europe."

"What about England?" Tiff's voice was dull and lifeless, like she'd rather be doing anything but having this conversation, yet was still determined to win it.

"Okay, except England," Grace conceded.

"And Ireland?"

"Fine! I give up. I know nothing about Europe. Are you happy now?"

Tiff dragged a chair closer so she could prop her feet on it, folding her hands across her stomach. "Yes."

"You're intolerable," Grace said. "Don't you have a migraine right now?"

Tiff dramatically flung an arm across her eyes, letting her head fall back onto the chair. "Yes! And this house is fucking ninety-five percent windows. Haven't these people heard of shades?"

"Says the girl who literally dropped an entire store's worth of metal onto a glass table," Grace muttered, her ears still ringing from the noise of it.

"I'm sorry my sickness isn't quiet enough for you," Tiff snapped.

So they were all in a mood.

In situations like this, Grace found it best to take one of two approaches: diffuse or escape. Even through the throbbing of her head, she realized there was an opportunity for both. The invisible lightbulb above her head clicked on.

"Why don't you go back to bed?" Grace asked, careful to frame it as a casual suggestion. Tiff didn't like being babied until she was sick enough to decide she *did* need it, at which time Grace needed to drop everything and help her. It was a delicate balance.

"We're supposed to be on vacation," Tiff whined. "I don't want to spend it sleeping."

"But you're not feeling well. Why don't you and Camille lie down for a little bit? I'll go get you guys some medicine, and we'll decide what to do after that," Grace suggested, her voice now steady and gentle. Like coaxing a scared animal out of its hiding place.

Tiff whimpered, kneading her knuckled into her temples. "You'd do that?"

Grace felt a gust of relief. Tiff was going for it. Grace's idea would work. She'd be able to make up for the previous night's no-show.

She stood and gave Tiff a hug, pulling her to her feet. "Come on. Let's get you into bed with your eye mask so the light doesn't bother you. I'll be back in a flash."

Tiff wrapped her arms around Grace's waist, squeezing her tightly. "You're such a good friend."

Grace swallowed the lump in her throat.

At least I used to be.

Once Tiff and Camille were safely tucked back into bed, Grace got ready as quickly and as quietly as possible. Josh had only a small window of time available today and she wasn't about to miss it. As it was, she was just happy he had responded promptly to her message this time. And she was fully prepared to reward him for it.

Finding her way to the bus was easy enough—Cancún geography was practically dummy-proof, even for someone with Grace's sense of direction. But she was so nervous about making sure she didn't miss her stop that she couldn't use her phone to distract her during the ride. Instead, she watched the scenery fly by, still trying to re-create the feel of Josh. It had only been a couple of days—how had she already forgotten what he *felt* like? Was he as warm as Daniel had been? Did his mouth feel as soft?

It wasn't the only reason she was rushing over to see Josh, of course. She missed him. Tiff was her best friend, but Josh had been her go-to person lately when she was upset. Or, at least, he usually was. Grace wasn't about to discuss her inability to stop viscerally flashing back to the night before with the person she was trying to win back.

Tiff, on the other hand, would be more than happy to hear Grace discuss exactly that, but nothing was as simple as

Tiff ever made it out to be. She couldn't understand the guilt Grace had over kissing Daniel at all, or that the guilt was just one more lie she had to layer on top of the ones she was already telling.

When she arrived at the hotel, Grace rode the elevator up to Josh's floor with a stomach full of butterflies. What if the spark they'd had was somehow extinguished by her (and possibly his) betrayal? Would he sense that she'd lied about not following him to Mexico? How could she possibly relax and enjoy her time with Josh, all the while knowing in the back of her mind that she still had to get back to her friends afterward?

He invited you, she reminded herself. He wanted to see her. It was everything she'd come for.

The moment Josh opened the door, Grace's nerves evaporated, and she fell into his arms. Nuzzling her face in the space under his jaw, feeling the roughness of his scruff against her skin, she couldn't believe she'd ever forgotten this. It was home.

Grace inhaled deeply with closed eyes, making sure she didn't forget this feeling again.

Josh gently petted her hair, one hand around her waist and the other on the back of her head. "Everything okay?"

She could feel emotion welling up, and she fought to keep it at bay. She'd risked too much to lose Josh over this. Conversations like the one she'd had in her head on the way over were exactly the thing Josh couldn't take on at the moment. This was supposed to be a simple visit, just to make sure *he* didn't forget what *she* felt like.

Grace separated herself and put on a dazzling smile. "It's almost lunchtime, but I'm guessing you didn't invite me over here to eat," she said saucily.

Instead of reacting the way she thought he would, Josh frowned. "Grace, talk to me. What's wrong?"

"Nothing's wrong," she lied, even more determined now to keep things ultra positive. Josh looked tired as it was, his thin face even more gaunt than usual and his energy low.

She pushed past him into the room, taking in the two queens (one visibly unused), the bathroom (only his usual toiletries), and the desk (always weirdly looking straight into a mirror). A completely regular hotel room.

She exhaled the breath she didn't realize she was still holding.

"Homey," she joked, kicking off her shoes and positioning herself atop the unused bed. Part of her was tempted to sit on his bed so she could get more of his familiar smell around her, but the bed that was made-up was better for her, aesthetics wise.

Josh let the door close behind him as he approached the bed, his mouth curved up in appreciation. "This is a very different dress from the one you showed me last night."

Grace gave herself a once-over—the baby-doll dress fitted across the bust but flared out over the hips. Her legs looked a mile long. "Is that a problem?" she asked.

"It's a problem that other people got to see you in it and I didn't."

He pressed his mouth to her, and Grace kissed him as vigorously as she dared, slowly pulling him onto the bed with her. She needed to consume him so that she'd never be without him. She needed to memorize every detail—to imprint his body on hers just to prove this connection between them still existed. She needed him to feel her love, but without all the yearning behind it.

He broke the kiss, and Grace scooted up toward the

headboard, forcing him to follow. "You get to see me naked, if that helps," she offered.

The way his eyes lit up—*that* was what Grace had come for—to see his eyes spark like that. It reassured her that she was still essential to him. To his well-being.

He sat back on his heels, eagerly taking her in. "It helps."

"I hope you weren't too lonely last night," she teased, pulling her dress off over her head. Josh's eyes were saucers now, taking in the soft baby-pink bra and underwear set as she hooked her leg over his shoulder.

"Is this new?" he asked, rubbing a hand along the outside of her calf.

Her chest twinged.

She'd worn it on Valentine's Day. It would be ridiculous to expect him to chronicle every time they'd had sex, but she was still disappointed he didn't recognize it. She had thought it was a pretty memorable night.

But Grace refused to let her face show it. "Maybe," she said teasingly.

Josh's hand stilled, his face losing all humor. "You didn't wear this for someone else, did you?"

"What?!" The thought of Josh getting jealous was both funny and incomprehensible.

But Josh was serious. "Did you?"

Grace slide her leg down to the bed. "Josh, I bought these for *you*. I wore them on Valentine's Day." Grace swallowed a lump in her throat when mentioning the holiday, but at least her voice didn't waver.

He relaxed and blew out a sigh of relief. "Of course. Valentine's Day." He stretched his arms out, going straight for her boobs.

"You know, there's a way you can stay up to date on my inventory," she said pointedly, lacing her fingers with his and pulling them above her head so that his body was stretched out over hers.

"How's that?" he asked.

Grace brought a finger to her chin as his mouth trailed along the side of her neck. "Hm, what would you call someone you see in underwear often enough to know if she's bought anything new?"

Josh's head snapped up. "Grateful?"

His wolfish grain told Grace he *knew* he was dodging her question, but his response had been so good she couldn't challenge it.

"Okay, how about this?" Grace was glad she didn't have to look at Josh while she said the next part. He probably felt her heart race as she gathered up her courage. "Are you seeing anyone else in their underwear?" she asked casually.

Easy. Breezy. Beautiful.

Grace was the Cover Girl of nonchalance.

"You know I wouldn't do that to you," he said, still hovering over her.

She didn't know that, obviously. The main feature of breaking up was *not* having to pledge fidelity.

"Not even Caity?" Grace had to press her lips together to keep from following it with "'The soy sauce we get in the States isn't even real soy sauce' Ruiz" in her mock Caity voice. Josh thought it was cruel for Grace to make those kinds of jokes about Caity.

Cruel. Like Grace was the fucking villain here.

"You see her every day now, don't you?" Her voice strained to stay casual. "Who's she staying with?"

Josh sat back on his knees again, frowning. "Do you think I'm lying to you?"

"No, jeez, it was just a question." Grace was a little annoyed he was making such a big deal over a tiny question she thought she was more than entitled to ask. He *did* just fly to a foreign country with the person in question after she was in his *bedroom* in the dead of night.

It was clear he wasn't buying it. "It's not *just* a question, Grace. I can tell you don't believe me. What do you want? A blood oath?"

Grace needed to get this rendezvous back under control. The last thing she wanted to do was upset Josh and spend her precious minutes arguing with him.

"I'm sorry," she apologized, reaching for him, but he stayed out of reach.

"I know you're frustrated with our situation," he said. His face and tone were sympathetic. "But we've been over this. It's not fair to you to make promises I can't keep. I'd rather be a good . . . whatever this is," he said, gesturing between the two of them, "than a shitty boyfriend. You deserve better than that."

"You're not going to be a shitty boyfriend." Grace propped herself up onto her elbows so she wasn't trying to argue from a lying-down position. She already felt like she was at enough of a disadvantage. "How is being a boyfriend any more of a demand than what we're doing right now?"

He ran his fingers through his hair, the tortured artist on full display. "Grace, I can't do this with you right now. I'm not trying to be a jerk, but I have the film and my dad and my summer project and I just . . . I'm already being pulled in a million different directions. You know how I feel about you. Can't that be enough?"

God, she wanted it to be.

Josh was right—he was being up front about what he could offer, and it was her own fault she kept hoping he'd change his mind. He wasn't there yet. But he also hadn't stopped having feelings for her.

The spark of hope inside her stayed lit.

"Remind me how you feel," she said with a sly smile, stretching out, giving him a full display of just what he was *not* committing to.

His eyes brightened back to their full hazel glory, the soft browns overtaking the green, as he ran his hands back up her torso. "I'm happy to demonstrate."

When it was all over, Josh rolled off her and headed into the bathroom to clean up, tossing her a small towel so she could do the same. He averted his eyes while she mopped up, and Grace belatedly wondered why she hadn't asked him to use a condom.

It hadn't mattered before, of course. She had already been on the pill and he said he'd tested early on, so they eventually stopped doubling up. But that was before he'd broken up with her and gone to Cancún with Caity "I have a photographic memory, so going off book is a snap" Ruiz.

Grace cleared her throat nervously as she gathered up her clothes. "We should probably start using condoms again. You know, just in case."

Josh shot her a sharp look, pulling a black T-shirt over his head. "Just in case what? I already told you I'm not sleeping with anyone else."

"Still," she said. "Condom-free is for boyfriends."

Josh shook his head, the rest of his clothes on before Grace had even had the chance to fasten her bra. "Fine. Punish me. I deserve it."

He did deserve it.

"It's not a punishment," Grace said, still struggling to get the clasp hooked behind her back. Her fingers were probably just a little shaky, her body still keyed up after their sex. She didn't expect orgasms and fireworks every time, but today had felt rushed, like he was in a hurry to get through it instead of enjoying the little time they had together. "I'm just trying to do what's right for me."

Without needing to be asked, Josh crossed the room and hooked her bra, dropping a kiss onto her bare shoulder. "I know you are," he said softly. "We both are. I just wish we didn't have to hurt each other in the process."

Privately, Grace didn't think him refusing to be her boyfriend, thereby impacting her entire present *and* future, was quite on the same level as her making him wear condoms, but she didn't want to start yet another argument.

"Maybe next time we'll make sure the hurt is consensual," she joked, strapping up her shoes.

Josh frowned as he turned her dress right side out for her. "I don't *want* to hurt you."

"I was kidding. You know? Like, *hurt*?" Grace swatted at his butt and missed, instead getting mostly his lower back.

Josh made a face. "Ow. I know some people are into that kind of stuff, but you're not, are you? Like, you want me to *hit* you during sex?"

He looked and sounded like she'd asked him to personally skin 101 puppies to make her a coat.

"It was a joke. Just forget it," she huffed, finishing up her shoes and pulling on her dress.

"Not really something people joke about," he muttered back. "I don't think it would look good for me if you show up at home with a bunch of bruises."

Right. Home. With her friends who had no idea she was seeing Josh at all.

The queasy feeling she'd had on the way over made a reappearance. But she managed to walk with him to the elevator, the ride down silent except the beep that signaled each floor they passed.

"I'm glad I got to see you," she said finally as they emerged back into the blazing sun.

"Me too," he said, pulling her in for another hug. "Am I going to see you again while you're here?"

She forced herself to pause instead of blurting out *yes*. "Will you have time?" She didn't want to get her hopes up for nothing.

"If I have anything to say about it," he said, pressing a kiss to the top of her head.

That sounded promising.

"Let me know," she said, tilting her face up for a real kiss. She wasn't going to let the visit end like this.

Josh obliged, and Grace squeezed her eyes shut again, certain she'd remember it this time.

CHAPTER EIGHT

"We could not talk or talk forever and still find things to not talk about."
***—Best in Show* (2000)**

Grace's ride home was quite a different experience than the ride there. She felt even more confused, her body newly sore. Seeing Josh was nourishing to her soul—feeling his body on hers like a weighted blanket had soothed her anxiety. But then there had been the rest of it.

He seemed jealous at the idea of her being with someone else. But when she lobbed it right back at him, he'd seemed annoyed that she even asked. He was especially touchy about Caity, like the idea was inconceivable. Granted, Grace probably should have brought up the condom conversation *before* asking about Caity so the two didn't seem directly related, but it wasn't an unreasonable request.

Then there had been the weirdness about what he thought was a request to hit her. First of all, it was a funny joke. She didn't appreciate having to explain it, thereby making it automatically less funny. But also, she'd never expected someone to react so negatively to something as tame as *spanking*. Maybe it was Tiff's influence, but very little shocked Grace when it came to sexual preferences, even if she'd never personally experienced them.

The reminder of her friends tightened the knot in her stomach, knowing she had to go back and pretend everything was fine and that she hadn't just had very confusing sex with her ex. How was it that he could make her feel both better and worse at the same time? Sure, he'd been glad to see her, and he'd all but promised he'd make time for her while she was in Cancún, but why had it taken her physically showing up for him to do it? He hadn't so much as texted her after he'd arrived, before he knew she was already there.

Then there was the sex itself. It was fine. Nice, even. But it lacked . . . sizzle. Maybe because her feelings were still a mess, but she hadn't felt the same connection between them that she normally did. He was gentle and loving and said all the right things, but without knowing where they stood, it had felt more like she was clinging to a rope he'd offered instead of the two of them weaving something together. That is, if she was going to get all poetic and gushy about it.

She made a quick stop at a pharmacy, picking up everything that seemed tangentially useful. Her Spanish wasn't really to the level of reading pharmaceutical labels, but *something* in the bag had to be of use. The fact that she'd used her own money helped ease her guilt just a fraction.

Taking a deep breath in front of the door and pasting on a cheerful face, she came in singing. "I'm ho-ome!"

Camille was already downstairs, her long legs folded up to fit in one of the cozy armchairs in the sitting room. Her hair was still a mess, but she looked much more alive than she had earlier. Her color had even returned—nearly up to a pale shade of beige.

"You were gone a long time," Camille remarked, and Grace tried not to stiffen.

"It probably just felt like that because time passes more slowly when you're hungover," Grace said, thrusting a bottle of Pedialyte into Camille's hands. "Drink. It'll help."

Camille didn't object, and Grace headed upstairs to rouse Tiff.

Tiff was already coming down the stairs, hair poufy, eyes half closed, and her mouth in a frown. "I'm up, I'm up," she grumbled, her feet dragging down each step dramatically.

"I brought you drugs," Grace cooed, fishing a package of what she hoped was extra-strength painkillers out of the plastic bag looped around her arm. If Tiff was still this drowsy, she wouldn't have noticed the length of time Grace was gone, which was a relief.

"You never bring me any of the good ones," Tiff pouted.

"Oh my God, Tiff, you can't just assume you can get hard drugs in Mexico, that's so racist."

Tiff's head jerked up in alarm, and Grace laughed with glee.

"Looks like that woke you up!" Grace cackled.

Tiff pushed her out of the way and stalked toward the

sitting room, depositing herself into the seat next to Camille. She sat sideways, her short legs dangling over the armrest. A big yawn later, Tiff folded her hands over her belly and dropped her head back. "I kind of like not being in charge for once. What's on the agenda for today?" she called out, not realizing Grace had already made it back to the sitting room as well.

"Agenda?" Grace asked.

She'd left lots of open space in their days in case Josh was free, figuring they could play each day by ear. After all, Tiff's migraines came and went, and Camille didn't know any better. Grace hadn't wanted to tie them to anything that required specific times. She was obviously going to spend time with her friends—she just didn't see the need to be so rigid about it.

Tiff shot up into a sitting position, her wild curls and fuzzy eyebrows giving her a slightly crazed look. "Grace Ling Johansson, please tell me you're joking."

"I'm not, Tiffany Mei-Hua Hong-Ahn. And once again, my middle name is Lynette. I'm half white, remember?"

Tiff waved a hand dismissively. "You know I don't think of you as white."

"So she does not have plans. Pffffft," Camille said, her voice drowsy. Her head rested comfortably against the padded wingback, eyes closed. "Tiffany, you must learn to relax. This is vacation."

"Exactly my thought." Grace beamed, grateful the suggestion came from Camille so it seemed less suspicious. "I figured we'd play it by ear since neither of you are in great shape."

"*Let me make the plans, Tiff,*" Tiff grumbled to herself. "*I'll take care of everything, Tiff.*"

The actress in Grace frowned at the poor impersonation.

"Sorry I didn't plan every second of every day," Grace

retorted, now feeling less guilty and more annoyed at Tiff's criticism. She wasn't a fucking travel agent.

She knew Tiff had a migraine, but Grace had her limits too.

"If you're really dying to go somewhere, into the *bright-ass sun*," she emphasized, "we can go shopping. There's a flea market nearby."

Tiff wrinkled her nose. "I'm not buying used stuff."

"Aren't you supposed to be all about saving the planet these days?" Grace asked. "Or else why have you been trying to push fava beans on us for the last two months?"

"I already gave up plastic straws, I can't be expected to do everything."

"I hope you are joking," Camille said.

"She is," Grace reassured her. "Sort of."

The fact was, Tiff was always going to live life like a person who had a lot of money. Maybe she *did* have deep passion for the environment, but her way of showing it was more of the "I drive an electric car" variety and not "I volunteer to pick up trash on the weekends."

Besides, between Tiff's dig about Grace's lack of planning and her "I don't think of you as white" comment, Grace felt justified in digging back just a little.

"Don't worry," she said brightly. "I know just what bus we can take to get there." Grace stopped herself in time before adding that she'd already ridden it that morning.

"I'm not taking the bus," Tiff said flatly.

Camille tsked in disapproval, her usual sign that she was going to offer a critique on American society. "I would think you Americans want better public transportation. In Paris, I take the metro everywhere."

Grace gave her a small round of applause. "There it is. I was wondering how long you could go without mentioning France's superiority."

Whenever Camille referenced the United States, it was always "your America" or "you Americans." As if every citizen needed to personally answer for each policy of its government.

"It is not my fault your country is so backward. No health care, no metro, but guns! Guns everywhere! Before I come, I have so many dreams I will be shot here."

"You still chose to come," Tiff pointed out.

Camille rolled her head to the side to make eye contact with Tiff. "My *parents* make me come."

"Stop pretending you don't love it. We may suck when it comes to social services and public health, but you forget we were with you the first time you tried string cheese. They won't let you back into France now that you admitted you like it."

At that, Camille bolted upright. "Ah! No! I only say it was fun to eat. Not the flavor!"

Grace shook her head solemnly. "I don't know, Camille. I've seen you drink wine out of a box."

"You have nothing else to drink that night!" she cried, a little more desperately. "Only cheap wine or vodka!"

"That sounds like a lot of excuses," Tiff said solemnly. "I've been keeping a list of every time you've smiled at a stranger. The elders would be shocked—*shocked!*—to see how friendly you've become."

Finally realizing they were teasing, Camille sank back to her original position. "Bah. You two always try to get me mad."

Tiff laughed and reached over to high-five Grace. "And it works every time."

Slapping Tiff's palm gave Grace a rush of relief. Tiff's mood had shifted, and the three of them were back on the same page instead of sniping at one another. People really underestimated the power of a little teasing.

That gave Grace the confidence to firmly assert, "We're going shopping, and we *will* be taking the bus. It's part of experiencing the local culture." She said it like it was decided, no argument tolerated.

"Aye, aye, Captain." Camille gave Grace a little salute and headed upstairs to change, Tiff doing the same (sans salute) a few moments later.

Having just seen Josh, Grace figured the rest of her day was probably free. And if she could tire her friends out enough now, she could maybe slip out again that night if Josh was free. She knew movie sets often shot long days, but if he'd been able to get away midmorning, it probably wasn't that taxing of a schedule. Also, he was essentially shadowing, not doing any *actual* work.

Okay, that could have been phrased a little more generously. But Grace was working just as hard as he was, having to live a double life to ensure the two most important spheres of her life didn't collide. She should probably be thinking ahead to the future—like, how she would reintegrate Josh into her life when Tiff wouldn't even allow her to speak his name in her presence—but right now Grace had all she could handle.

Shopping. Talking.

She could do that.

Besides, she couldn't text Josh for at least another six hours.

CHAPTER NINE

*"Of all the gin joints, in all the towns,
in all the world, she walks into mine."
—Casablanca (1942)*

The colorful and crowded flea market turned out to be just the thing to shut Camille up about the greatness of France. She oohed and aahed over every treasure presented to her and bought at least a half dozen tote bags, never bothering to negotiate the price.

"And you accuse *me* of wasting money," Tiff muttered to Grace, jerking a thumb toward Camille. "I swear, these ladies are colluding to raise the price as we walk down because they know she'll pay it."

Camille, in the midst of counting her change, stuffed it all back in her purse. "Oh, yes, you would like me to tell these people, 'No, sorry, I need this two euro, so you must give me discount.'" She gestured around. "They work for tourist money. So I give them tourist money. Why not? I have it. It's not a lot to me. But this is their job. I am not giving charity, I buy things in return."

"You're also driving up prices for locals," Tiff argued. "By haggling, it keeps things closer to their true value, but if they know they can sucker tourists into paying whatever they want, there's no incentive to sell it for cheaper to people who *can't* afford that price. That's why Asians haggle over everything. I once watched a man talk down the price of a dumpling in Vietnam. One single dumpling!"

Camille frowned. "I think maybe you take advantage of these poor sellers, no? Maybe this is why your people have less money in these countries."

Tiff's eyes went wide, and Grace recognized that her friend was on the edge of going feral. "Are you kidding me?" Tiff screeched. "*My people*, as you call them, are poor because of colonization and exploitation by white people like *you*, who travel there explicitly *for* the low prices and fetishization of both my culture and my people. My ancestors were forced to sell *themselves* as commodities just to survive, but please, speculate some more about the history of Southeast Asia."

"Whoa! Hey, deep breaths," Grace intervened, placing herself between them and pushing both Camille and Tiff back a step. "No need for World War Three here. Let's see if they sell those wooden penises you brought back from Bali." She hoped that by bringing up penises, she could distract Tiff enough to back off.

She should have known it wouldn't be that easy.

"Whose side are you on?" Tiff demanded. "You don't get to play both white and Asian on this."

Jesus Christ.

The meds Grace bought earlier must have had no effect on Tiff's burgeoning migraine because when her head hurt, she got *mean*.

"Thank you for the reminder that I'm not a real Asian. Subtle as always, Tiff," Grace said loudly, squeezing her hands together to keep herself from giving Tiff a boob punch.

"Shit, I didn't mean it like that," Tiff apologized, but Grace held a hand up to stop her. She was already on edge from seeing Josh earlier and had hoped that a relaxed afternoon with her friends would remind her that she actually was great and worthy and fun and all the other nice things they had said to her to make her feel better. Instead, she'd gotten not one but two jabs about being mixed.

"I'm going to need a minute," Grace said, keeping her head down so she didn't have to look at Tiff yet.

Camille grabbed Grace's arm and guided her into another aisle, Grace flicking a glance behind them to catch the guilty expression on Tiff's face.

"I'm fine," Grace said, shrugging off Camille's hand.

"You are upset?" Camille asked. "I don't understand. She is upset with me, but I am not upset. I did not say anything wrong."

Grace suppressed a sigh. The only thing worse than having to tell someone that the thing they said was racist was having to explain *why* it was racist. But if she didn't tell Camille now, it was bound to come up again.

"When you say 'your people' it makes it sound like Tiff needs to answer for things happening in Vietnam."

Camille frowned. "But she is from Vietnam. Like I am from France. I am not offended when you say this to me."

This was her penance, Grace decided. Having to keep patience through this conversation was the universe's way of punishing her for lying to her friends and sneaking off to see Josh.

She took a fortifying breath and kept her voice level so she wouldn't seem angry.

"Tiff isn't *from* Vietnam. She's from the US. Assuming that Asian Americans relate more to a foreign country than their own home is . . . really rude."

Camille's eyes widened. "I never think of it like this! I didn't mean to be rude."

"Well," Grace said with a shrug, parroting the ever-quotable line from *Ratatouille*, "'We hate to be rude, but we're French!'" She even did it in the same accent as the character.

Camille made a little show of using one fist to crank open the other one, her middle finger slowly unfurling like a growing plant.

Grace burst out laughing, relieved things were back to normal. "Did you just make a 'fuck you' jack-in-the box?"

"I do not like how French you sound with this accent." Camille sniffed.

Grace gave an exaggerated bow. "I'll take that as a compliment on my acting skills."

"For sure, you should. It's very difficult to get the right mix of sound and, *euh*, what do you call this?" She pinched the fingers on each hand together at the tips, swirling them as she lifted her chin haughtily.

"Snobby?"

"Bah." Camille gave Grace a little hip bump, refusing to agree. "I see you are not angry with Tiffany anymore?"

Grace swallowed thickly. The only thing she wanted to talk about *less* than being Asian American was being *half* Asian American.

As if Grace were a discount Asian. Watered down. Reduced to a percentage, where strangers looked at her like a puzzle to be solved. Did she even have enough features to "look" half?

Grace and Tiff didn't grow up talking about race because there hadn't really been a need. The entire Bay Area was pretty much just clusters of different Asian ethnicities. The nuances of each Asian subculture was the "diversity" she'd grown up with. Grace never *had* to talk about being half white because no one wanted to hear about it. Besides, what *was* white culture in the United States? Guns and police? Who also had guns?

But it didn't mean Grace never thought about it.

People would always look at her and know she was mixed. It didn't matter as much in regular life, except when people decided to use it against her like Tiff just had. Grace was proud of who she was and what she looked like; it was just a hard reality check every time someone identified her as "not the same."

She remembered worrying to Josh about her place in Hollywood—that she would always come second to girls who were *more* white or *more* Asian. He'd told her it was a blessing. An opportunity to "take advantage" of diverse casting because she'd be an "easier transition for white audiences." As opposed to Asian actors who were assumed to be foreign. Like Camille had done with Tiff.

The memory sat heavily in her chest. But there was no one to talk to about it.

"It's not worth being mad over," Grace said.

Tiff hadn't really meant it the way she said. She just didn't get why it was so hurtful.

Camille paused and then said delicately, "Maybe it's better to talk about, no? You are like sisters—you can be honest with each other. Nothing will break you up."

The words slammed into Grace.

For a few blissful moments, she'd forgotten about the enormous lie she was living. Then Camille reminded Grace of the one thing that might implode her friendship with Tiff—and she'd just had sex with him that morning.

Against her better judgment, Grace decided to risk a conversation about it. "This whole Josh thing has definitely come close though," she admitted, hoping Camille would take the bait.

Camille bit.

"You mean how she screams if you try to talk about him? Yes, I notice," she said dryly.

A gust of relief swept through Grace, and she pressed a palm to her chest. "Thank you! It's insane, right? Like, I can't even *mention* him?"

Camille shot her a look. "I think you do more than just 'mention.'" She even physically made air quotes with her fingers.

"I wouldn't have to if Tiff just let me talk about it," Grace argued. "Half the time, it's her saying a bunch of crap that I have to defend him against."

Camille arched a brow at that. "You are his lawyer?"

God, this was embarrassing, even for her. Vigorously defending the guy who broke up with her. Grace knew what her friends thought of Josh. But if she could just convince them he wasn't Satan, they might be able to see his good qualities for themselves. Right now, everything was being overshadowed by "the breakup." And the fact that he'd dumped her immediately after having sex.

"He never lied to me," Grace insisted. "He never said he

loved me, and he never promised me anything he couldn't deliver. It was my own fault for falling so far. So really, she should be mad at me. He didn't do anything wrong."

Camille stopped Grace with a touch to her shoulder, looking at her with so much pity that Grace wanted to die on the spot.

"Grace. I cannot tell you to not love Josh. But he did do wrong. A man who loves you cannot turn it off like—" Camille snapped her fingers for effect.

Grace wanted to argue more—insist that Josh still had feelings for her. She knew it. She'd *seen* (and felt) it that morning. But Tiff reappeared in their aisle, her face scrunched in guilt.

"Sorry I was an asshole. You still mad at me?"

Well, they were even now. Even if Tiff didn't know it.

"You're buying lunch," Grace said.

Tiff rolled her eyes. "When do I *not* buy lunch?"

Grace pointed to the first restaurant she saw—outdoor tables in glorious, glorious shade. They dashed over with the speed of girls who hadn't eaten all day and skidded to a stop at the maître d's stand.

"Carmen?"

Grace whipped around at the voice.

It was the hot guy from the night before.

She froze as their kiss played in her mind like the flashback of a movie sex scene. Her heart even started racing, her entire body reliving the moment.

He squinted with a tilt of his head, as if he still wasn't sure it was really her. "Wow, you look really . . . I almost didn't recognize you."

Tiff coughed loudly behind her, but Grace could only gawk at him.

He must have thought she was offended because he quickly added, "Not *bad* different. I mean, it's daytime. So you know, you'd be wearing different clothes, but it just threw me off. Especially the . . . Sailor Moon thingies." He drew little circles around the top of his head to indicate her space buns. "They're cute."

As he noted, she was back in her usual style. Tiff affectionately described it as "slutty Harajuku" and Camille mostly just shook her head, muttering, "So much color," anytime she was asked to weigh in on an outfit. Nothing about what Grace currently had on said *Carmen*. Definitely not the Carmen he'd met.

"Daniel, right?" she croaked. She sounded like a woman on the brink of death. A woman who would choose to replay that kiss instead of having the rest of her life flash before her eyes.

Why couldn't he have just hidden out behind a parked car or something until the coast was clear? It's what Grace would have done.

When they'd met, she'd been drunk and maybe a touch flirty. But looking at him now, the magnitude of Daniel's attractiveness and the size of her guilt over kissing him were roughly the same. She wanted both to fling herself at him and curse herself out for wanting to.

You came here for Josh, she reminded herself.

Grace couldn't help but notice that her voice of reason was very small and seemed very far away.

"Names," Tiff commanded, pointing at the two boys standing closely behind Daniel.

Daniel looked relieved that *someone* had said *something* and quickly regained his poise as he introduced his friends.

"This is Lúcio"—he said, pointing to a guy with a chiseled jaw and beautiful hair down to his shoulders—"a.k.a. Café a.k.a. São Paulito a.k.a.—"

"Tô Nem Aí," the third guy jumped in, causing all three of them to laugh and slap each other on their backs over their inside joke.

"And this," Daniel continued, clasping a hand on his other friend's shoulder, "is Andrés. They're both here playing at my uncle's soccer academy for the summer."

Daniel didn't speak English with an accent, but he did with Spanish, his friends' names rolling off his tongue like a seduction. Grace wanted to ask him to repeat them just so she could listen to him speak like that again.

"You do not have a nickname?" Camille asked Andrés.

"Maybe one day he'll be good enough to earn one," Lúcio joked, setting off another round of guy slapping and laughing.

Grace supposed this is what she and Tiff and Camille looked like when Tiff tried to do her boob-punching thing.

"This is Carmen," Daniel said to his friends, then gestured to hers. "And? I didn't catch your names last night."

"They weren't screaming it out of the cab like everything else?" Grace asked with a sardonic tilt of her head.

Her friends ignored her. "Tiff," Tiff said, her eyes on Lúcio. "And I've always wanted to go to Brazil."

Grace drew her eyebrows together. "How do you know he's from Brazil?" she whispered out of one side of her mouth.

"They called him coffee and São Paulo. I think it's a safe bet," Tiff whispered back as she and Lúcio made horny eyes at each other.

Camille rescued Grace from having to confess her inferior geography skills. "Camille," she said, leaning into each of the boys to give them air-kisses on each cheek. She had to bend her knees to get down to their level.

"So, what are you boys up to tonight?" Tiff asked, now magically next to Lúcio with his arm around her waist. "Maybe we should all meet up. I know Carmen here wants to."

Only then did Grace realize both her friends had used their real names, leaving her as the only one with a fake. "Well, well, well, *Tiff* and *Camille*," she said, grinding out each of their names between clenched teeth. "Aren't you both the picture of friendliness today?"

Tiff giggled at something Lúcio whispered to her, his face completely lost in the mass of her curls. "What can I say?" Tiff said, finally pulling her attention away from Lúcio for a moment. "We could all use some new *friends*, especially you. You know, to help us *grow* or *move on*?"

Tiff couldn't have been less subtle than if she'd waved two fucking neon air traffic controller batons at Daniel's dick like Grace was looking for somewhere to land.

"Uh, cool?" Daniel said. "I think?"

Grace shot Daniel an apologetic smile. "I'm sorry, she's new to speaking. And manners." It wasn't his fault her best friend was going rogue. Grace didn't want him to think she was rejecting him. Not that she was pursuing him either, of course.

God, even her internal voices were running little court cases in her head, defending every possible action from accusation. Josh had somehow gotten access to his own lawyer, even inside her brain.

"We should probably let you guys go," Grace said, intending to move out of the way for them to pass. Except that she and Daniel stepped the same way, causing their bodies to collide. Her soft parts melted into his hard ones.

"Sorry," she squeaked, pushing herself a few inches away, but not before noticing how his chest felt underneath her hands. She filed that little tidbit away to be pored over later.

Alone.

"You in a hurry to get away from me again?" he teased, his voice low enough that it was just meant for her.

Grace's jaw dropped. "That's not fair. I was already leaving last time."

"All right," he conceded. "But you never did let me get you that drink."

"I think you just want to see me drunk again."

"I think I just want to see *you* again."

"I'm not wearing that dress."

"I kind of hoped you wouldn't wear anything."

Grace nearly choked. She hadn't meant to flirt with Daniel. And she *really* hadn't meant to lose at it.

Judging by his grin, he knew it too.

"We should head back," Lúcio said with a glance at his phone.

"Tonight, then," Tiff announced with a clasp of her hands. "What's the plan? For the rest of us, I mean." She gestured to Camille and Daniel's friends. "Obviously you two have your own plans," she added with a glance toward Grace and Daniel, which sent a creeping blush up Grace's neck.

"Which I totally condone, by the way," Tiff continued, either oblivious to or uncaring of Grace's embarrassment. "Don't feel like you have to come with us. We can stay out *all night*, if you know what I mean." She added a theatrical wink at the end.

Grace prayed for a swift death. Preferably Tiff's.

This was what Josh disliked about Tiff. *She always has to make a scene*, he'd say. At the moment, Josh had a valid point.

"We're planning to go out, but we stay out later than eleven o'clock," Daniel said with a smirk, referencing Grace's earlier-than-expected exit the previous night. "But I don't know if it's the kind of thing you're into," he warned.

"Of course we'll be into it," Tiff snapped impatiently, barely waiting for Daniel to finish his sentence before she replied. "Carmen is into everything, isn't she?" She shot a knowing look at Grace, as if Grace was going to eagerly agree with her.

Tiff was in full Asian-auntie-mode now, trying to secure a hookup for her friend (that her friend had *not* asked for). Grace was half surprised Tiff wasn't waving condoms in his face and shoving the two of them into a closet and locking the door.

Daniel's eyes found Grace's again, a corner of his mouth kicking up into a smile. "Into everything?" he repeated.

He'd said it in a completely normal way, but the look he gave her was absolutely filthy. She went hot all over again.

At least this time, she knew he was trying to unsettle her.

Keeping her voice as casual as possible, she replied, "Why don't you tell us what this place is, and we'll let you know if we're interested?"

Perfectly neutral statement, no hint of flirting. In fact, she didn't even look at Daniel when she said it.

Still, Lúcio let out a low whistle and gave a little chuckle at the response. "We're going to a club called HRoof."

"It's the best club in Cancún," Andrés added earnestly. His accent was cute, but both his face and voice were so . . . young. Grace sincerely hoped he wasn't still in high school.

"I thought Coco Bongo was supposed to be the best club in Cancún," Tiff said.

Lúcio and Daniel snorted. "Maybe for middle-aged tourists," Daniel said.

"I was obviously kidding," she shot back. Tiff hated more than anything looking like she was somehow out of the know. It's why she spent so much time googling answers to questions no one else cared about.

Camille looked skeptical of both claims (though she always sort of looked like that). "What makes this roof club the best?"

Andrés was about to answer, but Lúcio cut him off.

"You'll have to come to find out. See you tonight!" he called, blowing them a kiss as he and Andrés started for the exit.

"Oh, we'll be *coming*," Tiff said with an air-kiss of her own. Grace closed her eyes again. She really couldn't bring Tiff anywhere. She wasn't fit for mixed company.

"So that's a yes?" Daniel asked.

Grace shrugged, playing the part of the cool girl who gets hit on by random hot guys so often it doesn't even faze her. "Like I said. We'll see."

Daniel smiled. "That's a yes."

"That's not what I said," Grace exclaimed, giving Daniel a little swat on the arm.

Not an excuse to touch him. Probably.

His grin only widened. "You'll be there."

Outrageous.

"I don't take orders from you," Grace said primly, watching his eyes go black at the idea of her doing exactly that.

"How about you go home and think about it," he said, leaning in closer to her ear, his breath lingering on her neck. "And when you come, because we both know you will"—his voice was so low Grace felt the sound waves in her body like vibrations—"wear lipstick. I want to see it all over me."

CHAPTER TEN

"So be prepared, be enthusiastic, and leave your bullshit attitude and baggage at the door because we don't need it!"
—Wet Hot American Summer (2001)

Grace spent the rest of the afternoon in a mid-grade panic. Since running into Daniel, she'd messaged Josh no fewer than four separate times.

It wasn't a good look.

The messages themselves weren't anything desperate—just check-ins and a picture of an old movie poster he would like and a question about his availability that evening. Because if he wasn't available, Grace didn't think she'd be able to get out of going to the club.

And she could *not* go to that club.

Her brain stayed a puddle (as well as other parts of her) for several hours after bumping into Daniel, frozen in some kind of horny ice jail. In her head, she could already hear Tiff correcting the very thought: *How can you be a puddle and frozen at the same time?*

If Grace saw Daniel again, she was going to have to spend her whole night flirting but *not* flirting, because she obviously couldn't *do* anything with him. The kiss the day before hadn't counted because it wasn't premediated (on her part), and flirting was technically allowed because Josh didn't get a say in who she talked to. After all, who knew who he was talking to on set?

Grace checked her phone. Still no reply.

She was being ridiculous. He was at work. Of course he couldn't message back whenever he wanted. He'd probably wait until production wrapped for the day. Anything else could be seen as unprofessional.

"I can't believe I'm going to say this," Tiff said, interrupting Grace's thoughts, "but I think maybe you need to stop drinking for a bit. Your eyes are doing that weird thing when you zone out."

Tiff took the shot glass out of Grace's hand and handed it to Camille instead, who still made the exact same face no matter which tequila she was trying.

The day's bottle was Don Julio 1942 (price tag: $180). Another tall, paddle-ish shaped bottle. It looked like it could tip over in a strong wind.

Grace tilted her head and squinted her eyes, trying to see through the amber-colored liquid. It was similar to the previous day's tequila, right? Wasn't tequila usually clear? Honestly, who knew there were that many types of it? And mezcal was somehow a completely separate type of liquor? With its own flavors too? But made from the same plant?

Standing up, Grace went a little light-headed and stumbled backward. Holy shit. Tiff was right. Grace was well on her way to being drunk, if she wasn't already. And they hadn't even left the house yet. Time was passing *so* slowly.

"Going to the bathroom," she said, excusing herself from the room.

"You're breaking the seal too early!" Tiff called back.

Safely inside the bathroom, Grace eagerly pulled out her phone, nothing but the blankness of her Zendaya wallpaper staring back at her. No messages—just a cotton candy pink–haired Zendaya in a purple ruffled leotard inside a circus hoop, looking like the absolute goddess she was.

Shit. Grace was running out of time.

She fake flushed the toilet and ran the sink as she typed out one last message to Josh.

Grace: going to a club called hroof, not sure i'll be able to hear my phone

Maybe this way, he might surprise *her* by showing up. Or he'd be so jealous at the thought of her out that he'd text and beg Grace not to go . . .

Fuck. She really *was* drunk.

"This is taking forever," Tiff moaned, trying to see past the group in front of them to gauge the distance to the entrance. "I should be in there and hooking up with Lúcio already."

Grace made a face. "Feels a little like you already started at the restaurant this afternoon."

"He's Brazilian," Tiff said, as if that explained everything. "They're very sensual people."

"That's . . . weird." Grace wrinkled her nose at Tiff's characterization, only half paying attention to the conversation. The other half of her was split between anxiously watching to see if Daniel had arrived and anxiously checking her phone to see if Josh had messaged her.

"We are not too far," Camille mused, apparently not paying attention to Tiff either. "I will go and talk to someone."

Camille stepped out of line and headed toward the front, ready to work her mysterious French magic that charmed every bouncer in existence.

Tiff turned her attention back on Grace. "You excited about the boy tonight?"

It took Grace a split second to realize Tiff meant Daniel.

She gave a sort of bewildered shrug. It wasn't possible for Grace to describe the situation she was in. Her confusion about Daniel was directly related to Josh. And Grace knew better than to bring up his name.

"Don't be nervous, babes," Tiff said, placing a hand on Grace's shoulder. "You look adorable. And if he was still into you this afternoon with what you were wearing then, he'll totally be into this."

Grace bristled at the backhanded compliment. "What the fuck?" Personally, she thought her cream-colored dress was plenty sexy with a short hemline and a generous keyhole over her cleavage. The fact that the dress had a little bunny face and ears on it didn't change that.

"Oh, stop. All I'm saying is that the stockings with the garters showing and red lipstick were good additions." Tiff gestured up and down her person. "You are still Carmen, don't forget."

Tiff suggestively waggled her eyebrows and Grace rolled her eyes. No way she was doing that again. She hadn't even really done it last time.

Not knowing whether she'd see Daniel or Josh had made it difficult to settle on an outfit. Grace needed to be sexy without being *too* sexy. Because she would probably eventually see Josh and she didn't want to show up looking like she'd been out looking for other guys.

But she also didn't want to look *not* sexy if she was going to have to see Daniel before then. Just sexy enough to keep things interesting.

Another phone check.

Every minute increased the probability that she was going to have to face Daniel again. Tiff had practically promised sex not only from herself but possibly on Grace's behalf as well. The guys weren't going to just *not* show.

"Let's go, we're in!" Tiff grabbed Grace's hand, pulling her out of her thoughts (and the line). Camille waved them over from the entrance.

"We go in now," Camille said with a smug smile, reserving a coyer smile for the bouncer, who shooed them through the door.

Inside was a carnival fun house. The dark corridor pulsed red, the timing of the vertical light strips beckoning them deeper into the space. That opened into a main room packed with bodies, colorful lasers beaming all different directions. A heavy beat of electronica permeated the whole club.

Already, it felt far too intimate. Dark corners abounded, the air heavy with hormones as people ground against one another. It would be much too easy to wind up in one of those corners with Daniel. Already she could picture the music lulling her into a trance, like at the foam party, and swaying against him until all of her nerves ignited.

"I need to get out of here," Grace mumbled, blindly pushing her way toward the exit.

She shouldn't have come without Josh, and she definitely shouldn't have come to see Daniel. She shouldn't have come at all. There was no possible way to end the night on a positive note. Grace was already losing, and she'd only just arrived.

"Where are you going?" Camille exclaimed. She was already vibing to the music like the true European she was, long arms raised and head lolling along to the beat.

"Is this about me embarrassing you at the restaurant earlier?" Tiff shouted over the music, following Grace down the hallway as they dodged incoming people like salmon swimming upstream. "I promise not to do it again!"

Grace felt somewhat guilty for letting Tiff think that was what had upset her, but right now she just needed to leave. She was almost to the door when a hand caught her upper arm and Grace found herself twirling into a solid (and now familiar) body.

Shit.

"Leaving already?" Daniel asked. "It's not even eleven this time." His eyes dropped to her lips, and his grin widened.

Yes, she'd worn the fucking lipstick. But he shouldn't just *assume* she'd worn it for him.

"I don't like electronica," she said defiantly, trying to prove to herself that she didn't care about some guy she'd met and kissed once. He wasn't worth throwing away all the time and effort she'd invested into her relationship with Josh.

"How can you not like this?" Andrés shouted, excitedly pumping a fist to the music. "I love this place!"

Nineteen, tops, Grace decided.

Tiff had already barreled her way into Lúcio, the two of them heading back, with Andrés trailing behind. Apparently Tiff wasn't worried about Grace leaving now that Daniel was here.

But Tiff didn't know Grace could still practically feel Josh inside of her. She needed to leave before she could forget it. As it was, the heavy bass extended even into this hallway, urging her body to inch closer to Daniel's.

He was freshly showered and glistening clean. The kind of clean that begged her imagination to think of him in nothing but a towel. His touch—just a hand wrapped lightly around her bare arm—further scrambled her brains. It was like she was being dragged away with her own hand clamped over her mouth, unable to scream for help from her conscience.

"Do you want to go outside for a minute? Get some air?"

The concern on Daniel's face told her his question was genuine. Not a ploy to get her outside and alone again. Probably.

But outside seemed worse. Outside, there was no one to interrupt or distract them from finishing what he'd started the day before.

Grace used all the mental power she had left to keep the reminder of Josh around her, wearing the memory of their sex that morning like armor. Shrugging off Daniel's hand, she turned back down the space tunnel. "Let's go get a drink," she suggested.

Safety in numbers. As long as she wasn't alone with him, she'd be fine.

As it turned out, sticking with the group was easy. Andrés and Lúcio were charming and funny and had the ability to argue without being condescending. Maybe that seemed trivial, but Josh was forever having to rescue Grace from hostile discussions with his fellow film major friends, many of them assuming a (female) acting major couldn't possibly know as much as they did about film. Josh, of course, always defended her and respected her opinion, but sometimes, Grace wished he just had fewer friends who were sexist assholes to begin with.

Daniel, for his part, maintained a steady presence near Grace but had so far kept his hands off and away from her. Instead, he made sure she and her friends were always included in the conversation, fetched drinks, and created a general radiance with his smile. The perfect gentleman.

So why did she keep hoping for the Daniel of the previous night to appear?

The discussion somehow devolved into a heated conversation about soccer, and Grace took the opportunity to excuse herself. She'd been drinking margaritas at a steady pace, and while she didn't believe in Tiff's "breaking the seal" theory, Grace *was* having to go back and forth to the bathroom quite a lot. (Upside: regular opportunities to check her phone.)

Another encounter with nothing but Zendaya's face on her phone all but obliterated Grace's hope of seeing Josh that night. It was already past one o'clock.

She cleaned her eyes in the mirror (no one who wore makeup ever "splashed water on their face" like movies showed), before fortifying herself and heading back. If she didn't need to keep checking her phone, maybe she could finally relax a bit.

Grace eased back into the space next to Daniel, noticing the soccer quarrel had escalated. Camille's voice, usually light and airy, had taken on the gritty quality of a French detective with forty years on the job. "How can you say South America has the best football when Europe has Ligue 1! Premier League! La Liga! Serie A! Eredivisie! Bundesliga! Primeira Liga!" Camille ticked off the names on her fingers, her drink sloshing over the edge as she argued passionately on behalf of her continent.

Andrés seemed equally upset, arguing back just as loudly. "But where are the best footballers from? Messi! Neymar! Vieira! Vinícius! All from South America!"

It was 50 percent shouting, 50 percent hands flying.

Lúcio wasn't as worked up about it, most of his attention always on Tiff, but he refused to let the conversation progress without advocating for his country. "And what country are all these players from?" he challenged. "Neymar? Brazil. Vinícius? Brazil. Allison? Brazil. Gabriel Jesus? Brazil." He looked at everyone, daring them to counter. When no one did, he rattled off more names. "Pelé? Ronaldinho? Ronaldo?"

That got a reaction.

"Ah no!" Camille shouted, banging her palm on the wall beside them. "You cannot name old players—we talk about now!"

Tiff leaned toward Grace and Daniel, her eyes widened. "I've never seen Camille like this. She's terrifying."

Grace nudged Daniel. "You're not going to jump in and defend the good ol' US of A?"

Daniel scoffed. "Please. I don't even root for them against Mexico. I've had three uncles play pro here; I'd be disowned if I cheered for anyone else."

"What about Taiwan?" she asked with a smile.

"They can win in something else. Soccer *is* Mexico."

"I'm bored with this conversation," Tiff complained. "Let's

go dance." She grabbed Grace by the hand, and without thinking, Grace grabbed Daniel's. The three of them snaked their way to the middle of the floor, where shot girls in silver dresses and blue wigs held up bottles and lighted sparklers, shooting off sparks in the semi-dark room.

"It's really too bad I love dick," Tiff shouted at Grace and Daniel, nodding toward the girls with the sparklers. "The girls in here are way hotter than most of the guys." With a glance at Daniel she added, "No offense."

Daniel laughed so hard that Grace took the drink from his hand, certain he would spill it otherwise. "This fucking girl. I like her," he told Grace.

"You would be the first," she quipped, handing his drink back to him.

Tiff shot a fake glare at Grace. "You fucking love me."

Grace placed a hand solemnly over her heart. "And that's *my* cross to bear."

Tiff laughed, tackling her with a drunk-girl hug, and Grace couldn't remember the last time she'd felt this happy. "We're in Cancún!" Grace crowed, embracing her own drunk-girl moment.

"Cheers," Daniel added, lifting his drink in a toast, which Tiff and Grace happily obliged.

"I gotta give it to you," Tiff shouted at Daniel. "You picked a really good fucking place."

Daniel lifted both arms up like a benevolent king. (Tiff could probably name which one.)

"What can I say? I have good taste." He shot Grace a grin, and her buzz ratcheted up a couple more notches. If this was what margaritas made her feel like, she'd drink them until the end of time.

The three of them bounced along with the music ("music") for a bit, Grace letting the energy of the space and the lasers wash over her like ocean waves. Daniel was careful to balance himself between Grace and Tiff so that Tiff wouldn't be a third wheel, which was unexpectedly thoughtful, and only made Grace want to get closer to him. This guy was like a dream list of qualities—finding out he could keep a rhythm too nearly undid her.

Maybe this was just the clubbing experience. Santa Cruz was all house parties and chill get-togethers. Maybe every guy seemed desirable after enough drinks and the right atmosphere. Just because this one moment in time was possibly the best thing she'd ever experienced didn't mean it was a once-in-a-lifetime kind of opportunity she'd regret not seizing.

Right?

"Going to the bathroom," Grace shouted at Tiff, desperate to escape for a second so she could put her head back right. Tiff nodded, but Daniel hadn't heard her.

"Where are you going?" he asked.

"Be right back!" Telling a guy she was going to the bathroom always seemed like TMI. Thinking about someone else peeing was not sexy.

But instead of letting her go, Daniel wrapped a forearm across her chest, pulling her back flush against his front with a thump.

Fuuuuuuuck.

Her mind blacked out for a full second as she absorbed the feel of his entire body pressed against her, head to toe. She fit against him perfectly.

"Did I tell you you can leave yet?" he rumbled into her ear.

Grace swiveled her head around to give him a piece of her mind, only to see the playful look in his eyes.

It was a game. Just a game.

"I already told you, I don't take orders from you," she chided.

He squeezed her a little tighter and leaned even closer into her ear, setting each and every one of Grace's nerves on high alert. "Hm, I think you *want* to take orders from me."

Puddle. She was an absolute puddle in the middle the floor.

"Pretty sure you already did," he added, releasing his arm from around her and nodding toward her cherry-red lips.

His challenge in stepping away from her was obvious. She was going to have to *choose* to let him boss her around. No more games until she opted in.

But Grace was a coward.

So she fled.

Safe inside the women's room, Grace sagged against the wall, trying not to think about the billions of germs she was touching.

This was so fucked.

She'd come to Cancún for Josh. *Josh.* This entire trip—planned and plotted for one reason, and it wasn't to let herself imagine the kind of things Daniel could (and probably would) do to her that Josh wouldn't (or couldn't). She hadn't come to comparison shop.

She flung off one final, desperate text to Josh.

Grace: wearing my bunny dress tonight, i know it's one of your favs

This time, Josh replied immediately.

Josh: Pics or it didn't happen

Grace: omg how old are you

Josh: Picture PLEASE

Josh: Make my night

Grace's face was flushed from the alcohol and more than a little sweaty, so she decided cropping out her face might be best. She sent him a picture of the bunny face, which happened to be just her boobs.

Grace: does this mean you're still at work

Josh: You're killing me

Josh: How much are you getting hit on right now

Grace: a LOT

She smiled to herself, imagining Josh getting jealous over the attention.

Josh: I hope you're not flirting back

Grace: why, you planning to come here and stop it?

Josh: NOT FUNNY

Josh: Don't do this to me

Grace: pretty sure i'm not doing anything to you right now

Josh: You known I don't like being teased

Grace: so come here and do something about it

It was a brazen challenge, but Grace was feeling a little brazen. She'd left Daniel (with great effort, she might add) to come give Josh one more chance for the night and instead, he was turning it on her like she was disrespecting him. There was no reason she couldn't be a tiny bit more direct about what she wanted.

Grace: are you still at work or not

It was a simple enough question. Either he was at work and couldn't see her, or he wasn't at work and he was *choosing* not to see her. She'd spent her entire day waiting to hear back from him. The very least he could do right now was finally give her a definitive answer.

Three dots appeared and disappeared several times, Josh clearly struggling to come up with a response. Finally, they disappeared for good. He simply left her question hanging.

She wanted to believe that this was all part of an elaborate ruse in which he really *would* show up at the club to surprise her, but she was neither drunk enough nor naive enough to think it. He wasn't planning to see her and she didn't know why.

If he'd just said he was working, she would've believed it. But he didn't. She supposed she should be grateful he was still upholding his promise never to lie to her, but that wasn't how it felt at the moment. It felt the way it always did—like rejection.

Grace had hoped (expected?) Josh would hear that he had competition and valiantly stand up to claim her. He'd nearly lost his mind that morning at the thought of her being with someone else. And yet.

A streak of anger shot through Grace. Who the hell did Josh think he was? He expected her to stay at home like a good little girl and wait for his call while he was off doing God knows what? Sure, he'd said he wasn't hooking up with anyone else, but that was hours ago.

Grace barged out of the bathroom with a new sense of purpose. She'd flirt as much as she wanted, guilt-free. After all, it wasn't like Josh was laying claim to her. And flirting wasn't hooking up; it was harmless. She was on vacation. And Daniel was like an adventure.

It was fine. It was all fine.

She found him back where they'd started, standing next

to Camille and Andrés, who had apparently called a truce and were now happily drinking together. Tiff and Lúcio were nowhere to be found.

"You good?" Daniel asked her.

Ha. She was the furthest thing from good. But she intended to fix that immediately. She wasn't going to let Josh spoil her otherwise great night.

"Just need another drink," she said with a smile she wasn't feeling yet. But more drinks always helped. Or so Tiff always claimed.

"Another margarita?" he asked.

When she nodded, he was off in a flash, returning with a delicious-looking salted-rim drink. This man was a fucking gem. And she had literally run away from him.

Well, then. She wasn't running now.

She made a show of licking the flavored salt off the drink before promptly downing half of it. Partly to soothe her nerves and partly to gauge Daniel's reaction, which was so far very promising. His posture was still relaxed, but his eyes had sharpened back to their previous intensity, burning holes into her.

Grace decided to reward him, running her tongue around the rest of the rim and taking the remainder of the drink in one gulp. It was a heady thing, watching him watch her like this. No thoughts about whether she was trying too hard or whether she should be playing harder to get—he very blatantly wanted her, and it was a fucking rush.

When she'd sucked out the last drop from her glass, Daniel took it out of her hands and set it aside with such efficiency, it bordered on comical.

"Let's dance," he said, leading her back to the floor. There wasn't even the chance to tell Camille where she'd gone, he swept her away so quickly. Not that she really minded.

Instead, she let the music ("music") and the alcohol and the lasers and the heat lull her into a happy space as she fell into a rhythm with Daniel. He made her feel small (in a good way), which wasn't an easy thing to do, especially considering he wasn't particularly tall. But between the muscles and the way he could simply move her by placing his hands in different spots on her body, she felt oh-so dainty. Another strike against her feminism, she supposed, but there was something to be said for feeling taken care of.

They were in the middle of a crowd, but somehow Daniel shielded her in a way that random people weren't constantly bumping into her. She stayed in a bubble of his making, feeling and seeing almost nothing but him as the beat thrummed through them.

Grace decided electronica was now her favorite type of "music." Europeans were vastly smarter than Americans because theirs was a beat you could absolutely fuck to.

"When am I going to get to kiss that lipstick off of you?" Daniel asked, sweeping her hair away from her neck, his lips so very close but not touching her.

Grace suppressed a shiver. "Oh, you thought I wore this for you?" she asked casually.

He seemed amused by her denial. "Even if you didn't, I'll still be the one who gets it off you."

Grace leaned away from him, needing his breath off her to keep her head clear. "You seem awfully certain of that."

He smirked, as if he knew exactly why she needed space. "I *am* awfully certain of it."

God, he was egotistical. It was hot.

Especially when she could drag it out.

"I don't know," she mused, looking around the club. "I'm not sure I've explored all my options."

He stepped back and gestured away. "Go ahead. Explore."

Another challenge. But for some reason, his didn't rankle the way Josh's did. Maybe because there was less to lose.

Grace moved to leave, as if she were indeed going to search for someone else, but Daniel pulled her back. His lips stopped millimeters away from hers, so close she could practically taste the sweetness of the rum and Cokes he'd been drinking all night.

Gripping his arms like she might collapse if she let go, Grace waited for him to kiss her like he had the night before.

This time, she was ready.

Waiting.

Wanting.

She held her breath, time suspended as she waited for him to put her out of her misery. He was *right there*.

But he remained exactly where he was, his voice low and hard. "If there *is* someone else you want to go kiss, you'd better go do it now, because once I start, I'm not stopping until I hear my name come out of those pretty red lips of yours."

Grace couldn't help it. She closed the last few millimeters and pressed her mouth against his, feeling like she might explode if she had to wait another second.

There was no excuse this time. She knew it. He hadn't ordered her to kiss him and he hadn't forced her to. But feeling his lips, soft and sweet and warm, she didn't care.

He pulled her in and angled his face, deepening the kiss and sending her mind into a tailspin. Josh had been against public displays of affection beyond holding hands, saying what they did was special and not meant for anyone else. But somehow, making out in an incredibly public space with hundreds of people around, it still felt pretty fucking special.

Daniel's hand slid up the base of her neck and into her hair, tugging lightly on the roots and sending threads of pure lust racing through her body. She was swimming in desire. Drowning in it. She clung to Daniel like a life preserver.

They kissed and kissed, Grace losing herself in space and time as the two of them fused together, sharing air and breathing each other in, pressing until there was no space left between them. Needing more, she wiggled against him and he moved a muscled thigh between her legs, giving her friction exactly where she needed it.

It wasn't nearly enough.

She pressed closer, needing him to consume her so she might finally be close enough to sate her hunger. Around them, people continued moving and dancing and drinking, but she and Daniel were rooted to the spot, a frenzy of just lips and hands.

If she didn't do something and do it soon, she really *would* end up pressed against the wall in a dirty bathroom stall, just like Tiff always wanted. If she was going to be a cliché, she could at least do it on her own terms.

Begging herself not to think too hard about it and to just lean into her temporary madness, Grace finally pulled away, panting, and uttered the words she never ever thought she'd say to a stranger.

"Do you want to get out of here?"

CHAPTER ELEVEN

"You know how to whistle, don't you, Steve? You just put your lips together and blow."
—To Have and Have Not (1944)

Other than Josh, Grace had slept with only one other person—her high school ex-boyfriend. He'd wanted sex, and she hadn't, so they'd broken up. But when they ran into each other the summer after freshman year, she felt ready to finally get it over with, and he seemed like the best option. They'd spent the rest of the summer hooking up, and when they'd parted again that fall, she told herself it was for the best.

She hadn't been in love with him or anything. But realizing she really hadn't meant much more to him than a warm, willing body had left her surprisingly empty. She held off on sex with anyone else until Josh.

It wasn't like she hadn't let anyone thoroughly grope her or given the occasional blow job (though Grace wanted to know what exactly made guys assume a girl would automatically swallow; a warning of some kind was standard etiquette)—it was still college, after all. But in keeping it to mouths and hands with everyone leading up to Josh, it had turned sex into something special and separate from the "other stuff."

It was probably the reason Josh was able to hurt her so much. Because every time she slept with him, it felt like she was giving him another tiny piece of her heart without knowing if she'd ever get it back. And while Josh had never given her the impression she was just another number to him, Grace couldn't help thinking she might be better positioned in their standoff if she could figure out how to care just a little bit less.

When their stop came, Grace pulled Daniel off the bus and bolted across several lanes of cars, practically shoving him through her front door to get him upstairs as fast as possible. The less thinking, the better. Just hormones and vibes.

"Hold on, hold on," Daniel protested, stumbling as she attempted to pull him toward the stairs.

"What's the holdup? You a virgin or something?" she taunted between kisses, refusing to take her lips off him for more than a second at a time.

"Virginity joke, good one. But some of us take off our shoes inside, or are you not that kind of Asian?"

Grace finally pulled back and saw that he was, in fact, taking off his shoes. She teetered on one foot, yanking off her high heels in mock disdain. "How dare you, sir. I just thought you were worth risking the outside ground germs for, but maybe not."

Daniel laughed and kissed her again, the two of them now exactly the same height.

"Are you . . . Do you . . . do a British accent when you're drunk? Because if so, I love it."

Grace slapped a hand over her mouth. "Oh my God, am I doing that again?"

Daniel arched an eyebrow. "So this is a regular thing?"

"Hell no, Josh *refused* to role-play." Grace's eyes went wide as she scrambled for a follow-up. "Oh fuck, I'm sorry, I didn't—"

"I'm *Daniel.*" He pointed to himself, the sarcasm showing in his smirk. "We met earlier?"

Grace's cheeks flamed as she buried her face in both hands. "I am so sorry. That's, like, rule number one of hooking up: Don't say someone else's name. I wasn't mixing you—we're—ugh. We're broken up." Her words stumbled over one another, trying to chase each other like enemies, sworn to make the worst possible impression of her. "I swear, he's not—"

Daniel pulled her hands away from her face. "Please. I'm not expecting I'm the first." Then, with a sly grin, he added, "How about . . . I keep you from mixing me up with this Josh guy?"

"I said I was sorry," Grace moaned in embarrassment.

"Subamos las escalaras," Daniel murmured, his hands still gently holding hers.

Grace's mouth curled into a half-open frown. "Huh?" It wasn't an elegant or sexy reply, but the sudden switch to Spanish threw her for a loop.

He leaned forward and kissed her in the space beneath her jaw, sending a shiver down her spine.

"Llévame arriba. Te haré olvidar a todos los demás. Solo trae yo a tu cama."

"I literally have no idea what you're saying, and I don't care, just keep doing it." Grace gasped, prying Daniel's lips off her and leading him up the stairs and into her bedroom, kicking the door shut with her foot.

"Luces encendidas," he commanded, flicking the switch and bathing the room in a soft yellow glow.

"Holy fuck do I wish I'd taken Spanish in high school now," Grace said as Daniel crouched down and ran his fingers up her legs, coasting gently over the sheer white stockings until they ended mid-thigh.

"I think we should keep these on," he said, tucking a finger under the garters that held them up, snapping them against her skin. Grace startled at the tiny flash of pain, but it quickly evaporated in the heat of his stare. She breathed her assent, and Daniel continued his journey upward.

He continued to murmur compliments she could barely hear, and in one smooth move, lifted her dress up and off her body, leaving Grace standing in nothing but her bra and underwear and a set of garters with stockings. His gaze burned the same path up her body as his hands had, the browns of his irises darkening, and she felt like she'd just tipped over the edge of a roller coaster.

It was all so much—his reverence, the rawness of her nerves, and the vulnerability of standing there in underwear and letting someone look.

Not just look—*consume.*

Daniel was devouring her with his eyes.

Unable to stand still any longer, Grace scrambled backward onto the bed, stretching herself out into the same position she'd used outside the club when they'd first met. It was a generally successful move, judging by both his reaction to it then and Josh's reaction to it that morning.

Shit. No thinking about Josh.

Daniel climbed atop the bed, prowling toward her on all fours, and Grace had a surge of panic. She was not at all ready for this.

Her body was, but her brain absolutely was not.

What had she been thinking? She should have stayed at the club where it was safe, sticking to just making out in a crowd of faceless people who would never know of her deception.

To cover her nerves, she kicked out a leg, intending to rest her ankle on top of his shoulder. It would give her an extra second to gather her nerves and serve as a kind of sexy "come hither." Unfortunately, in her inebriated state, she miscalculated the landing and kicked him square in the face instead, nearly knocking him off the bed.

"Oh shit," Grace exclaimed, her hands flying up to cover her mouth. "Fuck, I'm so sorry, oh my God."

Daniel hunched over on all fours, a sound somewhere between laughing and groaning coming from him as he rubbed a spot on his cheek.

"Are you okay?" Grace's face was positively erupting into flames. How many times could she botch a single hookup?

Daniel flipped his head up, wincing but still smiling. "Luckily, soccer players have pretty hard heads."

Well, at least she wasn't nervous anymore. But was humiliated better?

"Maybe you'd better let me take it from here," he said, prowling back until he hovered over her.

Grace shivered with relief. It was far better to have him calling the shots. Then she could just go along with it and enjoy the ride. No decisions to be made.

"But," he added, "you're going to give me directions."

Her eyes widened in alarm. "What?"

"You're going to tell me where to go," he replied, easily holding himself in a plank just above her.

Was he kidding? He looked like he could take her apart with nothing but his eyes and his tongue. What the hell did he need her help for?

"Um, how about . . . everywhere?" she suggested.

"Everywhere," he repeated.

"Everywhere . . . normal?" Grace had no idea where "abnormal" might be but figured it was prudent to cover her bases.

He looked like he was fighting a smile.

Shit. She was losing him.

Grace pulled his head down to kiss her, wrapping an ankle around his calf. When she was certain she'd kissed the humor out of him, she released him. "Is that enough to get you started?" she prompted.

His mouth curved up at the corners, his dimple little more than a shadow. "You know, you're the one who brought me here."

"I know. And yet you don't seem very appreciative," Grace replied.

"Oh, I appreciate it," he said, lowering his head and letting his lips just graze the hollow of her throat. "I just want to make sure *you* do."

"I appreciate it." She gasped, twisting her hands into the sheets. "I appreciate it very much."

He flicked just the tip of his tongue across the space, and she swallowed hard. He was torturing her.

"You cocky bastard," she breathed. "You just like torturing me."

"Do you want me to stop?" he asked.

"God, no."

He dipped his head again, this time tugging down her bra with his teeth before tracing her nipple with his tongue.

Grace sank her teeth into her bottom lip to keep a whimper from escaping.

"Now," he said, closing his mouth over as much of her breast as he could, then pulling off with a little pop. "Tell me what to do next."

"Why?" It came out like a moan.

He switched over to the other breast. "I promise, I'm very coachable. I have a whole MVP plaque to prove it."

"You seem to be doing pretty well on your own."

"Uh-uh," he teased, taking his mouth away and instead blowing a light stream of cold air across her nipples. "I want to make sure I'm not doing anything you don't like."

Grace felt like she might explode. "I like it all." She gasped. "Do whatever you want."

Another suck, followed by another stream of air. "Hm. That doesn't seem safe." Gently untangling her hands from the sheets. "Or very efficient." Every movement of his was so slow, Grace thought she might lose her mind. "What if I have to wander over your whole body, trying to see what makes you make that little sound?"

"What sound?"

In the blink of an eye, he'd grabbed her wrists and pinned them above her head. She gasped in surprise.

Daniel grinned. "That sound."

Fuck. Now *this* was foreplay.

"I think you just like to shock me," she said.

"I think I like how turned on you get by it," he replied.

"Who says I'm turned on?"

"Don't lie to me, cariño," he warned. "I have ways of finding out."

He slid his left hand down her body, across her stomach, and into her underwear. At the slightest touch, Grace's back arched off the bed and she let out a strangled moan.

"Mm. You want to rethink your answer?"

"You proved nothing," she insisted.

"So you *don't* like this," he said, flicking his fingers against her. A zap of pain shot through her, this time in her most sensitive area.

She gasped again.

"I swear to God, if you keep this up," she threatened, having zero idea of how she would even begin to retaliate. How did one pleasure-torture a guy? Just give a really slow blow job?

"You'll what? Kick me in the face again?" Daniel looked amused at the empty threat.

He skated his finger across her once more, this time his touch was back to featherlight. Grace moaned in frustration, struggling against the hold on her wrists as she tried to kick her legs up around his waist to pull him closer.

Daniel pinned her legs down with a knee across her thighs, her body stretched out and completely at his mercy. He looked her straight in the eyes, voice serious. "Do you really want me to let you go?"

She answered honestly. "Fuck no."

He smiled—not the sweet smile she'd begun to like, but the cocky grin she'd begun to like even more—the kind that told her he knew exactly what he was doing to her. "Good. Then whatever you do, don't say stop."

"Or else?"

He thrust his fingers into her, and she seemed to swallow all the oxygen in the room. "Or else I stop."

Daniel certainly knew what he was doing, and Grace found herself more engaged than she'd ever been before, trying to wiggle her body into the right places while dictating advice.

"More. Faster. Harder," she panted, bucking wildly, willing him to increase the pressure and speed.

"See? That wasn't so difficult, now was it?" he teased, finally rewarding her with the heel of his hand.

Grace let out a wail so loud she could shatter submarines, the internal and external stimulation exactly the combination she needed. "I'm going to die," she sobbed. "I'm dying."

"You're not dying, cariño."

"I am," she insisted. "If you don't finish me in the next two minutes I'll die."

Daniel smirked at her, and Grace knew for certain that he'd been holding back. "Hm. I *am* pretty competitive. I think we can do better than two minutes, don't you?"

She squeezed her eyes shut and clamped her legs together, anticipating the release of pressure in her abdomen. God, she was *so* close.

Instead, his touch went featherlight again, and Grace's eyes flew open in protest. "Wha—"

"Nope," he said, his face only inches away from hers, dark eyes staring intensely into hers. "You don't get to hide. Look me in the eyes or you don't get to come."

Grace's body flashed hot, and she moaned pitifully, unable to move under the grip of both his hands and his knee. She pressed her legs together even tighter, trying to get the tiniest whisper of an orgasm before she lost her grip on it.

She couldn't just stop and start like a car. If she didn't get it now, Grace wasn't sure God himself could get it back.

Daniel seemed unconcerned by her predicament, even removing his knee from her thighs to wedge it between her legs, forcing them apart and causing her to whimper again.

"Now. Let's try this again." His voice was low, fingers continuing to dip in and out at a slow pace. It was just enough to keep her riding the edge, but not enough to satisfy her. "Tell me what you want."

This time, Grace didn't want to play coy. She *couldn't*. "Make me come," she begged. "Please."

"Then look me in the eyes," he demanded.

She opened her eyes wide and stared into his as his fingers curled into her and pressed directly on the swollen spot inside of her, her body shattering into a million pieces.

The orgasm rolled over her like waves in the ocean, pulling her under for so long that she had aftershocks from the overwhelming experience of it, Daniel's eyes searing into her through the entire thing. It was the single best experience of her life, and she'd once stood next to Keanu Reeves on an elevator.

When she finally stopped convulsing, she could barely breathe, but managed to choke out, "Holy shit."

Grace was usually left stranded somewhere near the peak, unable to push herself over the edge without the aid of battery-operated devices. Yet this near stranger had fingered his way to her bliss in under ten minutes. Well, ten minutes and however long his kisses had taken. It had felt like an eternity at the time, but now all she could think was how much she wanted him to do that again every day for the rest of her life.

Every orgasm she'd ever had paled in comparison to what

she just experienced. She wasn't even sure she could call those orgasms anymore, they bore so little resemblance to what she'd just endured. (Yes, endured.)

Daniel released her wrists and placed a soft kiss on each one as he brought them back down to her sides.

"Well, Coach? How'd I do?"

Grace stared at him with stars circling her head like a cartoon character, eyes glassy and chest heaving like she'd just run an Olympic sprint. "How?" was all she could manage.

Daniel laughed as he rolled over onto his side, and Grace felt slightly embarrassed about the person she'd become with him—placing demands and threats like she had any claim to expectations.

"I'm sorry," she immediately apologized.

"For what?"

Grace blushed, the orgasm having magically dissolved most of her drunkenness. She had no ready excuse for why she'd been so . . . forward. "I just . . . it got heated and . . ."

She didn't know how to explain that she'd gotten swept up in all of it and that she wasn't usually so aggressive. She didn't want him to think she was the type of person who regularly brought guys home to have sex.

Yes, she'd done the hookup thing on occasion, but she'd generally been *very* sloshed, and it was mostly because the guy had really wanted to and it was easier to beg off with a blow job than to explain that she really just wanted to make out and do high school–level stuff.

Josh had been the first guy who was genuinely *nice* to her. He was the one who took her seriously, the one who listened to her opinions, and the one who hadn't rushed her into sex. After he'd been honest about his limitations, *she'd* been the one who agreed they could keep sleeping together without it complicating things.

Daniel was staring anxiously at Grace, watching her work through it in her head. "Was it too much? I was too rough. You're freaking out. Fuck."

"No!" Grace exclaimed, realizing her overreaction to his reaction was now making things worse. "I'm not freaking out," she reassured him, placing a hand on his arm. "I was just . . ." She flailed around mentally, trying to find something coherent to say.

Now was not the time to be thinking about Josh or the *niceness* of their relationship. Or rather, non-relationship. In fact, he was the last person she should have in her mind when she was here with this . . . this hot, muscly meathead with skin the color of sun-drenched earth and eyes so dark they had their own gravitational pull.

She regrouped.

"I was thinking about how I'm the only one naked here," she finished, pushing herself up into a sitting position. "Shirt off."

Daniel arched an eyebrow. "Yes, ma'am." He tugged off his black tee in that way only guys did—his hands grasping the back and pulling it over his head, showcasing all of his delicious muscles.

Grace never thought she'd be into someone so bulky and stereotypically *guy*, with the attitude and the sports and whatever else she didn't know about him but assumed. But seeing the black ink of the recognizable Formosan tiger that stretched across his broad shoulder and down onto his chest and back, she was quickly revising that opinion. Maybe she needed someone this big to be able to hold her down and *make* her come, as he'd just aptly demonstrated. Josh certainly couldn't.

No thinking about Josh.

She raised herself onto her knees and leaned forward, using her tongue to trace the lines of the tiger across the base of his neck and down his chest.

Daniel gave a little shiver, pulling aside his necklace to give her an unobstructed path. "Big fan of tattoos?"

"Big fan of this one."

"I knew it. You brought me here just to get a look at it."

"I could get a better look at it if you were on top of me."

"You in a hurry, mama?"

"Oh, are we going back to role-playing?" she teased. "Because I hope I don't look like anyone's mom."

Daniel grinned devilishly, transitioning back to Spanish.

"Voy a tomar las cosas bien y lento ahora," he murmured, crawling his way back on top of her, pulling her legs out from beneath and wrapping them around his waist. "No hay necesidad de apresurarse, tenemos toda la noche."

"Jesus Christ," Grace muttered, her hands fumbling against the zipper of his jeans that were infuriatingly still on. If she stopped for even a minute to think about how hot he was in this moment she might burst into flames.

"*Jesús Cristo*," he corrected, shoving off his pants and underwear (also black, tight, and hot as hell on him) all the way and rolling a condom on himself. "And if you think you need Jesus now . . ."

"Sure. Yes. Whatever," Grace panted, trying to pull him into her.

She locked her legs behind Daniel and tugged, pulling his length inside of her without warning. It wasn't exactly comfortable, straddling the line between good and painful, but Grace reminded herself that sex with someone new was always an adjustment. Daniel also required some, ahem, additional accommodation.

He stilled. "What's wrong?"

Grace tried to turn her grimace into a smile. "Nothing. Just getting used to you."

"Am I hurting you?"

Grace huffed. "Why do guys assume their dicks are so big they're going to hurt you?"

"I'm saying that because you stopped moving and you're making a face like you're in pain."

"Oh."

Grace wiggled her hips, trying to get comfortable. But everything about it just felt . . . wrong. Maybe it was the alcohol. It was probably dehydrating her. Shouldn't she still have some leftover moisture down there? Grace had never dared to try for back-to-back orgasms before. Maybe they were a myth?

"Do you want to try being on top? Might help you adjust to what you need."

Daniel's eyes were so earnest, like he was committed to solving the problem *with* her instead of simply dictating what would work best for him. He could have kept going, assuming the lubrication would come eventually. Josh had certainly taken that approach once or twice when they were short on time, and he was usually right. The only problem was that by the time he was done, Grace was finally warmed up and ready for real action.

But that wasn't the issue here—Daniel had made sure to take care of her first. Any lack of enthusiasm from her downstairs parts was her own fault, not his.

"Just give me a sec," she said, wiggling herself and taking a few deep breaths to try to calm her tensed muscles.

"Let me help." Daniel ran his thumb over the seam of her lips and on instinct, she took it into her mouth. It was warm and slightly calloused, and she had the urge to bite down on the tip of it.

When she did, he gave a strangled cry but didn't resist until she was done. Then he rubbed the now wet thumb across her clit, trying to get her more comfortable.

That little gesture undid her. Here he was, this random guy, giving more thought to her enjoyment than her own boyfriend had in months and months of sleeping together. Maybe Josh loved her, but he certainly hadn't noticed the responses her body had to different maneuvers the way Daniel had. Or maybe he hadn't cared enough to take notice.

To Grace's utter mortification, a tear slipped out and slid down her cheek before she had the chance to catch it.

Daniel immediately stopped everything and backed up onto his knees, his eyes widening with concern. "Oh shit, I'm sorry. We don't have to do this if you're not ready."

Grace swiped at her face, flaming with embarrassment. Why was her first emotion always tears?

"It's not that. I'm fine, really. It's probably allergies." She gave an unconvincing cough. "Really, I'm fine," she insisted. "Let's just do this."

But when she reached for him, Daniel was already climbing off the bed, pulling his shirt on in the process. "It's been a long night, and I should probably let you get some rest."

Damn it.

She'd tried to have *one* night of fun. *One* Josh-free experience where she could just enjoy herself and not break down into a garbage pile of emotions or spend the next day analyzing everything that was said and done for clues about *his* emotional state.

She'd done this to help her detach from Josh and instead let him ruin it. Some fucking actress she was.

But as always, the show had to go on.

Daniel was already going to think she was completely unhinged. No need to make it worse by explaining that actually, she was crying because she just realized her (ex-)boyfriend didn't care very much about her enjoyment of their sex together that she'd always thought was meaningful and precious.

Grace mustered up the breeziest expression she could, her rapidly blinking eyes holding back any further tears from falling. "Sure. Of course. No worries. Thanks."

Stop. Fucking. Talking.

Daniel hesitated at the door, having gotten dressed much faster than it had taken to undress, which was an extra blow to her already fractured ego. It was clear he was struggling to come up with something polite to say before dashing for the exit.

Grace decided to relieve him of the pressure. It was literally the least she could do at this point. "See you around," she lied, her bedcovers clutched against her naked chest to shield her from any further exposure.

Please let me never see you again.

Daniel nodded. "Yeah. Take care."

The moment he was out of sight, Grace collapsed back onto her bed, the relaxation of her earlier orgasm a distant memory. So much for forgetting.

CHAPTER TWELVE

"Houston, we have a problem."
—Apollo 13 (1995)

Grace didn't awaken until the next morning, her nearly dead phone alight with a single message from Josh.

Josh: Looks like you didn't miss me too much last night

He'd sent a link to her social media, where Tiff had tagged her in several photos.

Grace clicked over to the original post, where there were a slew of candid photos from the night before. Mostly selfies of Tiff and Lúcio, who Grace noted was exceptionally photogenic. But there were some of her *as* well—pictures Grace either didn't remember or didn't realize were being taken. One showed Grace laughing, head back and mouth open as Daniel stood close to her. The next was a face she'd made at Tiff, the camera flash reflecting off her forehead as she held a drink in each hand. But the one Josh must have been referring to . . .

It was dark, but still clear what was happening. Daniel leaning into Grace, his hand holding her hair off her shoulder as he whispered in her ear. It looked intimate.

Panicked, Grace swiped through the rest of the pictures, making sure that was the worst of them. Thank God Tiff hadn't gotten any photos of the two of them making out in the middle of the dance floor.

What the hell had Grace been thinking? This is why things were better conducted behind closed doors—you never knew who was watching or photographing you. No wonder celebrities were always complaining about the paparazzi.

Grace rushed to the balcony and flung open the doors, screaming silently into the hot, salty air. All that effort, all that progress with Josh . . . only to be brought down by a dark-ass photo taken from thirty feet away on zoom.

She looked at the pictures again, a mix of feelings swirling through her.

In all of them, she looked . . . happy. Deliriously so. And that made her remember just how fun the night *had* been. That is, until she cried.

Now, that happiness morphed into guilt. She'd actually taken someone home. Not just someone—the guy in these very photos. Josh was looking at a practically real-time account of her vacation fling. None of it would have even happened if he'd just fucking texted her back.

Grace had been awake all of five minutes, and already her head was throbbing. And now she had to go face her friends.

"Morning," Tiff chirped, already nursing a steaming mocha courtesy of self-trained barista Camille. "Where's the boy?"

"Gone. Didn't you notice there weren't any guy shoes in the entryway?"

"Who am I, fucking Sherlock Holmes? When we got home, I tried to open your door, but it was locked. I assumed you were still together in there."

"Well, we weren't."

Tiff and Camille exchanged looks at Grace's clipped responses.

"Someone should look a little more happy, no?" Camille teased. "Or is he bad like his football taste?"

"Yes, Camille, because that's exactly what the rest of us use as a barometer for sexiness," Tiff said. "Though I did get a glimpse of that soccer ass, and whew, girl, I am not mad at that. We should find out if UCSC has a soccer team."

"Thanks for your approval," Grace said sarcastically. "By the way, can you not tag me in random pictures without asking?"

Tiff frowned. "What are you talking about?"

"The ones from last night. I don't exactly want a bunch of pictures of me with some random guy just floating out there on the internet."

Tiff laughed, wiggling her fingers like she was performing magic. "Ooh, not the *internet*. Who cares? They're not even scandalous."

"It doesn't matter what they are. I don't like it," Grace snapped.

Another glance between Tiff and Camille.

"Did something happen with the boy last night?" Tiff asked.

"This isn't about him or last night," Grace insisted. "It's about basic courtesy."

"Jeez, okay. I won't do it again. Sorry."

Grace relaxed a fraction, finally slumping into a chair at the table as Camille slipped a steaming mocha in front of her. Grace inhaled deeply before taking a sip, the concoction tasting a bit like . . . cinnamon?

"Did you change your recipe or something?" Grace asked Camille. "It tastes different than usual."

Camille beamed at the recognition. "I use the chocolate I buy yesterday at the market. Mexican chocolate. It's good, no?"

"Delicious," Grace agreed, indulging in another tiny sip. "Sorry for my freak-out. Guess I woke up in a mood," she joked weakly. She knew it wasn't Tiff's fault that Josh had seen the pictures. Or even that she'd taken them in the first place. After all, Grace was technically single. She wasn't *technically* doing anything wrong.

But it didn't make her feel any less like crap.

Tiff, luckily, recovered quickly. The upside of having a moody best friend was that she was just as forgiving of Grace's mood swings. "Does this mean you're ready to talk now? I want all the dirty details, and they'd better be dirty because I'm not trying to stereotype, but that boy looks like he could put the 'lover' in 'Latin lover.' Lúcio does."

"Let's hear more about that," Grace said, hoping to steer the conversation toward Tiff's exploits instead of her own. It still felt too raw to talk about.

"Nuh-uh. I'll tell you after you tell me."

Grace's friends must have already agreed not to let her wiggle out of questioning because Camille pressed on. "So . . . Daniel goes himself or you ask him to leave?"

Tiff whacked a hand against Camille's bony arm, nodding vigorously. She was *way* too amped up about this interrogation. "Good question, Camille."

"I know," Camille said with irritation, rubbing the spot Tiff hit.

Grace forced down a big gulp of her mocha to stall for time, the drink scorching a path down her esophagus.

"Did you at least see the rest of his tattoo?" Tiff asked, too impatient to wait for Grace to start speaking. "And is he circumcised or uncircumcised? Because Lúcio is *not*." She waggled her eyebrows.

"Jesus," Camille muttered, covering her face. "Why create this ego alter if you don't use it? You make me pretend an accent all night, but you stay the same as you always are."

"Not last night," Tiff protested. "Only Grace was stuck being someone else. Which seemed like a good thing?" Tiff raised her eyebrows expectantly at Grace. With all the waggling and raising and furrowing, Tiff looked like she was trying to invent an entirely new language out of just her eyebrow movements.

"It was fine," Grace answered vaguely.

Hot. Intense. And then horribly, horribly embarrassing.

"You are not telling us everything," Camille chided.

"You're not telling us *anything*!" Tiff exclaimed. "Enough. Spill it."

Part of Grace wanted to put up another argument—to insist she didn't owe them anything. Except she did, actually. She owed them this entire trip, which they still believed was in service to getting her over Josh. They deserved to hear about what happened with Daniel.

Grace heaved a sigh. "He left on his own." Another

moment of hesitation, then Grace vomited out the whole story as quickly as possible, her hands covering her face when she admitted the thought of Josh had brought her to tears.

"I wasn't, like, full-on sobbing," Grace rushed to explain. "It was just a couple of tears, and I told him I was okay, but I guess he got weirded out and left. I don't blame him."

Apparently, it was even worse than Grace had thought. Tiff uncomfortably twisted the rings on her fingers while Camille simply stared.

"Needless to say, I won't be seeing him ever again," Grace joked, laughing nervously to fill the dead silence that settled in the room.

"You thought about *Josh*?" Tiff burst out.

Of course. An entire story's worth of material and that was the detail she focused on.

"It's natural, no?" Camille replied. "He was not so long ago, it takes time to recover."

"It's not that," Tiff said. "I'm not saying I expect her to get over him right away, even though it's been *weeks*. I just mean, how the hell can you be with someone who looks like Daniel and still conjure up *Josh*?"

Great. Her friends were discussing her recovery like she wasn't even in the same room.

"It's not like I meant to," Grace interjected. "I was just drunk and it was really overwhelming."

Camille nodded like she understood. "I see the way you two look at each other. Like you are hungry. Maybe it was too much."

"Too much sexual attraction? No such thing," Tiff said. "I saw the two of you too. It did not look like you thought about Josh a single time you were with Daniel."

Well. Grace certainly wasn't going to try to convince Tiff that she *was* thinking about Josh. That she'd come all the way down here *for* him, in fact. So instead, she just shrugged. "At least it's over and done with. It still counts as a hookup, so I've officially rebounded."

It doesn't really count, Grace whispered secretly to herself. She had barely even touched Daniel. Just because he did things to her didn't mean she did them back. And that five seconds of him being inside her really shouldn't count as sex (unless she were to apply Tiff's standards, in which case everything they did was sex).

The fact that Daniel had used a condom (without prompting) gave her more relief. No risk of STDs.

"And if you did see him again?" Tiff asked.

"I'd finally be convinced I was cursed?" Grace replied.

Camille waved away Grace's comment. "Pfft. So you have one bad experience. Who does not have this? We are adults. Who knows? Maybe you get another chance later." Camille waggled her eyebrows, clearly having learned Tiff's new silent language.

"You're not understanding. I started *crying* while he was *inside of me*," Grace emphasized. "No guy wants sex that badly, especially when that's all it is."

Abruptly, Tiff reached across the table and punched Grace in the boob.

"What the fuck?!" Grace bellowed. She clutched a hand to her chest before Tiff got any ideas about targeting the other one.

"Do you hear yourself?" Tiff demanded, still leaning over the table threateningly. "God, Josh really fucked you up. Do you really think sex is the only thing you have to offer?" She hit her hand against the side of her head. "This boy has been chasing you from the beginning. He obviously liked you or he would have tried to fuck you the first night. Who cares if you did something embarrassing during sex? Guys do that all the time! Do you think they just stop putting themselves out there, apologizing for their limp dicks? No! They just say, 'Oh, this never happens to me,' and move on."

Camille nodded vigorously. "It's true. They all say this. Even if it happens all the time."

Tiff shot Camille a questioning look, which Camille again dismissed with a flick of her long fingers.

"Ah. He was too old."

"Too old to get an erection?" Grace asked in disbelief. "How old was this guy?"

Tiff waved a hand between Grace and Camille, drawing the attention back to herself. "Hey. We can talk about Grandpa *Misérables* later. No changing the subject."

"I don't even remember what the subject was," Grace innocently lied, hoping desperately to get off the topic of Daniel, Josh, or any of her other failures.

Tiff tilted her head and pursed her lips in a way that said, *Nice try*.

"Whatever," Grace pouted. "Either way, I'm not doing that again. He left—no, *ran out!*—while I was still naked!"

Camille and Tiff both grimaced. "Not great," Camille said at the same time Tiff said, "Yeah, that wasn't ideal."

"But everyone gets a one-time pass to be an asshole," Tiff quickly added.

"How many passes do we give you, Tiffany?" Camille asked innocently, earning her a boob punch from Tiff.

"Ow! Why do you do this?" Camille moaned, clutching her chest.

"Oh, please, I can barely find your boobs. I think I punched your clavicle."

"Why are you so set on Daniel anyway?" Grace asked, unable to resist. Was it just that Tiff wanted Grace as far away from Josh as possible? Or did her friends see something she was missing?

"It's not just Daniel," Tiff confirmed. "Though I still think you should give him another chance"—Tiff held up her hand to keep Grace from arguing—"*if* we happen to see him again."

"We won't," Grace insisted. "And if we do, I'll just hide."

Tiff continued, ignoring the interruption, "I also don't think it's healthy for a vagina to get so used to one person. Especially if that person is vanilla. It's like that whole 'don't make that face or it'll freeze like that' thing. What if your coochie gets frozen to the point it'll only fit Josh's skinny dick?"

"Seriously, what is wrong with you?" Camille asked.

"I never said Josh's dick was skinny," Grace pointed out.

"Oh, okay, so beefcake Daniel *doesn't* have a thicker dick than vampire theater boy?" Tiff challenged.

"Oh my God," Camille muttered under her breath. She collected all their mugs with a ducked head and took them to the sink.

"I'm done talking about dicks," Grace announced, slapping her hands on the table and rising to her feet. At this point, it wasn't even worth it to find out the details of Tiff's night. She just wanted to get as far away from this conversation as possible.

"I'm *never* done talking about dicks," Tiff replied. "And I will continue to talk about them until you assure me that if you get the chance, you will let that boy give you another orgasm, because the orgasm gap is real, and this is the way we fight back against it."

"*Mi* orgasm *es su* orgasm?"

Tiff raised a fist in the air. "Fight the power. *Si se puede.*"

Grace knew Tiff was partially kidding, but she wondered if other women really approached their hookups so . . . mercenarily. Maybe what was really bothering her about her mess-up with Daniel wasn't just the embarrassment but that she didn't hold up her end of the deal. He'd gone home with her expecting sex. Or at the very least, getting off in some way. But she was the only one who had. The imbalance of it made her uncomfortable. Like she was in his debt somehow.

"I'm not joking, Grace," Tiff insisted, kicking her little feet up onto the now vacant chair beside her so that she was boxed in like a magician's assistant, ready to be sawed in half. She stuffed the last bite of toast into her mouth. "You getting off without him getting off has shifted a tiny part of the power in the universe." Crumbs sprayed out of her mouth as she talked around her food, garbling the words but still managing to sound authoritative about it.

Grace rolled her eyes. "Yes, blue balls will cure the world of the patriarchy."

Tiff shrugged. "It's what they get for making that up to pressure girls into sex in the first place."

"I just feel kind of . . . I don't know. Guilty?" She was nervous admitting it aloud, but Grace wasn't sure what else to do with the emotion. She was juggling too much—the secret about Josh's whereabouts, the secret of keeping Daniel from Josh and vice versa (though she supposed she'd already screwed that up), and now, the secret of just how deep her shame went about all of this.

Grace had never considered herself some kind of pearl-clutching Puritan, but the past few days really made her question that. She even felt a little embarrassed about how *much* she'd enjoyed being with Daniel. Why did her brain insist on interpreting everything that felt good to her as shameful?

Camille frowned. "What do you mean guilty? About Daniel?"

Grace rubbed her ear. "I just mean, he came home with me expecting sex and then he left after getting nothing. It feels unfair, you know? Like I tricked him somehow."

Tiff tried to punch her again, but Grace was too quick and protected her chest.

"Tiffany, stop!" Camille admonished her. She turned to Grace. "You were crying, yes?"

Grace winced at having to address the embarrassing moment again, but nodded.

"Drunk? You want him to try to sleep with you, even while you are like this? Ask you to do things for him even though you are upset? Make him feel better but not yourself?"

"Well, not when you put it like that . . ." Grace replied slowly.

"But you expect this to happen?" Camille continued.

Grace pressed her lips together, not wanting to answer the question. It was obvious what her friends thought. And it was obvious Grace hadn't realized until right that minute that the expectation to suffer through sex until the man came was deeply, societally fucked. But still, there was unspoken etiquette to consider.

"Shouldn't hooking up be an even and fair exchange of services?" she asked. "Otherwise how do you make sure one person isn't always getting cheated?"

Camille looked at her with her most pitying look yet, and

Grace had the urge to simply walk into the ocean. But it was Tiff who spoke up this time.

"This isn't your job, Grace. You're not a sex worker. You don't owe anyone anything. If they give you something and expect something back, that's on them. Sometimes you come out ahead, and sometimes you don't, but that's life. We all have shitty encounters. I'm not about to give some guy head just because he did it first, especially if it sucked. You have the right to bail at any time, for any reason."

Camille nodded vigorously, but her eyes still held the same sympathy. Like Grace was a small child, learning about sex for the first time. Poor, naive Grace.

Shame replaced guilt, her insides shriveling the way they had the night before when she'd cried. Her friends thought she was weak.

Worse, so did she.

Grace had always thought it was noble to agree to Josh's wants and needs, sacrificing herself for the greater good of their relationship, even when she didn't want to. She did it to show him she cared—that she loved him. But why hadn't her wants and needs been taken into equal consideration? While she was looking out for him, why wasn't he looking out for her?

"I'm not sure most guys see it the same way," Grace said lightly. After all, if she believed this and Josh didn't, what would it matter?

"Who cares whether they do or not? If they don't, fuck them," Tiff said belligerently. "Better yet, *don't* fuck them."

Camille, thankfully, was a bit more thoughtful. "This is true, many men do not see our pleasure as important. But that is why we must, no? If a man thinks this when you begin, he will never change his mind."

"He might," Grace said, still determined to believe there was a way to patch the huge crack in her relationship with Josh that was just exposed. "Don't you think guys approach sex differently between a random hookup and, like, a girlfriend?"

"Of course!" Camille replied. "But even with someone for one night, they should give you respect, no?"

"There are plenty of guys out there who aren't selfish assholes," Tiff chimed in. "I think you need to get back out there, try again." Tiff was clearly hatching another plan to get her friend laid—properly this time. Grace needed to stop her before she gained steam.

The last thing Grace needed right now was sex. From anyone. She needed a lecture from Tiff about Josh even less. Her friends probably already suspected Grace's questions were about him. If she kept talking about it, Tiff would end up hating Josh even more than she already did.

"I think I could use some decompressing," Grace said quickly. "Maybe some yoga?"

Tiff looked surprised. Grace hated yoga, and Tiff knew it. She'd tried it exactly once before promptly announcing she'd never accompany Tiff to another class. There was just a lot of . . . stretching.

"Ooh, I love yoga," Camille exclaimed. (Of course she did.) "Maybe we can do it on the beach?"

Tiff attempted to call Grace's bluff. "I've heard about yoga classes where they have you do them on paddleboards in the water."

"I'm game if you are," Grace replied sweetly, refusing to break eye contact. "We're here to try new things, aren't we?"

Tiff narrowed her eyes, still suspicious of Grace's diversion.

But she also wasn't going to pass up the chance to force Grace into doing her least favorite activity. Tiff seemed to be convinced her mission in life was to push Grace out of her "comfort zone" (a.k.a. normal activities that normal people participated in). "I'll make some calls."

CHAPTER THIRTEEN

"Why are you wearing that stupid man suit?"
—Donnie Darko (2001)

To Grace's relief (and Camille's disappointment), Tiff hadn't been able to find a yoga instructor who specialized in paddleboard classes on such short notice. But a regular certified instructor arrived within hours, bearing mats for all of them. Grace lobbied to keep the activity indoors, but the woman spouted something about the position of the sun and the energy from the water or whatever else and convinced Tiff and Camille to outvote her.

"I can't believe she charged you *per person*," Grace said quietly, struggling to plank her body in the soft sand as a bead of sweat dripped off her forehead. She'd wanted to escape the great French Inquisition about her sex life at breakfast but was now having second thoughts about her strategy.

"Tell me about it." Tiff grunted after each word, trying unsuccessfully to adjust her bikini bottoms mid-plank. "I hope whoever's flying the drone that's going to discover you enjoys my spectacular wedgie right now."

"Now back to downward-facing dog," the instructor intoned, stretching her lean body easily into the pose. "Really feel that stretch through the back of your legs as you drive your heels down into the sand."

"You really missed out on that yoga class you dropped," Tiff panted, pushing the back half of her body up into the pose. "We did this with partners who were supposed to make sure your hips were lifted so they'd stand directly behind you and grab your hips. Like straight up acrobat doggy-style. So fucking awkward when I got paired with that weird guy with the scraggly beard you said looked like an ugly Nick Miller."

Grace tried to hold in her laugh, which only succeeded in making her arms shakier, the decidedly muscle-free limbs already struggling to hold her weight. "I'm trying to picture how low he had to crouch to make that position happen."

"God, look at that bitch," Tiff whispered, gesturing toward Camille, who was folded over like a circus performer, each bony joint sharp and angular.

Grace chuckled, happily dropping out of the pose to grab her phone, which had buzzed a number of times in quick succession.

Josh: What are your plans tonight

Josh: We might be wrapping early

Josh: We could meet up?

Josh: Maybe grab dinner?

Grace's smile grew as she read the messages. Suddenly, it didn't seem to matter how hot it was or how sweat had forced her bangs to cling to her forehead, surely clogging her pores.

Josh: Unless you have another hot date with some guy you just met

Jesus. Why? Couldn't he have just asked her to come over, no underhanded dig required? Grace had assured Josh she wasn't sleeping with anyone else and she'd (mostly) kept that true. He really had no reason to distrust her. A photo standing near someone wasn't sex.

"Why the fuck did we plan this for the hottest part of the— Hey, who are you texting?" Tiff hissed and flung a handful of sand toward Grace, who finally tore her eyes away from the phone.

"What the hell?" Grace whispered back, wiping sand off herself and her mat (though that was really a losing battle).

"Why are you on your phone? We're supposed be suffering through this together."

"You *like* yoga," Grace reminded her.

"I like it when there's not sand blowing in my eyes during it," Tiff grumbled, shoving an errant curl out of her face, failing, then trying to blow it off her forehead by contorting her mouth into different shapes. "Whose terrible idea was this?"

"And now we rise into sun salutation," the instructor continued, her body stretching seemingly forever upward.

Grace glanced over at Camille, who once again looked the picture of fitness, unbothered by both the heat and sand. Grace made a mental note to never do anything remotely athletic near her again.

Another buzz.

Josh: I need to know if you're coming or else I'm going out with the crew

There should be no hesitation. Sure, Grace had entertained some uncomfortable thoughts about him during her conversation with her friends. But she'd also been excited when his texts came in just now. Her head was a mess. Grace needed to see him to sort it all out.

Grace: i'm in, just lmk when and where

Josh: Is your mom going to be ok with that lol

Grace looked up from her phone to see Tiff frowning at her. But why? It was clear Grace was smiling. Why didn't her best friend want her to be happy?

Grace: she's definitely not

Grace: but she's a big girl, she'll live

Josh: Ok big talker

Josh: Can't wait to see that

Grace chuckled lightly to herself at that. Josh always teased her about not standing up for herself. She knew he was right, but it was also why she'd (mostly) stopped complaining about her problems with Tiff to him. The two of them just had too much animosity toward each other to stay objective. Josh thought Tiff was judgmental and controlling; Tiff thought Josh was a vanilla fuckboy who was using Grace. The only thing they had in common was that they both thought Grace was too much of a coward to do anything about either of them.

"You're not even pretending to follow along anymore," Tiff said, trying to scold Grace while wobbling in tree pose.

It was true. Grace was simply kneeling now, phone shamelessly in her hands. But Josh was a bigger priority than practicing her balance. If she didn't lock down plans, Grace risked losing him for the night. It wasn't a difficult choice.

“I’m on break,” she said, shrugging.

Grace: if you could only see me right now

Grace: i’m out here with guns blazing high noon ready for a showdown

Grace: i’m damn near john wayne but without all the racism

Josh: Pic or it didn’t happen

Grace almost texted back a comment about how he’d seen enough photos of her for the day, but she didn’t want to reopen *that* conversation. The less said (or thought) about the previous night (and Daniel), the better.

Grace: no way i’m sweaty and gross

Grace: we’re doing beach yoga

Grace: it’s a nightmare

Josh: I bet you look hot

Josh: Send me a pic

Before Grace could respond, Tiff darted over and snatched the phone with a triumphant little laugh.

“Got i— Oh my God, you’re texting *Josh*?” Tiff bellowed.

With Tiff’s momentary paralysis, Grace grabbed her phone back, holding it against her chest protectively. “For the record, *he* texted *me*,” Grace said. “I was just answering a question.”

“So the fuck what?”

“All I said was that we were doing beach yoga.”

“He’s your ex! He doesn’t get to know what you’re doing!” Suddenly, Tiff sucked in a huge gasp of air, her eyes bugging in revelation. “Oh my God. That’s why you were so mad about the pictures of you with Daniel! I *knew* I should have blocked that vile rodent.”

Fucking private detective Tiffany Hong-Ahn. Good luck to any guy she dated in the future who might even *think* about cheating on her.

Still, there was nothing Grace could do but continue to deny it. "He has nothing to do with that, it's just basic courtesy to acknowledge other people's texts," she insisted. (It really was.)

"Give me the phone," Tiff demanded, thrusting her palm out. "This entire fucking trip is to help you get over him, and instead, you're what? Making excuses to him about why you're going out as a single, unattached person even though he's the one who dumped you? Don't you have any self-respect?"

That one stung.

"I'm not making excuses about anything," Grace shot back. Her good mood was officially obliterated, sacrificed at the hands of a person who claimed that nothing but the brutal truth was the true mark of friendship. As if talking to Grace like a human being would somehow diminish Tiff's message. As it was, Grace heard it loud and clear: She was a loser for wanting someone who didn't want her back.

"Fuck," Grace said, pushing the bangs off her face, only to feel them land back on the sticky target that was her forehead. "It was one text."

Tiff looked at Grace with utter disgust. Like Grace was actually repulsive to her. "It's never just one text with you."

"Tiffany, please. Let's go inside and get some water," Camille urged, she and the instructor finally surrendering the lesson to the drama going on next to them. "Everyone cool off, it is very hot."

"Don't bother." Grace stood and aggressively brushed the sand off her legs, wishing she were hitting Tiff instead of herself. "I'll go. I have enough *self-respect* to leave when I'm not wanted."

"That's new," Tiff muttered, not even pretending to say it quietly enough that Grace wouldn't hear it.

"Grace, no," Camille implored. "Tiffany does not mean it this way."

"Yes, I do." Tiff smirked, folding her arms across her chest. She looked like a fucking Bratz doll.

"Well, there you have it," Grace said to Camille. For Tiff, she bit out a sarcastic, "Thanks for the support."

Stomping back to the house, she heard Tiff yell, "You just wasted two hundred and fifty dollars!"

By the time Grace finished showering, Josh had sent her the location of a restaurant to meet at. But it was hard to summon her earlier excitement.

The fact was, Tiff wasn't completely wrong. Grace *was* making excuses to Josh about her activities, even though it was his fault she was single in the first place. But Tiff also had no idea how complicated the situation really was. Grace was trapped in this kind of limbo where she and Josh had regressed back to the early stages of dating, but with the developed feelings of a long relationship. How could she be expected to just cut ties and erase everything between them without any kind of real closure?

Grace had no idea what to think of her relationship with Josh anymore. All she knew was that she still wanted to see him more than she wanted to see anyone else, and if that made her pathetic, so be it. She couldn't just give up now. Not after all the time and emotions she'd invested. She was determined to see it through to the bitter end, no matter which way it went.

She refused to have regrets about what could have been.

There was a soft knock on her bedroom door, followed by Camille's gentle voice. "May I come in?"

Grace threw the door open for her and flopped onto the bed, mentally preparing herself for some kind of intervention or mediation, no doubt. Sometimes it felt like college was one giant sitcom, where every conflict was amplified for drama and someone always had to learn a lesson at the end.

If only it wasn't always her having to do the learning.

"I don't want to talk about Tiff," Grace said before Camille could say a word.

"I am not here to talk about Tiffany," Camille reassured her. "I just come to check on you."

Grace rolled her eyes. "To see if I have any self-respect left?"

Grace knew she was absolutely playing the part of the bratty teen on the sitcom, but she couldn't help it. She was going through massive emotional turmoil, and all her best friend seemed to care about was whether Grace would fuck someone new.

Camille stayed safely tucked against the wall, as if Grace were a wild animal harboring unpredictable and possibly dangerous behaviors. "That was not nice to say. But we are worried about you."

"What is there to worry about?"

Camille shot her a knowing look, and Grace had to look away to conceal her guilty face.

Of course her friends were worried. Even Grace was worried.

"If Josh is good for you, I will be so happy," Camille said. "But you are sad all the time because of him."

"Not *all* the time," Grace protested weakly. "I've been plenty happy since we've been here, even though he's been texting me."

"Maybe this is because of Daniel, no?"

Grace scoffed. "Please. Last night was one of the most embarrassing things I've ever experienced, and I once accidentally shouted 'ménage à trois' in history class instead of 'coup d'état.'"

Camille giggled at the French mix-up but pressed on. "But this is the first time I see you smile in weeks. Cannot be by accident?"

Grace had to admit that Daniel *had* been a nice distraction, even though it ultimately ended in disaster. He'd made her feel good about herself for the first time since she and Josh had broken up.

She sank back into the pillows, making sure to flip her wet hair from behind her shoulders so that it fanned out around her head. "It doesn't matter. Daniel or no Daniel, this is vacation. At some point, I have to go back to my real life."

"And Josh is real life?"

"He's . . . I don't know." Grace stared at the ceiling for a few moments, trying to find the right words to convince her friend of something she wasn't even sure about herself. "More real than this. He cares about me enough to check in and see how I'm doing."

Camille remained silent, which caused Grace to nervously fill the space with more explanations. "And he's always been up front about his limitations. I mean, he's not promising me anything. But he still cares about me and wants to make sure we stay on good terms, you know? Keep *some* kind of relationship? Shouldn't that be a good thing? As opposed to guys who run around talking shit about their ex the minute they break up?"

Josh had always been so *good* to her. It was part of the reason she never said anything bad about him, even when she was angry about how he'd slept with her immediately after breaking up with her, or how he'd continued to keep her at arm's length. Grace knew he'd never say a bad word about her, no matter what. Even with this stupid Daniel fiasco, she wasn't worried he would call her names behind her back or spread rumors about her sleeping around.

Maybe it was a low bar, but the fact was he still cleared it. She'd seen guys Tiff hooked up with do far worse. The idea that Tiff could even attempt to judge Grace for this was laughable.

Camille worried her bottom lip, always taking an extra moment before speaking. "I am friends with some exes. Some I am not. But I think it is too difficult to decide so soon. You must have space. Separation." She mimicked splitting her hands apart. "Then you decide. This is why we come here."

God, Camille could really twist the knife in Grace's gut, even without knowing she was doing it. Grace rubbed her ear, wishing she didn't *have* to lie to her friends. "I just want everything to go back to the way it was before."

Before Josh broke her heart. Before Tiff forced her to get over him. Before all the lies.

Grace must have looked sufficiently pathetic because Camille came over and perched gingerly on the edge of the bed. "And you are sure you are happy before?"

"Yes, of course. Yes." But even to Grace, her words rang somewhat hollow.

Was she happy with Josh? Before all the "I don't have time for a girlfriend" talk?

There had been dates to the movies with bowls of ramen after and visits to the campus galleries to decide which pieces were their favorites and walks around the arboretum as they shared dreams of their futures in Hollywood. But there had also been arguments. About her friends. His friends. His possessiveness. His unwillingness to commit to things ahead of time. Getting him to agree to go with her to the LA Film Festival had been a feat unto itself.

And then he canceled. For Caity. Without telling her.

Would he have told her? If she hadn't stopped by his house that night?

Grace had thought it was really only semantics—that she and Josh spent nearly the same amount of time together now as they did "before." It was why she'd been so frustrated with Josh's insistence that he couldn't commit to making time for her, because the fact was, he already was. But maybe the distinction was important.

Girlfriends had power. Girlfriends could demand answers. Right now, Grace had no right to anything, too afraid to lose even the status she currently held. Josh decided everything, and her only options were to either go along with it or not. And if she didn't, she would lose him—for real this time.

Ironic that Josh and Tiff despised each other so much, considering how similarly they sometimes operated. An ultimatum didn't need to be spoken for it be given.

"Tiffany would like to go for dinner early. You are coming with us?" Camille asked.

Grace was supposed to meet Josh. She wasn't completely sure she still wanted to, but she'd already agreed to it. "I'm going to stay in tonight. I could use some extra sleep."

Camille raised an eyebrow. "The whole night? Not just dinner?"

Grace faked a little yawn, hoping that might be more convincing. "All this sun has really taken a lot out of me. I'm just going to crash."

Camille nodded, though she looked a little disappointed. "I hope tomorrow is better."

Grace laid in bed silently until she eventually heard the closing of the front door, Tiff complaining the whole way out about Grace's absence.

CHAPTER FOURTEEN

"There's no crying in baseball!"
—A League of Their Own (1992)

Grace was a wreck on the bus ride over. First, it had taken an eternity to decide on an outfit. Then there had been her *Turning Red*–style plan to make it look like she hadn't left the house. Yes, she'd stuffed pillows under her covers like a preteen sneaking out. But there was a very real chance Tiff and Camille could come home before her and, despite her begging off, might still invite her to hang out.

Then there was the heat. Even with the windows open, the bus was stuffy, and her amped-up anxiety had Grace sweating buckets. Bangs were really not conducive to hot weather. At least her hair was up this time, twisted into a simple bun on the top of her head with a big bow around it.

Josh was waiting for her when she arrived, and Grace couldn't deny the little skip in her heart when she saw him. Whether or not she still wanted to be in love with him, she just was.

She fell into his arms, and he held her like he always did, the tug of familiarity so goddamn comforting. Maybe she *didn't* have any self-respect.

Grace was the one to end the embrace, pulling back and putting on her cheerful *Everything is great* face. "Should we go inside?"

Josh reached for her and pulled her back into him. "What's the rush? We have all night."

She wasn't going to argue against extra affection, though the timeline did need to be clarified. "Well, not *all* night," she said.

This time, Josh pulled back. "What, you have a curfew?" He laughed. "What happened to your big talk this afternoon about standing up to Tiff?"

"It has nothing to do with Tiff," Grace said, more than a little defensively. "I'm supposed to be on a girls' trip. I can't just ditch for a guy."

Yes, that was exactly what she was doing right now. But it wasn't to spite Tiff.

"Oh, now I'm just *a guy*?" Josh asked, clearly offended by the not-inaccurate descriptor.

Grace sighed. This night was not off to a great start.

"Let's just eat," she said. "This place looks really cute."

She was lying. It didn't look like anything from where they were standing. They were basically roadside in a gravel parking lot with no sight of the actual establishment.

Begrudgingly, Josh led her down a steep set of stairs to a pretty little deck with tables overlooking the lagoon that sandwiched Cancún's hotel zone into a little peninsula. Grace was glad she lied earlier. It *was* cute.

A server handed them each a menu as they were seated. Grace thanked him and opened it to start reading, but Josh kept his eyes squarely on her.

"What really happened last night?" he asked, before shaking his head. "Wait, never mind, I don't want to know." He opened his menu but immediately closed it again and set it down. "No, I do. What happened. Who was that guy?"

Grace pretended not to understand, keeping her eyes firmly on the menu. "What guy?"

"You know what guy. The guy from the pictures."

"I've never had tostones before, but they sound good. Do you want to split them?" For all her supposed non-adventurous eating ways, Grace had been pleasantly surprised to find she'd enjoyed everything she'd eaten in Mexico thus far. It was a lot more than just tacos—though those had also been great.

"Stop avoiding the question," Josh insisted. "Did anything happen with him?"

Josh sounded . . . jealous. And instead of feeling excited about it, Grace found she was a little annoyed.

"I don't even know what you're asking. Can we just decide what we're going to eat? I don't like making the server wait for us."

Josh dismissed her concern. "It's their job to wait for us until we're ready. Just answer the question."

"It's rude, and it messes up the whole flow of their service," she argued. "We can order first and talk while we're waiting for our food. It's not like this is a matter of life and death."

Josh frowned, but when the server appeared and Grace put in her order, he begrudgingly did so as well. "And two margaritas," he added.

"None for me, thanks," Grace said, correcting him.

"Yes, she'll have one," Josh insisted.

"I don't want one," Grace said, more forcefully this time, and directed at Josh.

But he paid her no attention. "Just bring us two." He flashed a smile at their server, who wisely disappeared.

"Since when do you not like margaritas?" Josh asked.

Since last night.

Grace wasn't sure she'd ever be able to drink another one without thinking of Daniel and the way those margaritas had emboldened her to become someone she didn't recognize. That was exactly what she did *not* need right now.

"I just don't feel like drinking," she said. Best to keep things simple. She was already juggling so many lies.

Josh squeezed her thigh, and her traitorous body warmed at the contact. "You look like you could use one. Loosen up a little, maybe take the edge off that bad mood."

"I'm not in a bad mood."

Josh shot her a *Yeah right* look. "You forget I know you."

Grace settled back into her chair and realized that yes, maybe she *was* in a tiny bit of a bad mood. But why? Other than her argument with Tiff earlier, which was hours ago, there was nothing to be upset about.

She was out on a date with Josh. He'd invited her here. This was even a step beyond their last meeting. It was almost everything she wanted.

And yet, Grace found herself rolling her shoulders, trying to get the tension out of them.

"You want me to massage your shoulders?" Josh offered.

Josh gave really good massages. She'd give him that.

Grace remembered once reading some article aloud to him, where 84 percent of men said they massaged their partners with the intention it led to sex. They'd both thought it was funny at the time because that was generally what happened between the two of them. Thinking about it now was . . . unsettling.

But she *did* want the back rub. And he'd offered. And they were in a public place, so there wasn't even the possibility that it could lead to sex.

Not that she was avoiding sex with him.

Forcing herself to be bold, Grace flipped her chair around so that her back faced him. "Thanks."

Josh seemed surprised. "Really?"

"Do you not want to?"

"No! I do," he said, rubbing his hands together briskly to ensure they were warm.

A thoughtful gesture.

Then he pulled the neckline of her strawberry-print blouse over her shoulder, and his warm hands hit her bare shoulder.

Grace shooed his hands away, pulling the sleeve back up before settling in.

Starting again, Josh tugged down the same shoulder.

"Forget it," she huffed, attempting to move her chair back to its original spot.

"Stop being so dramatic," Josh chided, pressing a heavy hand on the back of the seat. "I'll keep the shirt up, okay?" He began massaging through her shirt but kept mumbling under his breath, easily heard since he was directly behind Grace.

"I wasn't even showing anything. And you didn't seem to have any problem showing skin last night," he sulked.

"You know what?" Grace said, firmly standing up and pulling the chair with her. "I don't want a shoulder rub." She loudly dropped her chair back in its original spot, the plastic legs rocking back and forth until they settled.

Josh shot a furtive look around the restaurant. "Don't make this a whole scene," he hissed.

"No, *you* were making a scene by acting like I committed a crime by going somewhere without you in my regular clothes that you know I own, even though you were the one who didn't want to see me last night."

God, that felt good to say.

It must have hit its target because Josh straightened up and apologized. "You're right, I'm sorry. I'm being a jealous idiot for no reason. I know you would never cheat on me."

Grace bit her tongue to keep from pointing out that it wouldn't be cheating because they weren't actually together. At least he wasn't harassing her anymore. And he'd apologized.

The food arrived, and Grace dug into her fish tostada (amazing) and the tostones (better than french fries) she'd decided to order, even without Josh's agreement to share them. "How's the margarita?" she asked.

"Awesome." He held the glass out. "You sure you don't want to try?"

Grace shook her head. Setting aside the fact that she absolutely could not even look at another margarita right now without getting flashbacks, she needed to stay sober. Alcohol made her overly sentimental, and when it came to Josh, sentiment was not her friend—he was always laser-focused on the future. If she truly wanted him back (and she was *fairly* certain she did), Grace needed to show him how she fit into *that* life. In which case, it was helpful for *him* to keep drinking.

"Tell me everything about working on set," she said, truly enthusiastic to hear about it. Whether or not he'd ditched her, the opportunity to work on a real film set was amazing, and she wanted to experience it, even vicariously.

"It's a lot less glamorous than it seems," he admitted. "There are long hours, lots of standing around or just fetching stuff. It feels like we're always waiting on someone or something."

Grace's eyes still sparkled with excitement. "But still. A movie! And you get to work with Hélène! She is so badass."

Hélène was something of an inspiration for Grace, being biracial and "unconventional" in that she came to film after having a successful singing career. Grace's high school French teacher had introduced the class to her discography, and Grace had been a fan ever since.

It didn't hurt that Hélène was also known for her outlandish outfits and brightly colored wigs. A girl after Grace's own heart.

"She's cool," Josh agreed. "But the project isn't something I would ever pick. It's . . . I don't even know how to describe it. Experimental? Really . . . *out there*."

"Out there can be good though," Grace said. "Look at *Everything Everywhere All at Once*."

Josh grimaced in a way that made it clear he didn't agree.

"You said it was good!" Grace exclaimed.

"I said it was different," Josh corrected.

"Different *is* good."

"It is *sometimes*. That just wasn't one of them."

"You're really telling me you disagree with the quality of the most awarded movie of all time?"

Josh shrugged. "I think it rode a wave of feel-good vibes to a lot of those. It makes for a good story: an overlooked older actress, a comeback from a wholesome child actor, a predominantly non-white cast, and an LGBT character? It was like a checklist of things that win accolades."

Grace slumped back in her chair in disbelief. "You think *EEAAO* was awards bait?" She shot back up to sitting. "Are you joking? They literally had an entire segment with hot dog hands. Hands!" she cried, shaking her own. "Made of hot dogs! What checklist was that on?"

Josh gave a look around the restaurant before shushing Grace. "This is why I wasn't going to say anything—I knew you were going to get like this."

"Get like what? Invested?"

"It's just a movie, Grace."

Grace scoffed. "I can't believe you of all people are saying that. What happened to all that 'movies are transformative' talk?"

Another glance around their surroundings. "Can't we just agree to disagree? All I said is I don't like a movie, and you're acting like I killed your dog."

"You didn't just say you didn't like it," Grace shot back. "You basically called it overrated."

Josh gave a deep, suffering sigh as he dropped some bills on the table and offered his hand to help her stand. "Let's drop it. I never should have said anything."

Grace took his hand, but she didn't want to drop it. She was still struggling to put her finger on why his words bothered her so much. Was it that he couldn't seem to appreciate a piece of art that was deeply meaningful to the Asian American community (especially aspiring actors like herself), or that he'd purposely withheld his opinion because he didn't like her reaction?

The truth was, she had cried a lot through the movie. Maybe Josh was right that it hadn't been the time to start a debate about its merits. And he certainly wasn't the first guy to run away from her tears.

The reminder of the night before flooded her brain, causing Grace to nearly stumble over the last step leading to the street. Her friends had said there was a basic level of decency for hookups. So was Daniel the anomaly? Or was Josh?

"Hey, let me ask you a question," she began, grateful she could stay half a pace behind as they walked toward the bus stop. She didn't have quite enough courage to look him in the eye as she said the next part. "What would you do if you were having sex with someone and they wanted to stop midway?"

Josh stopped to face her, bracing his hands around her biceps. "What are you talking about? Is this about that guy? Did something happen with him?" His eyes were filled with concern.

"What? No! It's just a question."

Josh continued staring and Grace shifted her hands into her hair, pretending to fuss with it. "Why are you asking?" he asked. "Where did it come from?"

"It's a hypothetical."

Josh scoffed, resuming the walk to the bus stop. "I'm not answering a hypothetical."

"Why not?"

"Because it's pointless. So, what? We can argue about something that's not even real?"

Grace mulled that over for a moment, wondering if she was looking for reasons to demonize Josh or if it was truly a red flag that he wouldn't answer. He did that a lot, now that she thought about it. He simply opted out of answering things if he thought his answer would upset her. Or he ended things with an "agree to disagree." God, she hated that phrase.

She decided to press the issue.

"So would you? Stop?"

Josh looked at her with full offense. "Seriously? You're really asking?"

"Yes."

Josh shook his head in disbelief. "Yes. Obviously. If she tells me to stop, I'd stop."

Grace tugged agitatedly at her ear, trying to pinpoint what exactly she wanted to ask Josh. It was just something about the wording of his answer. Was she being petty? He wasn't a writer or anything—she shouldn't expect him to perfectly express his feelings all the time.

But she couldn't shake the feeling. Something was making her uncomfortable, and for once, she wanted to follow it instead of squashing it down.

She needed his answer.

The bus screeched to a stop in front of them, but Grace pulled his arms back. "No, thanks," Grace called to the driver, waving him off.

The bus pulled away in a cloud of exhaust. "What was that?" Josh exclaimed.

"What if she didn't say stop?" Grace pressed, shoving down her discomfort about forcing this conversation. "What if it just looked like she wanted to stop?"

Josh raked his hands through his hair, his frustration evident. "What are you talking about? What does that even mean, 'looked like she wanted to stop'? Like no, I'm not going to force someone to have sex with me, Grace. But I'm not a mind reader. If someone doesn't want to have sex, they should just say so."

Grace's insides were a mess. It felt like her brain, stomach, and heart had all been run through a tumble dry and she wasn't sure where each of them belonged.

Another bus pulled up, and the two of them boarded, Grace choosing a seat across the aisle from Josh.

It was clear he was just as agitated, one leg bouncing in the aisle and his hands clasping the headrest of the empty seat in front of him. "What's going on?" he asked. "Why are you asking me this stuff? Is Tiff trying to poison you against me again? You know I'd never force anyone to have sex. That's disgusting. Everything we do is consensual."

"Is it?" she wondered aloud.

"Are you serious right now?" Josh swung his body around so that he faced her straight on, both legs now blocking the aisle. "Is this about yesterday? Because the way I remember it, *you* came on to *me*. I didn't *force* you to have sex with me."

He was *pissed.*

"I know you didn't, that's not what I'm talking about," she reassured him. But it was, in a way. Because while he hadn't been the one to talk her into it the day before, she'd also known that it was expected. He'd invited her to his *hotel room.* What else were they going to do there? Talk? That hadn't gone especially well thus far.

"I don't know what you want from me," Josh said. "I feel like you came here tonight just so you could pick a fight, and I have no idea why."

"I'm sorry," Grace apologized. "That's not what I was trying to do."

"Then what *are* you trying to do?"

Grace didn't have an answer for that. She only had more questions. But she suspected she was figuring it out.

"Remember the night you told me you couldn't be in a relationship?"

Josh sighed. "What now?"

"Do you remember it?"

"Of course I remember it. But if you're here to argue about it again, I'm telling you now I'm not up for it."

Grace shook her head. "It's not that. It's just—do you remember everything that happened?"

Josh knit his eyebrows together, as if trying to remember. "Yes? I think so. Why?" he asked warily.

It wasn't as if Grace really wanted to revisit her worst day in recent memory. For one thing, it was humiliating. Did she really ask Josh to take her back so often he assumed that was what she was about to say?

"I know I was a mess during that conversation," she admitted slowly. "But why didn't you just tell me to go home afterward?"

"I don't understand. Grace, what are you asking?"

"I'm asking why you had me stay there if you'd just broken up with me."

Josh raised his eyebrows. "What did you want me to do? Open the door and shove you out?"

Grace let out a sound of frustration. "That's not what I mean."

"Then say what the hell it is you mean because I'm not a goddamn mind reader!"

Josh's anger shook something loose. Grace turned into the aisle, her knees knocking Josh's to one side.

"Why did you have sex with me that night while I was in that state?" she asked.

Either Josh didn't remember, or he didn't think it was

an issue. "Why did *I* have sex with *you*?" he asked, eyebrows nearly up to his hairline. "Like you had no say in it?"

"That's not what I said," she argued. "I'm asking why you *wanted* to have sex with someone you just broke up with."

He looked at her like it was a ridiculous question. "Grace, we've been having sex this entire time. *Now* you suddenly have an issue with it?"

"I've always had an issue with it!" she burst out.

The words hung between them for a moment, until a loud ding caught Josh's attention. He looked up just as the bus coasted to a stop in front of his hotel.

He didn't ask any follow-up questions or invite her in this time. Instead, he just stood and shook his head, like her saying the words aloud was a damn shame. As if she'd ruined the illusion that everything between them had been fair and balanced. "I don't know what you're trying to do," he said, "but next time, figure it out before you decide to blame all your problems on me."

He stepped off the bus, and Grace waited for the usual twinge of worry that happened anytime she disappointed Josh. But this time, it didn't come.

CHAPTER FIFTEEN

"If anyone orders Merlot, I'm leaving.
I am not drinking any fucking Merlot!"
—Sideways (2004)

The tension between Grace and Tiff hadn't disappeared by the next morning, likely because Tiff had caught Grace sneaking in the previous night. Tiff had still been miffed about what had happened during yoga and hadn't bothered asking Grace where she'd been, but Grace, with her guilty conscience, had offered up an excuse anyway.

"Walking on the beach." Ha. Grace knew that, even with all her acting skills, she wasn't very convincing, especially since she was dressed up with a full face of makeup on. But it was all she could come up with on the spot, and she hurried to her room before Tiff could issue any follow-up questions.

Now, as Tiff sat across the breakfast table, frostily consuming her mocha (if such a thing was possible), her friend had switched into passive-aggressive mode.

"So. What do you have planned for all of us today?"

Translation: Did you actually plan anything?

She hadn't.

Grace had spent most of the previous night tossing and turning, not asleep enough for peace but also not awake enough to figure out what the hell she was going to do about Josh.

"Well." Tiff's words were clipped. "I thought something like this might happen. Luckily I already thought of something."

Grace frowned. Tiff hadn't trusted her to actually plan this trip?

Camille prompted her. "Yes?"

"We're going to Isla Mujeres. It's a nearby island."

Camille, ever the Frenchwoman, frowned and nodded to show her agreement. "I like this plan." Only the French could frown when they liked something.

The name stirred something in the back of Grace's mind. She'd heard it before, but couldn't remember where or in what context.

"What should we wear?" she asked.

Tiff's tone remained strained. "Maybe the outfit you put on to 'go for a walk on the beach' last night. That seemed about right."

Oof.

"How will we get there?" Camille asked, deciding to ignore the tension in the room. "Transportation ferry?"

Tiff dropped her scowl for a second at that. "I love that you just casually say shit like 'transportation ferry' now. Your parents aren't going to know who the fuck you are when you go back."

Camille laughed, the tinkle of her voice like a bell. "I was so angry when my parents first send me here. I argue with them for weeks, so sure I would be miserable. But now I am here, I don't want to go back!"

Grace's face lit up. "So don't! You should stay!"

Camille looked at Grace like she had just claimed Wisconsin made better cheese than France. "And give up free tuition in France?"

Oh. Right. A country that actually gave its citizens things. How nice that must be.

"It's not like you can't afford it," Tiff pointed out.

"This is true," Camille admitted.

"And we only have one year left," Tiff continued. "That's only, like, what, seventy grand or so?"

Grace watched the two of them continue to discuss huge sums with utter casualness. Grace was eternally fascinated by the decision-making process of the rich. How many more options they had! If Grace's choices in life were doing something that cost another *seventy thousand dollars* or not doing that thing, there would be no choice. She was already in more debt than she'd probably ever be able to pay back in a lifetime, and that was *with* her parents chipping in what they could.

Grace had already accepted the sad fact she might never make enough money to sustain herself with just acting. Hollywood wasn't exactly known for its racial diversity—especially BIPOC people who didn't fit existing stereotypes. Grace didn't know martial arts or have a tiny body and a meek voice or speak Chinese (because, who was she kidding, Taiwanese didn't make it into movies) or even look East Asian enough to qualify for any of the usual parts that were offered. If she was smart, she would set her sights on the Hallmark Channel and make a career out of being the best friend/office mate/overly friendly neighbor of the white heroine.

But it was now a post-*EEAAO* world, and Grace wanted to believe it might be different for her. She wanted to be able to dream as big as everyone else.

Ironically (was that the correct usage of "ironic"?), it was Josh who had first supported her. Of course her friends were supportive in words, but Josh had offered actual, concrete help in the form of expanding her film horizons and giving feedback before auditions. He'd understood her dreams and how hard she was working to achieve them.

Maybe that was what had bothered her about the previous night. For him to watch something that centered Asian voices and starred Asian characters with heavily Asian themes and think it was only being lauded for PC reasons? It was . . . upsetting. If he wasn't able (or willing) to grasp the significance of it, what did that say about how he truly viewed her potential?

Luckily, Tiff's voice cut into her thoughts before Grace could start spiraling again.

"We're leaving in twenty minutes," she said with a sharp look at Grace, who was, admittedly, the slowpoke of the group. "If you're not ready, we're leaving without you."

A short time later, Grace, Tiff, and Camille stepped off the "transportation ferry" onto the receiving docks of Isla Mujeres.

The trio struggled to stay together as they were jostled by other groups of disembarking passengers.

A stroller rammed into Tiff without so much as an apology from the parents. "Where do these people think they are? Disneyland?" Tiff grumbled. Her mood had improved ever so slightly on the ride over, but the crowds were quickly erasing that margin.

"No manners," Camille agreed. She turned sideways and narrowly avoided being crushed by a stampeding family reunion group wearing matching neon orange T-shirts.

Grace's heart sank just a fraction when she noticed they were Asian. It always did that. Was it hypocritical to hate having to answer for an entire race, yet want these strangers to represent their ethnicity?

"There." Tiff had pulled them through the ferry terminal and was now standing next to the road, pointing across the street to a host of golf cart rental businesses.

"This is cute." Camille delighted at the motorbikes and golf carts whizzing by.

Grace raised her eyebrows. "You found that with alarming precision. How long ago did you plan this?"

Tiff ignored the questions and handed Grace a wad of pesos and pointed her toward the door. "Camille and I are going around back to check things out. Go in and rent us a cart for the day."

Grace didn't even have time to point out Tiff's lack of the word "please" before they disappeared. With a sigh, Grace pulled the door open and stepped inside of what felt like a vacuum of heat, only just now appreciating the slight breeze she'd left behind outside. At least she got a break from Tiff.

She understood why Tiff was pissed. Between texting Josh

during yoga and getting caught sneaking home after feigning sleep, Grace *was* being a shitty friend. But she wished Tiff would just fucking yell at her like she normally would. Then they could move on and Grace could stop feeling guilty.

She wasn't even sure she'd see Josh again. After what happened the night before, she wasn't exactly clearing her schedule for him. Maybe a day off would help clarify her thoughts.

There was no one behind the counter, so Grace queued up behind the only other person in the tiny lobby—a well-built guy with wide shoulders, back muscles for days, and truly spectacular calves. She wondered if this was the same way men objectified women, or if it was only about tits and ass. In fairness, this guy's ass was also noteworthy. He was wall-to-wall muscle, each defined by the warm, golden highlights across his otherwise medium-brown skin. Between Daniel and this guy, maybe she liked meatheads after all.

Grace felt a pang of regret about the way things had ended with Daniel. She'd known from the beginning it was only ever supposed to be a onetime thing—that running into him again was on the "struck by lightning" scale of improbability—but some part of her still silently hoped she would see him again anyway. To think she'd spoiled it all over Josh.

Josh, who would never force someone to have sex but who wouldn't rule out pressuring them into it and getting mad if they refused. Or finishing even if his partner was uncomfortable or in pain.

Ugh.

She'd been considering the fact that she too had bought into those same normalcies; that maybe she couldn't hold Josh totally accountable for not knowing better when this was all anyone knew. But then she remembered Daniel.

And how he'd known better.

Grace ground the heel of her hand into her breastbone, hoping to ease the ache there. The customer in front of her got his keys and Grace stepped to the counter with her head already turned. She wanted to see what nice-body guy looked like from the front. Except the guy she'd been objectifying didn't just look like Daniel. It *was* Daniel.

Her heart stopped beneath her hand. Either she had the best luck in the world, or the worst. Had she somehow summoned him? Did she possess those kinds of powers?

He managed to overcome his surprise first. "I'm starting to think you're stalking me."

Grace flushed with embarrassment, finally grateful for the coverage her new bangs provided. "What? No! How do I know *you're* not stalking *me*?"

"I was already in here when you showed up, so . . ."

Grace performed a discreet quality control check, retucking a bra strap into her bright blue polka dot dress and adjusting her tidy little red bowler hat. She wasn't in the bandage dress, that was for sure. This über short Wednesday-esque silhouette with bright platform sneakers was even a step down from the space buns, which ranked below the bunny dress with garters.

Every time she ran into him, she got one notch less hot.

The polite thing to do would be to step aside and let him leave—she could crumple into a ball and die after he left. But the tiny selfish part of Grace insisted she at least say *something*.

Just in case.

"Aren't you supposed to be playing soccer or something?"

Yes. Sports. Excellent entry.

Provided she didn't have to ask any follow-up questions.

Daniel casually rested his elbow on the counter, and Grace

couldn't stop herself from sneaking a peek at his chest. She knew what was underneath that shirt. "We schedule by level; ours is later this afternoon."

"'Ours' meaning Lúcio and Andrés?" she asked.

"Impressive. You're one of those people who remembers names."

"You mean taking five seconds to respect someone enough to commit their name to memory? Mindy Kaling said being 'bad with names' isn't a thing; it's a choice you make."

The deep tones of Daniel's laugh sent little butterflies through Grace's stomach. "That might be true. But I'm bad at them anyway." He grinned.

The man behind the counter cleared his throat, reminding Grace why she'd come here in the first place. How had Daniel managed to set her at ease again?

"Driver's license, please."

"Oh! Sorry." She handed it over without a second thought.

"Grace Johansson," the man read aloud, typing it into his computer.

Oh shit.

Daniel cocked his head, his dark brows furrowed. "I know I just said I don't remember names, but I'm pretty sure you told me your name was Carmen."

Instinctively, Grace reached for her earlobes, tugging on them furiously as she tried to figure out the least embarrassing way to explain. "So . . . funny thing," she began, stretching out the words in hopes that someone would interrupt them and she'd never have to finish that sentence.

The problem was, she wasn't ready for them to get interrupted yet because then he would leave. Besides, he looked fairly determined to make her admit it aloud. She sighed, accepting defeat. She would probably end up as that one weirdo Daniel recalled if asked about horrible hookup stories.

At least she was memorable, Grace supposed.

"Yes, I gave you a fake name, okay? It's a stupid thing we did because it seemed funny, and it's safer than using your real name with total strangers. And since we were on vacation it didn't seem like it would matter . . ." She trailed off, her ears still held in a death grip.

Daniel let her flounder for a minute before shrugging in indifference. "Makes sense. I bet you attract a lot of weirdos, walking around looking like that."

Grace straightened up in indignation. "You think I bring it on myself because of what I wear?"

"Whoa. Hey. Dial it down about eight thousand levels. I was trying to say you look hot. And you stand out."

"And you mean this in a good way?" Grace knew she was shamelessly fishing for more compliments, but the truth was, she sometimes had her doubts over whether it was worth it. Daniel was right—she attracted a lot of weirdos. The sexual harassment alone was enough to make her reconsider certain items of clothing some days.

"Yeah, but who cares what I think? Or what anyone else thinks? You're the one wearing it."

Grace relaxed a fraction.

"And for what it's worth," he added. "I think the name Grace suits you better. This"—he gestured up and down at her ensemble—"doesn't really say Carmen to me."

"Yeah, well, that's why I was in a completely different outfit the first time you met me."

The curve of his smile told Grace he remembered exactly

what she'd been wearing when they'd met. "That . . . also makes sense."

Grace couldn't help wondering which persona he preferred.

She was a masochist that way.

"She's really more of a nighttime kind of persona," she babbled, apparently unable to stop herself. Maybe she had a humiliation kink.

The rental man blessedly returned, handing Grace a key and directing her around back to collect her cart.

Daniel held the door, and the two of them stepped out into the fresh air together, like escaping a jail of staleness and embarrassment. Grace just hoped the guy working the counter had a good laugh later when he retold the story to his friends and family. She had a feeling he didn't really have much to do in the back room, but got a kick out of listening to their incredibly awkward interaction and making Grace suffer as much as possible for maximum humor.

Well done, sir.

She was saved the hassle of having to explain to her friends the nearly impossible chance that she'd run into Daniel again because she found them already huddled with Lúcio and Andrés.

"Tiff and Camille," Grace whispered out of the side of her mouth so Daniel would know their names.

"Tiff! Camille!" Daniel exclaimed, greeting them with the warmth and jubilance of old friends. "Good to see you both again."

"You remember," Camille said, looking impressed.

Daniel shot a wide, dimpled grin at Grace, and she rolled her eyes, the whole interaction so normal it felt like they'd done it a million times before.

Tiff sat on the back of a golf cart next to Lúcio, her fingers combing through his gloriously thick shoulder-length mane. "I always wanted hair like this," Tiff marveled. "You can run your fingers right through it!"

Camille tried slapping her hand away. "Jesus, Tiffany. You cannot just touch people like this."

"You . . . don't seem surprised to see these guys," Grace said slowly. Had Tiff orchestrated another run-in with Daniel?

She tried to catch Tiff's eye, who was too busy giving Lúcio what appeared to be a full-on scalp massage to notice. It was weirdly intimate.

"No one is rubbing my head," Andrés joked with a hopeful look at Camille.

The look Camille gave him left no room for misinterpretation.

"We can't all have good hair, brother," Lúcio said, running his own fingers over his head as if to prove it. "You can sit next to me and keep doing it while I drive," he said to Tiff, who probably would have whether or not she had explicit permission. He held up his hand, and Daniel tossed him the key. Tiff and Lúcio shifted into the front of the cart. Camille glanced between Grace and Daniel, and with a resigned sigh, grabbed Andrés's hand and pulled him onto the back of Lúcio's cart.

Grace stayed rooted to the ground, her panic level rising again. How would Daniel react to her friends' scheme? Being polite to her for a few minutes was one thing—but now they'd be trapped together? For an indeterminate amount of time?

She sent a frantic look toward Tiff, silently asking if they were really going to leave her alone with Daniel. Again. And whether he was okay with it.

Or at least, that's what she hoped she was communicating.

Tiff rolled her eyes. Refusing to respond silently, she said, "Not everything is about you, you know. But you're welcome." They took off with a squeal, and Grace didn't know whether to kiss her friends or murder them.

Daniel took the key dangling from Grace's frozen hands and pulled her toward a waiting golf cart. Robotically, she climbed in, hoping to all things holy she could survive encounter number four intact. Daniel turned the key in the ignition and shot her an easy grin. "Well, looks like it's just you and me."

CHAPTER SIXTEEN

"'Surely you can't be serious.'
'I am serious . . . and don't call me Shirley.'"
—*Airplane!* (1980)

Grace sat quietly in the passenger seat, the wind rushing against her face, as Daniel drove around the island. He pointed out all the little roadside stands selling shells or freshly cut fruit, offering to stop if there was anything she wanted to look at more closely or buy. But mostly, Grace was in awe of the scenery.

It was different from the glitz and glamour of the Cancún hotel zone, built and maintained for tourists like her. Here, the income inequality was visible everywhere—massive, impeccably maintained houses with imposing fences next to houses that were little more than husks of concrete with plants growing through the cracks. Impossible to ignore.

She was shielded from so much of that where she grew up. Tucked away in one of the "nice" suburbs, most of the families tended to be upper upper middle class. Grace's parents had scrimped and saved to buy a house in that school district, hoping that the surrounding environment of excellence would somehow propel Grace into a more successful future.

Something like guilt clawed at her. "Is it, I don't know, *bad* that we're here?" she wondered aloud.

Daniel slowed the cart to a crawl, the wind rushing by the open vehicle surprisingly loud. "What do you mean?"

"It's just . . . some of these houses, all the roadside stands selling the same stuff . . . it makes me wonder if it's really helpful for us to be here, spending money, or if it's just . . ."

"Destroying the local culture and turning the entire island into a tourist destination?"

Grace blinked in surprise. "Yeah. How did you know I was going to say that?"

He chuckled, a sad sort of chortle, his head shaking. "My parents moved us to Hawaiʻi when I was thirteen. It's pretty much the same there." He pronounced it the way she assumed it was supposed to be pronounced. Ha-vai-ee.

"There's a big push to become an independent country again, especially to get the US military out of there, but most everything is owned by non-Hawaiians. I don't know how it would ever survive now without kicking out all non-Natives and just taking back the land."

"Which would include you," Grace realized.

"You know, it's funny. Before we moved, I thought I'd fit

right in because of the way I look. Pretty much everyone on the islands is mixed, and I didn't really stand out because I wasn't white. But I didn't blend in either, and they made sure I knew my place. I'll always be a malihini, which means, like, a newcomer. A foreigner."

He said it casually, with no trace of bitterness in his voice.

"Don't get me wrong," he continued. "I think Native Hawaiians totally have the right to be pissed that people keep showing up and taking their land from them. Especially when a lot of the poorest people in Hawai'i are the ones whose people are actually *from* there. They have a lot of the same problems here. Just look at all these mansions on this island." He waved an arm around. "I don't know who they're owned by, but I'm willing to bet at least some of them aren't from Mexico. They let these houses sit empty or rent them out for crazy-high prices while the people who live here kill themselves working just to afford to live."

Daniel shook his head and gave a sigh. "I don't know. It just sucks all around. It's hard to feel like you're on the right side of things when you're the type of person they want gone."

It was the most Daniel had said to her . . . ever. It was probably more than he'd said in their last three encounters *combined.*

It was wonderful. Grace didn't want him to stop.

Flirting was great, but this . . . this was even better. She felt like he was letting her dig down into his soul, talking about things Grace didn't talk about with *anyone*.

"It's not like it was your choice to move there," Grace pointed out. "You were just a kid."

Daniel shrugged. "Doesn't change people's opinion though. My first year there was pretty rough."

It was hard to imagine anyone disliking Daniel for any reason—he seemed too nice. Not in a pushover-type way, but he had an easygoing, friendly attitude that Grace would have assumed would fit in well in Hawai'i.

But what did she know?

"A few years ago, I went to China with Tiff and her parents," Grace said. "I don't know if it's really the same because we were just visiting and not moving there, but I guess I thought going there would feel . . . different. Like a connection or something. I know I'm not Chinese," Grace rushed to clarify, fully aware of the political decision to clarify to people that she was Taiwanese and not Chinese. "But it was my first time ever going to Asia, and I guess I was just surprised everyone there saw us as foreigners. No different from the average American."

Daniel gave her sort of a sad nod. "I think it's the same."

"Is it still like that for you?" she asked. "Or does it feel more like home now?"

Daniel shrugged. "It's *a* home. But I have a home here too. I don't know, I'm comfortable everywhere, but I don't know if anywhere feels like home. I think of home more like wherever my family is, instead of a particular place."

Grace smiled. "I like that. Then it doesn't matter where you move, as long as you're with the right people."

"Don't get me wrong, Hawai'i is great. I have friends there, and my parents and two sisters still live there. And I don't think anyone really cares that we're not *from* there. Most people who live there don't have Hawaiian blood. But it's still this . . . *thing* that's always present—the people who do and the people who don't. I don't know how to explain it."

"I think I get it," Grace said. "Like everyone I grew up around was some kind of Asian. But most of them were a hundred percent of whatever they were. And even though no one really cared that I was only fifty percent, it was like you said—just this thing that was always present but not really acknowledged. Except sometimes my friends would do this thing where they'd be like, 'Why do white people love to go fruit picking?' or some shit and then look at me to answer like I should know. But that was about it."

Daniel laughed. "Only white people pick fruit? I think I have some relatives down here who might disagree."

"They mean those U-Pick farms where you pay to go pick it and then pay more for the actual produce you picked."

That only made Daniel laugh harder. "People *pay* to pick their own fruit?"

Grace shrugged helplessly. "I guess so, I've never done it. But there are a ton of those farms in the Bay."

"Capitalizing on all the rich people in the area, smart." Daniel nodded.

"You guys should do that in Hawai'i. Can you imagine how much they'd pay to pick pineapple?" The lightbulb above Grace's head switched on, and she gasped excitedly. "Oh my God, just think. It could be a covert operation to get all the white people into the service and farming jobs while the actual Hawaiians make the money!"

Daniel chuckled. "Perfect. All we need is a few million to start."

He'd said *we*.

Grace's heart skipped a beat.

"I have fifty bucks in my checking account, how much you got?" she said.

Daniel shot her a side glance. "You trying to find out if my family's rich? How Taiwanese of you."

Grace burst out laughing. "I was making a joke!" she exclaimed, swatting his arm.

Daniel pretended to be hurt, leaning away from her to protect himself. "Hey! What's with the hitting?"

"You're lucky it's just my hands. That's what my mom would always say. Apparently my ahma's preferred weapon was wooden spoons."

"My mom is, like, third generation. Totally Americanized. No hitting of any kind. But my abuela?" Daniel whistled. "I've been threatened with the chancla more times than I can count."

"Maybe you should have stopped being such a bad kid."

He shot her a wicked grin. "What's the fun in that?"

Grace had to look away before he saw her blush again. She didn't even know if he was making an actual innuendo or if she just couldn't get sex off her brain when he was around.

She cleared her throat as she cast around for a subject change.

"So, what do you want to be when you grow up?"

"Damn, still trying to find out if I'm going to be a doctor?"

Grace laughed heartily at that, warmed by the knowledge that they shared enough of a background to make "in culture" jokes. Daniel 1, Josh 0.

"Fine. What does the Mexican side of your family want you to be?" she asked.

"Are you kidding? I already have a sister in med school. You think they're not dying to have *two* doctors in the family?"

Grace shook her head. "Who knew you were such a stereotype?"

"Let me guess, you're going to be a pharmacist. No wait, an accountant."

Grace laughed, trying to imagine her parents insisting on such traditional careers. It had been a struggle for them to accept her love for the performing arts, sure, but that was more about the money and less about the prestige for themselves. "Believe it or not, I'm majoring in theater. I want to get into movies."

Talking about her acting wasn't something she did very often. Grace was everything an actor wasn't supposed to be when it came to craft—self-conscious, reserved, and intensely private. Josh insisted that she tell as many as people as possible to create her "network," but Grace always felt awkward about it. People looked at you differently once you said you wanted to act. Like you couldn't be trusted to be genuine, or that you were some naive country girl who was in denial about her prospects. Grace had seen *La La Land*—it was better to just keep her dreams to herself.

But with Daniel, it seemed easy to open up. He'd already seen her at her worst and hadn't written her off, and as far as she could tell, didn't spend a whole lot of time judging. She didn't know if he was just naturally easygoing or if the Hawaiian way of life had rubbed off on him, but it was a nice change from the hypercompetitive undercurrent of the Bay Area.

"Movies are cool," he said, relieving Grace of any anxiety she had about telling him. "What kind are your favorite?"

She answered without hesitation. "Dramas. Especially historical ones. Those always have the best costume design."

Daniel nodded at her current ensemble. "I should have guessed that."

"I think it would be fun to experience a different era," Grace said dreamily, imagining herself twirling around a candlelit ballroom in a gown and long gloves. "But you know, without all the racism. And sexism. I mean, going back to pretty much any point in time in the US is impossible since people like you and me wouldn't even have been allowed to exist."

"True," Daniel agreed, pulling into a parking space. "I don't usually judge people, but when a white person's like, 'My family goes back six generations in Texas,' I'm definitely side-eyeing them 'cuz you know which side of the Civil War they were on."

Grace made a sound somewhere between a laugh and a cough, too surprised to even think of a comeback. Daniel 2, Josh 0. With Tiff as a best friend, it was hard to rattle Grace with a shocking joke.

Daniel took the opportunity to walk them down to the very tip of the island, where nothing lay ahead but bright blue water.

"Well? What do you think?" he asked, spreading his arms out.

Grace thought it had all the trappings of a romantic epic—sweeping cliff, colors at 100 percent saturation—even the wind that could create a dramatic swell out of any thin fabric. If she and Daniel were dating in real life, him bringing her here would make her think he was about to propose. The view was *that* beautiful.

Except Grace's life was more like a rom-com, where she'd be the girl who opened the small velvet box on her birthday to find earrings instead of a ring. Also, this wasn't a date, and she and Daniel weren't a couple. She needed to shift her brain away from anything remotely romantic.

"Tell me about the academy," she prompted, setting off along one of the trails that traversed the area. The greenery around them reached no higher than her knees, leaving an unobstructed view of the water from all angles.

Hands stuffed into the pockets of his salmon-colored shorts, Daniel casually lifted a shoulder. "Not much to say about it. I've been coming here since I was a kid. Now, I come less to train and more to just spend time with my family and help out with the kids' classes. I train pretty heavily during the year, so summer is kind of my downtime to rest and relax before it all starts up again."

"Awww, that's so sweet," she crooned, flattening her palms over her heart. Grace pictured Daniel surrounded by tiny humans and her heart melted just a little bit more. Not that she had any interest in kids, but it was impossible to resist a guy who could charm those sticky little monsters.

Daniel flushed, clearly embarrassed. "Okay, okay, you don't have to play it up for my sake. It's not like I'm adopting them; I just run drills and stuff."

"Still. I'm sure your uncle appreciates it."

"He and my aunt don't have any kids of their own, so they treat all the kids who come here to play like they're theirs. They put everything they have into it."

That garnered another *aw* from Grace.

Daniel laughed at her sincerity. "It's that easy, huh? Just talk about my family and you go all softhearted?"

"I'm an only child of only children. Tiff is pretty much my only family outside of my parents. Well, and her parents too, I guess. But they both work a lot, so I don't see them that much more than my own parents." The Hong-Ahns may have had tech money, but it wasn't the same as the people who came from generational money. They still had to actually show up to work to keep getting paid.

Daniel shook his head in disbelief. "I have so many relatives, I'm not even sure I can count them all. My mom is one of eight and my dad is one of twelve. I'm one of five. And that's before we even reach the second and third cousins or the aunties who aren't really aunties."

Grace remembered how confusing that had been as a little kid.

"All sisters, right?" She remembered their conversation from the night they met.

"Yep. All older."

"That tracks. You seem like a guy who's been trained by a bunch of women."

"You have no idea. I wasn't even allowed to talk when one of them was going through a breakup." When Grace raised her eyebrows in question, Daniel explained. "Because it's always the guy's fault and I'm the representative of all men when bad shit happens."

Grace nodded. "That seems fair. It's really the least you can do."

"So you probably agree with them that it's my job to get ice cream and painkillers during PMS. That was always a big event in our house. Synched cycles and all that."

"Definitely."

Grace kept a straight face, but privately she was amazed. She didn't know of a single cis guy who willingly discussed *periods*, let alone *knew* things about them. She'd been asked by more than one guy (including a male professor) why she couldn't just "hold it" until there was a more convenient time to change tampons.

"Any other important life lessons they teach you?" she asked.

"Always be prepared for tears." He paused. "Guess I failed you on that one, huh?"

Grace's jaw dropped. Did he seriously just bring up her crying incident?

She gave Daniel a shove, sending him stumbling into the greenery. "I can't believe you said that!"

Daniel laughed, holding his hands up as he stepped back onto the path next to her. "I was kidding! See? Always the guy's fault."

It *was* pretty funny, but Grace refused to let him off that easily. "I hope your sisters still give you progress reports." She sniffed.

"Oh, definitely," he agreed cheerfully. "I'm told it's a lifelong journey."

Grace tsked. "You poor thing. Having four whole people in the world occasionally gang up on you in a society that tells them that your existence is more important than theirs. I'm sure it's been a complete struggle for you, looking like . . . this." Grace drew big circles in front of his face and body, unable to articulate just how attractive he was, and just how much more men were rewarded for that trait.

"I think you're calling me hot," he said, the dimple in his cheek appearing.

Grace rolled her eyes. "You already know you're hot. You don't need me to tell you."

Daniel grinned bigger. "Yeah, but you did anyway. You better watch out or I'm going to get a big head with all these compliments."

"You already have a big head. And I'm not complimenting you. I'm just stating facts."

It was true. He was empirically beautiful.

If she, Tiff, and Camille could all agree on it, it must be true. They all had such wildly different tastes.

"Keep 'em coming," Daniel urged, pretending to preen. He slicked his hands over the sides of his head and brushed off his shoulders. "What else is great about me?"

Grace laughed. He was ridiculous. "I'm not giving you any more."

"That's all I get? Just my looks?" He pretended to look offended. "Not my skills? My personality?"

"Remind me what your skills are?"

Daniel's lips curled up into a slow, melting smile. "So *that's* what you want to talk about."

Grace froze as panic shot through her. "Wait, no. I was just kidding."

"Too late."

"It's not too late. See? Here we are, *not* talking about it."

"I'm definitely talking about it."

"No, you're not," Grace argued, lunging at Daniel to clamp a hand over his mouth.

Sure, she'd gotten a good joke in, but at what cost?

Grace struggled to keep her hand in place as he finally pried it off, his other hand keeping her just out of striking distance.

"Hm, what should I start with?" he mused, easily ducking and weaving away from her hand as she tried in vain to stop the conversation from happening. "How soft your skin is? Or how about how demanding you get when you're turned on? Or the mean left-footed kick you have?"

Grace gave up fighting him, instead opting to bury her face in her hands. "Just kill me now. See? This is why one-night stands are supposed to be one night. Because someone sees you do something absolutely mortifying while naked and then you have to avoid them for the rest of your life."

She should have calculated the distance to the edge of the cliff so she could fling herself off it to escape this. So much for her do-over.

"Hey." Daniel stopped his teasing, gently prying her hands away from her face. Grace's head stayed ducked in shame, but he bent down until she finally met his eyes.

"I really, really liked seeing you naked," he said. "If you die, I won't get to see you naked again."

Her head shot up. "Hey!"

Daniel grinned, his dimple lighting up his whole face and easing Grace's embarrassment. "Only kind of kidding."

Grace scoffed. "Yeah right. That's why you left so fast your pants weren't even buttoned by the time you reached the door."

Fuck. Apparently her embarrassment had eased too much. She'd really said that aloud.

Daniel grimaced, coarsely rubbing the back of his neck. "Yeah. Sorry about that. It was kind of a dick move. I was sorta drunk, and I didn't know what to do—"

"What are you doing?" she cut in. "I'm the one who's supposed to apologize. I brought you home and then *cried.*" Honestly, she could still cry just thinking about it again.

"Would it help if I told you you're not the first girl to cry on me?" he asked.

Grace's eyes went wide. "Really?"

"No. But I could tell you that."

Grace shoved him again. Harder this time.

"Hey now, violence is never the answer."

"It *could* be the answer," Grace said. "Depending on the question."

Daniel's eyes gleamed mischievously. "Oh, *I know*."

Grace blushed as she turned away. The whole conversation had been an emotional roller coaster, but that last bit pushed her over. The freefall of Daniel looking at her like that put an honest-to-God quiver in her vagina.

Would it be a terrible idea to try a second time? Already, she'd cut back on thinking about Josh. In fact, since she'd seen Daniel in front of her at the golf cart rental, she hadn't thought about Josh at all.

Daniel stopped walking, turning to Grace with an expression that looked . . . torn.

"I know how I can make up for the other night," he announced.

"Are we really still talking about that?"

"Mental stamina," he said, tapping the side of his head with a telltale smirk. "Soccer gives you more than just physical skills."

Okay, so this was a sex thing. Interesting.

Maybe he'd been considering another try too.

Grace smoothed her hands down her skirt, the buzzy feeling beneath it intensifying. "I'm listening."

"First, I wanna know that if you decide to bully me again, you're not going to push me off the cliff." He pointed to the water below.

She peered over the edge. It was maybe twenty-five feet to the water. Not lethal. "No promises."

"Fair enough. Okay, for the question . . ."

"There's a lot of lead up into this, should I be making a drumroll?"

He gave his head a little shake, as if to say to himself *Here goes nothing*. Then he turned his dimple on her, the full force of *that* look making her head swim. "How do you feel about outdoor sex?"

CHAPTER SEVENTEEN

"I'll have what she's having."
—When Harry Met Sally (1989)

Grace trailed Daniel down a set of stairs, her heart nearly beating out of her chest. Surely he was kidding. The closest thing to a building she'd seen was a small ruin of what used to be a temple, and even that was roped off and in full view of anyone on Punta Sur. She might have fantasized before about having sex in a place where she could be caught at any moment, but with the actuality of it staring her in the face, it seemed . . . okay, still thrilling, but also more terrifying than expected.

Holy shit, were they really going to do this?

Gone was the leisurely stroll of the upper level, where

Grace had time to look and appreciate the view around her. Down below, they were on a mission. She followed Daniel around rocks and over cracks along the path as waves crashed alongside them.

"You in a little bit of a hurry?" she joked as Daniel dragged her along, pivoting away from a girl posing for quinceañera photos.

"Hell yeah, I am. I don't know how much more time I have with you."

She knew this was just a fling, but the comment sent flutters through Grace's heart.

Hormones, not feelings, Grace reminded herself. It was best not to get the two mixed up.

They wound their way around the bottom of the island until they reached a dead end. Grace was out of breath and flushed, but Daniel gave her no time to rest, pressing her toward the shielded enclave created by a hollow in the rock. They were kissing before her back even hit the wall.

"Ouch!" The ridges of the curved wall were sharper than they looked. "I'm not sure there's enough space in here."

"Don't worry, baby, I'll make it fit," he murmured, pulling her closer.

Grace laughed, a full, hearty laugh that threw her head back. Even in a heated moment like this, with sex solely on his mind, Daniel could still make it fun and put her at ease in this entirely unfamiliar situation.

Josh treated sex with a kind of seriousness, like it somehow meant less if they laughed or she used the word "fuck." Grace used to think that made it special—made *her* special.

But Daniel, his lips making their way down her throat as he pulled her tighter, seemed to direct a never-ending loop of electricity that changed every time it passed through her. He'd created custom patterns of blinking holiday lights inside her and Grace had no way of knowing which body part he'd illuminate next. She felt special because he gave her exactly what she wanted—what she hadn't even known she'd wanted.

Grace pulled his face up to hers and sealed her mouth over his. She felt him sink into the kiss, as if the familiarity of her mouth had relieved him of the fear he might never kiss her again.

It was a fear Grace knew well.

She kissed him with a renewed sense of urgency, and Daniel's hands moved across her hips and down her ass before gripping the backs of her bare legs, pulling them up to wrap them around his waist without ever breaking the kiss.

"Jesus Christ," she panted, out of breath from kissing but shocked by the move he'd just pulled off. Come on, not even an extra little hitch to get her over his hip bones? How fucking strong was he to make it that smooth?

Grace squeezed her thighs together. Daniel grinned at her, as if he knew exactly what she was thinking and that yes, he too was proud of it. "Tell me what you want."

She dug her teeth into her bottom lip, not quite sure she was brave enough to say it. Grace was already starting to have more feelings for Daniel than she'd intended. She was clearly fooling herself if she thought she could ever restrict things just to sex when it came to him. The fact was, Grace wanted Daniel to *like* her.

She hedged. "What you promised me earlier."

But he wasn't going to let her get off that easily.

"Be more specific. I like it when you get a little bossy."

Did that mean Daniel was expecting her to turn into Carmen again? After all, she was the one he'd gone home with.

But he'd also met the regular Grace. And he seemed equally excited about her.

Maybe with Daniel, she and Carmen were one and the same. Maybe she didn't need to play the game and pull back because she caught feelings. Everything they did came with a ticking clock. It was like he said—she had no idea how much more time she had with him.

She didn't want more regrets.

Heart racing, Grace leaned forward and pressed her breasts against his chest as her lips barely skimmed the shell of his ear. "I want you to fuck me," she whispered.

His breath hitched, and she swelled with pride. She did that to him. Grace had made this magnificent specimen of a man so turned on that he'd actually stopped breathing for a moment. Even with all her awkwardness and stumbles, Daniel liked her enough to keep coming back.

He kissed her again, more ferociously this time, his hands grasping her ass as though his life depended on it, before breaking away. "You worried we're going to get caught?"

"Yes." She didn't add that the prospect of it somehow added to the thrill of it all. Terrifying, yes, but less so, knowing they were in it together. She trusted Daniel to keep them both hidden.

His eyes flashed hot, his dimple creasing his cheek. "Then make sure you keep your eyes open."

With that, Daniel hoisted her even higher, until her legs were on his shoulders and his hands were curled around her thighs, leaving his mouth free to . . . *oh*.

He released a hand and tugged her underwear to one side.

"Eyes open," he directed, ducking beneath her skirt and pressing his open mouth to her.

There was zero chance Grace would be able to keep her eyes open. Already, she was tilting her face up to the sun, needing the warmth on her eyelids to balance the warmth from below. She could feel herself swaying and clutched at his hair, not able to concentrate enough to keep herself steady. Below her, Daniel shifted his stance to rebalance them and keep her from falling off. But his hands remained tightly locked around her bare thighs, and his mouth didn't stop for a second.

He was so good at this.

How was he so good at this?

This was professional gymnastics-level oral sex (were there even professional gymnasts?), and Grace had never been happier to be wearing a skirt.

A ticklish little flick of the tongue reminded her that she was supposed to be on lookout. She reluctantly opened her eyes and took a cursory glance around.

No one.

Thank goodness. She'd only just started relaxing enough for tension to build. Stopping now would be cruel, especially when this was the one thing a mechanical device couldn't replicate.

Daniel shifted again, tilting her back ever so slightly as his tongue found its way deeper, sliding all the way forward until his teeth grazed her clit.

Grace let out a hiss. "Be careful with the teeth," she yelped.

Daniel changed course, sucking hard to create pressure, and Grace had to hold her mouth shut to keep from moaning, her other hand buried in his thick, wavy hair.

Grace couldn't even remember the last time she'd let

anyone go down on her. Josh offered to occasionally, but he put so much pressure on whether he could make her come that it wasn't worth the stress of it. The constant questions about how close she was or how much longer she was going to take made it literally impossible for her to come. She usually just declined up front to save herself the trouble.

But Daniel. Sweet, wonderful Daniel!

He made it feel like this had always been the destination, not just a place to stop on the way to somewhere else. Every point where his body made contact with hers was like a pleasure center, where even her thighs were turned on by being forced open and spread apart for him. There was nowhere for her to hide.

Grace had never been one of those petite Asian women who guys fetishized, and while she was mostly fine with her body, there was something impossibly sexy about a guy who was strong enough to hold her up as if she weighed nothing more than a couple of dumbbells. Especially when he could do *that* with his mouth at the same time. Good God, how was he even breathing?

The tension in her lower belly continued to build, and Grace had to force her eyes to stay open when she wanted nothing more than to sink into this feeling and let it finally carry her over the mountain of self-doubt she generally lived atop. She was *so close*.

Biting down on her lip to stifle another moan, Grace rolled her head to the side and locked eyes with . . . a kid?

A big kid, but a kid nevertheless.

Fuck.

She tapped urgently on Daniel's head, which he took to mean that she was close. Instead of stopping, he managed to somehow get *more* intense, which did not help.

"Someone's coming," she hissed, realizing that didn't help clarify the problem. "Someone can see us," she tried again, this time a bit louder.

Daniel peeked out from under her skirt and, with as little effort as it had taken to hoist her up, he pulled her off his shoulders and set her back down on her feet. Just in time for them to face their unwitting audience.

The entire quinceañera group—daughter, mother, father, and photographer—was staring back at them. Well, that wasn't quite true. The photographer was averting his eyes, pretending to fiddle with something on his camera and checking the spare bag slung over his shoulder. The daughter looked confused (bless her fifteen-year-old heart), the mother scandalized, and the father maybe a tiny bit impressed.

There was a full five seconds of horrendously awkward, uninterrupted eye contact, where none of them was able to look away from one another but also didn't know what to say. It was a dead end.

Literally.

Which meant Daniel and Grace had to squeeze *past* the entire group to exit.

Grace attempted to discreetly adjust her underwear back to a place where it wasn't just a fancy tourniquet, cutting off circulation to her labia, but there really wasn't a way to do that without drawing even more attention to what they'd just been doing. The fact that she was still turned on wasn't helping.

She squeezed her legs together to keep them from shaking.

Daniel attempted a weak cough before mumbling, "Solo mirando." Another cough that was more like a choking sound as he amended, "Ah, *turismo,*" before leading Grace past each and every person in the quinceañera party.

Single file.

"Happy birthday," Grace managed to say weakly as she shuffled by. "Beautiful dress."

Daniel and Grace waited until they'd rounded the corner before dissolving into laughter, sprinting around and up the stairs to where they'd started.

"That's the most awkward thing that's ever happened to me," Daniel said.

Grace was still gasping for air, partly from laughing, partly from running, and a lot from simply having held her breath for the past three minutes. "Really? In your whole life?"

Having run out of covert options, she finally reached under her skirt with both hands and firmly tugged her underwear back into place. Ahhh. Circulation.

"Your luck must be rubbing off on me because I've been through more uncomfortable situations this week than the rest of my life combined."

She knew Daniel was joking, but his comment managed to burrow into Grace's ever-expanding heap of guilt. She kept dragging him into the mess she called her life, not even sure she was unattached enough to be hooking up with him in the first place! She'd spent the previous night out on a date with her ex, whom she'd been actively trying to get back together with.

Her face must have given her away some of her thoughts because Daniel looked at her with something like panic. "Listen, I'm sorry, I know it was my idea—"

Grace cut him off. "Oh my God, why are you apologizing again?"

"I . . . don't really know," Daniel admitted. "But you looked like . . . that," he said, gesturing to her face. "So I thought maybe you were freaking out about . . . that." He awkwardly gestured toward the stairs.

Great. She'd made it awkward for both of them.

"No!" she exclaimed. "I'm not . . . I just . . ." She blew out a sigh and tried again.

"That," she said, gesturing to the stairs like Daniel had, "was . . . good."

"Good," he echoed.

Fuck. Her vocabulary was failing her.

"No, not good."

"*Not* good."

Grace gave a strangled sound. "No. It was . . ." She didn't have the words to describe it.

Fantastic.

Transcendent.

Life-changing.

"It was great," she settled on. "I just don't get why you'd keep doing this."

Daniel cocked his head to the side. "Are you mixing me up with someone else? Because I don't remember doing that with you before."

It was so easy. She just needed to ask him why he kept prioritizing the pleasure of a girl he barely knew and would never see again. Why he kept giving her chance after chance when she fucked up absolutely every single one. Why he was even interested in her in the first place when she hadn't done a single thing for him. Perfectly straightforward.

What came out instead was her exploding, "I just want to know what your deal is!"

"What my deal is?"

This conversation was never going to end. He was going

to just keep repeating her nonsensical comments until they both died or until he got frustrated enough to shove her off the cliff.

Honestly, it was the ending she probably deserved. That was the kind of movie people would break out into applause for. Filmed in black and white with subtitles for a foreign language and it would be an Oscar contender.

"Like, do you do this with everyone?" she asked, still too aggressively. She couldn't shut it off. The anger she had for herself only had one outlet, and right now, it was pointed toward Daniel, as if all of this was his fault.

"Are you asking if I regularly bring girls to this exact spot so I can give them oral? Because no."

"Be serious."

Daniel threw his hands up. "How am I supposed to be serious when you're somehow mad at me after that? I have no idea what I did to piss you off!"

"I'm not mad!" Grace exclaimed. She sighed, scrubbing her hands over her face and bringing her voice back to a regular volume. "I'm not making any sense. I know. I'm sorry. I'm just . . . God, I'm being an absolute fucking weirdo. I'm sorry. Forget it. Ignore me. Please."

Daniel pulled his phone out of his pocket and checked the time. "I should be heading back now; we have practice in a bit. I'll call the guys and have them meet us at the dock so you can link back up with your friends."

Grace nodded and followed him to the golf cart, half a pace behind. He didn't bother holding her hand this time, and she didn't blame him. Once again, she'd ruined an otherwise perfect experience, and for what? So she could uncover whether he was secretly a Josh in disguise? If he planned to lure her in and make her fall in love with him, only to turn around and use her in the exact way he promised he never would?

There was no heart to break with Daniel—no relationship to end. In a couple of days, this whole thing would be a distant memory and all she would have to show for it was an argument over why he didn't treat her worse.

They drove in silence and Grace panicked the entire time, wishing there was some way to fix this mess. She knew she should just thank the universe for another chance with Daniel and leave it at that. As nice as he was, everything between them had also been incredibly casual, with no insinuations about the future. She needed to part on friendly terms, salvage what was left of her ego, and go back to her regular life, now armed with the knowledge that both oral sex and semi-public sex were, in fact, things she could very much be into.

Still, a tiny voice in her head whispered doubts. *This isn't you. You're just doing this to impress Daniel, the way you did with Josh.* After all, she'd been convinced before this week that she enjoyed slow, mushy sex. Even if it had never turned her on the way sex with Daniel had. Daniel made her feel like she could ignite a rainforest in the middle of April.

But Grace couldn't deal with anything more, so instead, she laid her head back against the seat and let the island fly by her as she savored her last few moments of being whoever she was with Daniel.

CHAPTER EIGHTEEN

"Carpe diem. Seize the day, boys.
Make your lives extraordinary."
—Dead Poets Society (1989)

Grace spent the boat ride back to the mainland filling in her friends with what happened at Punta Sur. Tiff shrieked and squealed so loudly and often that other passengers started moving away from them.

"I knew that boy was stacked, but holy Jesus. Holding you up to his face while he eats you out? God tier," Tiff marveled.

"I am not religious, but all the oh my Gods and Jesuses when we talk about this," Camille said disapprovingly, shielding her face as though she was embarrassed to be seen anywhere near this conversation. Never mind that Grace had definitely heard Camille discuss the duration of lesbian sex versus hetero sex *at length* in a public restaurant before (pun intended).

"It was . . . unbelievable," Grace agreed, allowing herself to get the tiniest bit giddy again. How long had it been since she felt this kind of glow? The last time she'd gushed to her friends about something like this was . . . after the first time she'd had sex with Josh. Hm.

"Do you think it's just the excitement of someone new?" Grace asked tentatively.

"No way," Tiff replied without hesitation. "You were *never* like this about Josh. Not to mention, there's no way his scrawny-ass arms could even hold you against a wall, let alone hoist you on his shoulders."

Grace rolled her eyes at Tiff's jump to get in yet another dig against Josh, though she couldn't disagree. He hadn't even been able to help her and Tiff rearrange the furniture in their house. But she hadn't chosen him for his physique.

"Isn't it sort of, like . . . un-feminist of me to want to feel small though? Should it really matter that Daniel can pick me up so easily? Why do I find it so hot?"

That, her friends didn't have a quick answer for. Grace looked anxiously at each of them, hoping they would find a way to reassure her that it was fine and normal.

Camille was the first one to answer. "I think this is the culture of *les hétérosexuels*. This idea of big man, small woman."

"Totally. We've been brainwashed into idolizing traditional gender roles," Tiff agreed, always eager to find a hypothesis she could latch on to. "Think about it. The reason guys even have an Asian fetish is because they think we're all these little exotic dolls they get to keep and play with."

"Yeah, maybe . . ." Grace said vaguely.

She knew it was silly to keep comparing Josh and Daniel, but she couldn't help it. Daniel was supposed to be just a vacation hookup. A fling. But at the moment, he was the one she couldn't stop thinking about.

Grace was a different person when she was with him. She was bold, and she enjoyed sex in a way she hadn't before. With Josh, it had been all about creating a connection—getting *him* to feel connected to *her*. It wasn't that she minded the sex, but after their conversation the previous night, it was becoming clear that he wasn't exactly exerting himself to make sure she felt connected to him.

With Daniel, there'd been a natural ease between them from the start. She didn't feel like she had to be on alert around him—she could just be herself. Plenty of their time had focused on sex, sure, but they'd also talked about other things. In fact, she'd talked about things with him she'd never discussed with Josh at all—some she hadn't even discussed with Tiff.

She and Daniel had undeniable chemistry. But that happened between costars all the time (if it didn't, gossip magazines would probably be obsolete). Was what they had just a product of this vacation? This setting? Or did it extend beyond that?

Or the real question: Did she want what she felt with Daniel to affect what she felt for Josh?

"I should have asked him for his number," Grace lamented. Not because she wanted to use him as a distraction, but because she could finally admit she wasn't ready to be done with him.

Camille and Tiff exchanged looks, the two of them clearly having a silent conversation Grace didn't understand.

"What?" she demanded.

Tiff leaned forward, her elbows on her knees and her hands

folded beneath her chin as she examined Grace. "What would you do if you had it?"

Grace shrugged, flustered by the unexpected follow-up. Why did it matter? "I don't know. Just to have it. In case."

"In case?"

She could tell the truth. She could admit that, despite knowing there was no real future with Daniel, she still wanted to get to know him better. She wanted to excavate his brain and find out who he was beyond the few details he offered. She wanted to spend enough time with him that she understood what his different faces meant. She wanted to know what made him smile and what sparked his passion. To know if he treated everyone with this amount of care and respect. She wanted to know if he was actually a *nice guy*.

But she also knew Tiff, and her inability to focus on anything more than the excitement of the moment. She was like the dog, Dug, in *Up*: deeply loyal but constantly distracted by whatever seemed most fun. And Grace developing feelings for someone she might never see again was decidedly not fun.

"I heard there was an orgasm gap and that it was my duty to close it," Grace quipped.

Tiff gave a screaming cackle that was several octaves above comfortable, her poufy black hair swirling wildly around her like an old witch whose potion had just been drunk. "I knew you'd get there eventually!" She tapped a few buttons on her phone with a flourish. "I just sent you his contact info."

Grace never ceased to be amazed by her best friend's resourcefulness. "How?"

Tiff scoffed. "Please. I'm like Mama Matchmaker over here, setting you up on dates you didn't even ask for."

"Mm-hm. I'm sure it's been such a hardship for you,"

Grace said. "I believe you told me earlier that not everything was about me?"

Tiff rolled her eyes. "You could just say thank you, you know."

"*Euh,* I would also like some thanks for always being left with Andrés for you two," Camille added, raising a hand like she was bidding on imaginary friend points.

"I thought you two had a lot in common," Tiff said. "You're always arguing about *something.*"

"He is okay to talk to," Camille admitted. "But he is like a little boy. There is no attraction for me."

Grace winced. She'd been so concerned about not getting caught with Josh and everything going on with Daniel that she hadn't even noticed they'd permanently fifth-wheeled Camille. On a trip that was also meant to be her going-away vacation.

"I'm sorryyyy," Grace moaned, leaning over to give Camille a hug. "You're so right. We totally abandoned you."

"Je suis désolée, mon amie," Tiff crooned, joining the hug.

Camille shuddered. "You see? I need to stay so you can finally learn how to correctly pronounce French words."

"I'll have you know, I got an A in French," Tiff said.

Camille shot her look. "Be serious."

"Fine, B-plus," Tiff admitted. "But technically, I had an eighty-nine point eight percent, and the teacher hated me, so he wouldn't round it up to a ninety. Tell her, Grace."

"Camille, you have no idea how many times I've had to relive this story," Grace said, barely looking up from her phone.

Tiff punched Grace's boob.

"Fine, if you think my French sucks so bad, why don't you teach me some? But I want slang. Give me the good stuff."

Camille frowned. "What is 'good slang'?"

Tiff shrugged. "I don't know, something I can use a lot."

"How about 'oh my God,'" Grace suggested, her eyes still glued to her phone. "You say that about once every five seconds."

"Oh my God, I do not!" Even Tiff had to laugh at that. "Okay, fine," she conceded, "but I already know that one. Oh mon dieu!"

"You sound ridiculous," Camille said with a shake of her head. "No one says it this way. Try *la vache*."

Tiff repeated the word several times until Camille was passably satisfied with the pronunciation.

"Now, let's get into the good stuff," Tiff said, rubbing her hands together with a gleam in her eye. "I need to know every way to say 'fuck.'"

Grace tuned them out, her eyes still fixed on Daniel's number in front of her. It was so tempting, just sitting there, like a cartoon pie cooling on a windowsill. What if she inched just a little closer to tasting it? Maybe send an unserious text just to see if he would respond? What would she even say?

He was much kinder at their parting than he needed to be, considering Grace had managed to pick a fight with him over absolutely nothing. He'd pulled her in for an unexpectedly sweet hug and knee-weakening kiss, tilting her hat to cover their faces from their friends. It had been . . . romantic.

But then the boys had left, and Grace had no idea if she'd ever see him again. Granted, they'd already bumped into each other three times before, but wouldn't he have given her his number himself if he'd actually wanted to see her again? Or asked for hers?

A message popped up on her phone, and Grace's heart jumped into her throat.

Josh: How much longer are you here?

She couldn't suppress a sigh of disappointment. Two days ago, she would have been setting off fireworks over an unsolicited text like this. Now it just made her tired.

Luckily, her friends were too engrossed in their language lesson to notice what was going on. They were still discussing variations of "fuck."

Grace: we leave tomorrow

She was almost relieved to be done—to leave this place that was causing her so much stress. But the end of vacation also meant the end of Daniel. She would have no reason to text him once she was no longer in Cancún.

Josh: Aw, too bad

Josh: I'm busy tonight

Grace rolled her eyes a little. She hadn't even asked to see him, and he was already blowing her off. After their argument, Grace wasn't entirely sure how things stood. All she knew was that she was past begging him to spend time with her.

Chasing him down here had been a mistake. She couldn't entirely regret it, especially considering her afternoon with Daniel, but it was probably best if she started taking Josh's words at face value.

He was busy. He wasn't prioritizing her.

Sure, maybe it was work-related. Or maybe it wasn't, but Grace found the reason why didn't seem to matter quite as much anymore. He'd made it clear that he could carve out time for her if he really wanted. He simply didn't want to.

It was a heavy reality.

On the other hand, it really required heaping amounts of audacity for Grace to even *ask* Daniel to make time for her again. Not to mention the explanation of how she got his number in the first place. What was the etiquette on texting someone she'd already sort of had sex with if he hadn't given her his number himself?

Approaching stalker territory, that's where.

Grace imagined Tiff giving her a punch to the boob for disparaging herself. After all, texts were relatively safe. He could always choose not to respond if he was sick of her or thought it was weird she tracked him down. It's not like she knew where he lived and could show up to embarrass him in front of some other girl like she had with Josh and Caity "I cried the day I had to choose between painting and theater" Ruiz.

Then again, Daniel seemed much less concerned about public spectacles. He was the one who suggested they mess around in broad daylight—something Grace couldn't imagine Josh even *considering*. He'd barely tolerated public hand-holding.

It was funny. All this time she'd thought there was something wrong with Daniel to be so easygoing, but maybe it was Josh who was wrong by being so uptight.

Before she could lose her nerve, she texted Daniel.

Grace: need to know your whereabouts in case you "happen to be" where i show up so i know for sure you're not stalking me

Grace: this is grace, btw

Within seconds, Daniel texted back.

Daniel: couldn't make it look like an accident this time huh

Daniel: about to have dinner with my aunt and uncle

Grace: how old are you and why are you eating on a senior citizen schedule

Daniel: welcome to the Mexican life

Daniel: breakfast is fruit and we don't eat lunch

Grace: where's my passport i'm getting out of here

Daniel: don't worry, we usually eat again before bed

Grace: ok that helps

Grace: i'm on board with any culture that encourages night time snacking

Daniel: my mom always has a hard time adjusting when she comes here. She started carrying her own snacks everywhere bc she says they don't feed her often enough

Grace: stop starving your mom she's clearly hungry

Daniel: how are you taking her side, you don't even know her

Grace: believe women daniel

Daniel: wow

Daniel: WOW

Daniel: you really went there

Grace: i'm a feminist

Daniel: clearly

Grace: weren't you going to eat

Daniel: I think I've done a lot of that already today

Grace: wow

Grace: YOU really went there

Daniel: i'm picturing your face right now and it was worth it

Daniel: it's ridiculously easy to embarrass you

Grace: fucking sadist

Daniel: you wish

Grace let out a gust of breath at that last message. She had to hand it to Daniel—he could whip her up into a frenzy (pun intended) with the littlest comment. There was that damn chemistry again.

She would do it. She would invite him out with them. Why not? She wanted to see him. It was her last night. It was worth the risk that she might mess it all up again.

"Hey, what's our plan tonight?" Grace asked, looking up at her friends.

Neither of them answered, Tiff instead gaping silently at Camille.

"Uh, what's going on?" Grace asked. Were the two of them in a fight? How long had she been checked out of the conversation?

Tiff pointing accusingly at Camille. "She . . . did you know? She's friends with Hélène! And she's here! In Cancún!"

A cold wave of fear hit Grace, her hands going clammy. What were the cosmic chances that Camille somehow knew someone working on the same project as Josh?

She tugged nervously at her ear. This seemed like a bad sign.

"As in the pop music superstar a.k.a. most beautiful woman to ever walk the earth?" Tiff stared expectantly at Grace for a reaction, mistaking her silence for ignorance. She punched Camille in the boob. "How could you not tell us?"

Camille slapped away Tiff's hands and braced her arms over her chest. "I tell you now. And if you continue to hit me, I will not invite her to meet you tonight."

Tiff threw her hands up in surrender. "I'll be good, I swear. Just let me take one photo with her. Wait, no, one *good* photo. I need to make sure my face doesn't look like a gigantic moon next to hers. I'm so close to hitting thirty-six hundred followers, and this will totally put me over the top."

Camille tsked. "I already tell you, no one celebrates this number. Three thousand followers, yes. Four thousand, yes. Three thousand, six hundred? Come on. Be serious."

"You made plans with Hélène tonight?" Grace asked nervously.

"*We* made plans with Hélène tonight," Camille corrected her. "I told her we would meet for dinner."

Grace nodded, still in a daze from the news. She was going to meet an actress. An actual, working, *celebrity* actress. And a half Asian one at that! Grace had a million and one questions she'd love to ask, but all she could focus on was the fact that Hélène was working on Josh's project. What if that somehow came up?

"I know she's famous, babes, but you look like you're about to throw up. You're never going to make it in Hollywood if that's your reaction to celebrity proximity," Tiff said.

"It's not that." (It was kind of that.) "I was . . ." Grace trailed off. What would she even say? That she'd hoped to spend her last precious hours in this country with a guy she'd only just met? She could already hear Camille's voice in her head: *Come on. Be serious.*

This was an opportunity for Grace to actually ask the things she'd been wondering about the industry. People couldn't *buy* access like this. (Though Grace was certain that Caity "I only believe in holistic medicine" Ruiz would certainly try if it were possible.) But most important, this was the exact kind of thing Josh had bailed on her for. Career before relationships. Maybe Grace should follow his lead and keep her focus where it needed to be.

Meanwhile, her friends were still staring at her, waiting for the rest of her thought. "You were what?" Tiff asked impatiently.

Grace shook her head, pasting on a happy face. "Nothing. I would love to meet Hélène."

CHAPTER NINETEEN

"Look at me. Look at me. I'm the captain now."
—Captain Phillips (2013)

By the time they made it home, the three girls were exhausted. Grace's Punta Sur high had been replaced by seasickness, Camille was the color of a semi-ripe tomato, and Tiff was nursing the beginnings of a migraine. But the prospect of meeting Hélène propelled Grace through her shower and makeup, changing outfits more times than she ever had for a date. Straight men were under the mistaken impression that women dressed for them. When, in fact, they would never be able to provide the highly specific flattery that came from truly understanding the difficulty level of what was achieved in makeup, hairstyling, and clothing. Grace wanted to make sure Hélène was judging her on the most "Grace" outfit possible.

Meanwhile, Tiff had decided to nap before dinner, while Camille spent the time sipping white wine to "rehydrate." Grace had no idea if everything Camille said about French culture was true or only true *for her*, but between the two-hour lunch breaks and collective riots for anything deemed unfair to the masses, France sounded pretty fucking great.

A few shots of Tres, Cuatro Y Cinco tequila (in which Grace was the tres, Camille the cuatro, and Tiff the cinco) and a quick trip down the strip later, all three girls arrived intact to meet Hélène for dinner.

Camille performed the requisite introductions and Grace managed to keep it together as they were seated at a wooden table outdoors. Hélène was . . . luminous. As if she literally *glowed* in the early-evening light. Closely cropped hair—almost shaved, really—and a sculptural yellow blouse that defied the laws of gravity. If Grace were more certain of her skull shape, she would absolutely go full *G.I. Jane* to be more like her.

She couldn't tear her eyes away. Maybe this was just how really beautiful people looked up close. Grace was grateful she sat next to her instead of across to keep the creepy staring at a minimum.

"I'm planning to just order a few of every type of taco," Tiff announced, her body already swaying from the drinks they'd had at home. "Does that work for everyone?"

Grace skimmed the menu, which was literally only tacos. No wonder Tiff was thrilled.

"This place is cute, Hélène," Grace commented. "How did you find it?"

Hélène smiled, and Grace swore she could feel actual heat

radiating from it. Hélène was a literal star, burning hydrogen at a rate that could warm everyone in the restaurant. "Everywhere I travel, I like to venture out and find places to eat," she said. "I haven't had much free time during this project, but I ate here the other night." Her voice was smoky and warm, like expensive bourbon sliding down your throat. "Camille mentioned to me you are studying theater?"

Grace nearly choked on her water. "She did?" Grace turned to Camille. "You've talked about me with Hélène?"

"Of course," Camille said, as if it were completely normal that a celebrity not only knew Grace existed but also knew a whole fact about her. "You are important to my life, no?"

Grace found herself a little misty-eyed at the unexpected compliment.

"Do you hope to be a theater actress?" Hélène asked Grace.

"Film, actually."

Hélène gave a little smile. "Ah, you are a romantic."

"Everyone loves movies," Grace replied. "Isn't that why you stopped touring? To make this movie you're working on?"

"It's true," Hélène confessed. "I loved the cinema as a little girl. But I have not been a romantic for a long time," she chuckled.

Grace grimaced at the trace of hardness in Hélène's voice. "Is Hollywood any better than the music industry?"

This time, Hélène broke out into a loud laugh. "This is like asking me to choose between a crocodile and an alligator. They are the same in different ways. In both, I must make my own way."

"What do you mean?"

"I am a Black woman. Black and Chinese, with French nationality, but the world sees me as Black first. Always. When I wanted to start movies, I couldn't find anyone to help. Too many Black actresses, they would say. There are not enough roles. So I created my own. I thought, I can write music, why not a movie?"

Grace laughed in disbelief. "Sure. Just make your own movie."

"Yes," Hélène said simply. "This is what we must do. You will go to audition after audition where they say, 'Thank you, but you are too Black, you are too Asian, too white. You are too pretty, too ugly, too fat, too thin, too old, too tall.'" She rolled her wrist as if to say and on and on. "You must first know who you are and what you are capable of. This movie? It is all *my* money. I must believe in myself so others will believe in me."

Her self-assurance was so solid it bordered on unnerving. It wasn't bluster or posturing—it was clear Hélène had truly built herself atop an unshakable foundation. It was probably a big reason why she was able to become a star in the first place. Josh was forever reminding Grace that she needed to toughen up or, as he put it, 'Hollywood will eat you alive.'"

The tacos appeared, and Grace temporarily shelved the serious talk while they all ate as if they hadn't seen food in days. But she continued to mull over Hélène's advice.

"Holy shit, these sesos ones are amazing," Tiff raved. "Camille, I can't believe you really don't want a bite of this."

Tiff held her taco up, and Camille made a face. "What kind of meat is this one?"

"Cow brain," Tiff replied happily, taking another big bite out of it as Camille made a gagging face.

"The French are weak," Tiff garbled, her mouth still full.

"Can I ask you a question?" Grace blurted out.

Hélène was mid-bite, but nodded her assent.

"How do you know what you're capable of if you never get a chance to try?" Grace asked. It was terrifying, opening herself up like this. She felt like she'd stripped naked in the middle of the restaurant. "If I'm going to get rejected outright over and over again because I'm mixed, how am I ever supposed to gain the kind of self-confidence that makes other people believe it?"

Hélène cocked her head toward Grace, not bothering to set down her taco. "I don't tell you this to discourage you. I'm telling you to *warn* you. So you can prepare. There will be so much rejection. More rejection than you have ever faced in your life. They say no just *looking* at you. You will hear no so many times you will wonder why you keep trying. It feels hopeless."

Grace had thought she'd adequately steeled herself for it, but Hélène managed to terrify her anyway. She'd cracked open Grace's chest and seen her deepest, darkest fears, then announced it was far worse than anything she'd imagined.

It wasn't so much *what* Hélène was saying as it was *how* she said it. There was an intensity to her words. Like she was entrusting Grace with a secret mission that would self-destruct in seconds.

Luckily, Hélène continued, so Grace didn't have to scramble for a response. "If you hold tight to who you are, what you value"—she tapped her fingers against her chest—"you don't spend your time with regrets. You know what you are willing to do and what you are not willing to do. It can mean you take work you hate because you hope there will be work you love after it. Or it can mean you walk away from opportunities that will force you to be someone you cannot live with. But only you can answer this."

Grace knew they were discussing the industry, but she couldn't help but feel like Hélène was, in fact, extolling advice for life.

Across the table, Tiff and Camille continued to get drunker, totally unaware of their friend's mini existential crisis.

When Camille caught Grace's eye, she circled a finger over the top of Tiff's head. "Will we do something about this?" Tiff was sucking the spilled bits of meat directly off the table with loud, slurping noises.

Grace laughed. She couldn't help it. Her friends were so ridiculous it was impossible to maintain any kind of serious thought.

Tiff lifted her head for a moment. "I'm preventing food waste!"

Camille waved a hand in the air to get the host's attention. "Les serviettes, por favor!"

"I'll bet this isn't what you thought your night would be like," Grace laughed to Hélène.

"I like that she is serious about climate change," Hélène said, licking the juices off her fingers like a mere mortal.

Face still on the table, Tiff sent Hélène a salute.

"Sorry," Grace apologized. "But can I ask you one more question about your job and then I'll be done? I swear I won't ask you anything else." (A blatant lie.)

"Of course."

"Is it worth it?" Grace asked. "It seems like every step of the way has been a fight, and even as this hugely famous person, you still face a lot of the same kinds of discrimination as you did in your regular life. Like, if you could go back in time, would you choose to do this again?"

Grace held her breath, hoping that Hélène didn't see Grace's question as a weakness or unwillingness to grit it out. She knew it wouldn't be easy—for every successful actor there were probably a thousand (okay, ten thousand) failed ones.

But she loved acting, and for once, she was doing something she felt she could really excel at. Grace had spent a lifetime learning how to conform to a character—she just hadn't realized it until recently.

Hélène mulled over the question before answering. "I love my life," she said slowly. "I am proud of my achievements and how strong it has made me. I love music, I love performing, and I cannot have a life without them. But . . . if I had a daughter?" She paused. "I don't know if I would want the same for her."

"Ooh, like those tech execs who don't let their kids have social media." Tiff nodded knowingly.

Grace cocked her head. "That makes sense in a drunk Tiff kind of way."

"Thank you!" Tiff said, lifting her glass up to toast.

Grace didn't think she and Hélène were suddenly friends or anything, but it was nice to have another person who seemed to just *get* her. Funny. Between Hélène and Daniel, Grace was having a real identity reckoning in Cancún.

Hélène checked the time. "I don't like to stay out late these days, but I have a party I need to stop by if you all want to come?"

Grace tried to play it cool. They were *stopping by a party* with a movie star. NBD.

"Hell yes, we want to come," she exclaimed. Then: "Oh. Shit."

"What is it?" Camille asked.

Grace gnawed on her lip, nervous to even admit it aloud. "I was kind of hoping to maybe see Daniel at some point tonight? You know, since this is our last night."

What was she looking for? Permission? Consensus?

Luckily, Hélène wasn't offended that she might not be Grace's first choice. "Invite whoever. It's on the beach, plenty of space, very casual. Here."

Hélène gave Grace the address, and Grace sent it on to Daniel.

Grace: tell me if you're not cpr certified so i don't accidentally pretend to drown

Daniel: my mouth to mouth technique is definitely certified

Grace: it turns out i do have limits and its that joke

Daniel: are you saying we need a safe word

Grace: lmao

Grace: see you there later?

Daniel: yes

Grace couldn't help but smile at the phone. There it was: yes. No "I'll try to make it" or "maybe I'll swing by" vague bullshit.

Just . . . yes.

Would Daniel ever stop knocking her off-balance? Grace had spent her twenty-one years on this earth acclimating to men's allowable behaviors before he came along and showed her those were all lies. It was disconcerting.

The server appeared, and Hélène snatched the bill out from under Tiff's delayed reflexes. Tiff was only able to put up a weak fight at best, while neither Camille nor Grace even noticed. (Not that Grace would have been able to afford paying for everyone anyway.)

Camille stretched her arms and let out a huge yawn. "I think the tacos make me tired."

"I'm sure it has nothing to do with the *several* glasses of wine you had before coming here and drinking a bunch more," Grace said.

Camille attempted to sit up but nearly wobbled off her stool. "Yes, I am sure too," she said with a serious face.

"You're too sober," Tiff warbled. She called for a round of shots.

"I already paid," Hélène said with a sharp look.

Tiff pulled out her credit card out with a victorious grin. "I'll just have to get this one."

After a couple more rounds, the group headed over to Hélène's party on the beach. Two massive bonfires were already built, the logs standing nearly as tall as Tiff. The sky wasn't quite as dark as expected for the time of day (blessed summer hours), but the fire blazed high with heat. As Hélène promised, it was incredibly casual. Grace had expected bartenders and hors d'oeuvres but instead found clumps of people standing around coolers of alcohol. She wondered if she might recognize any other famous people.

"We didn't even need to leave Cali for this," Tiff muttered quietly, clearly disappointed by the low-key vibe.

"Grace, come, let me introduce you," Hélène offered, taking her hand and leading her across the sand toward some people. "This is Antoine," Hélène said, releasing Grace and clasping a hand on his shoulder. "He is the lead grip on production. Always good to know the crew because they are the ones who make everything run. Antoine, Grace is studying to be an actress."

Antoine shook Grace's hand, and she was sure she gave him a smile as was appropriate, but nothing he was saying registered. It was as if the entire scene had gone blurry, and Grace watched the message slowly come into focus.

This was a crew party. For the people who worked on her film. Hélène's film. Josh's film. Josh could be at this party. Why hadn't that occurred to her?

Cold dread trickled down her spine.

This couldn't be happening. They did not end up at the *one* place where they might run into the *one* person they absolutely could not run into. Grace clutched at her chest, keeping her eyes trained on Antoine with a smile as her entire body went hollow.

The conversation ended, and Hélène pulled Grace over to meet the director next.

"It's okay," Grace protested weakly, trying to shake her wrist out of Hélène's grip. "You don't have to do that."

Hélène scoffed, refusing to even slow down and let Grace catch her breath. "How do you think anyone gets anywhere in this industry? In all industries? If we want to see more people like us, we must help them get there."

Damn. Grace was on the verge of tearing up at the thought that Hélène thought she—Grace!—was worth investing in, after meeting her for only a few hours. But there were more important factors to consider at the moment.

"We don't all have to go," Grace said, trying to urge Tiff and Camille away as they got closer to who had to be Caity Ruiz's dad. Naturally, Caity "I've been a board member of a children's dramatic arts nonprofit since I was eighteen" Ruiz was standing next to him.

"Carlos!" Hélène leaned in and gave the director an air-kiss on each cheek. "I want you to meet a friend of mine, Grace. She is studying to be an actress."

Grace and Caity's dad shook hands, Grace acutely aware of just how exciting and how short-lived this moment was about to be. As if she'd heard Grace's thoughts, Caity turned at that moment. But so did the person tucked behind her, invisible at first glance.

Josh.

Emotions rioted through Grace. Jealousy that he was with Caity, anger that he hadn't invited her, disgust for the same reason, and a shot of pure joy, the way she felt every time she saw him. If her brain had been working to get over Josh, her heart hadn't quite gotten the message yet.

Grace looked over her shoulder at Tiff at the exact moment Tiff noticed Josh. "What the *fuck*?" Tiff bellowed, her head moving back and forth between Josh and Grace. They both stood frozen, matching looks of alarm on their faces.

"Shit," Grace whispered, whirling around with all the logic of a kid playing hide-and-seek. *If I can't see you, you can't see me.*

Her eyes immediately found the space between Josh and Caity.

The two of them weren't holding hands. They were standing apart. Had they been this far apart when she'd first spotted them? Or had they jumped apart when her back was turned?

Why, in this terrible moment, was that her first thought?

"Oh my God. Oh my God." Tiff paced around, the heels of her hands pressed into her eyes. "I am such a fucking idiot."

Grace put herself in Tiff's path, trying to pry Tiff's hands open. "Please. Let me explain."

"Oh, no, you don't," Tiff growled, shaking her hands free of Grace. "You don't get to explain this. You don't get to look me in the eye and fucking *lie* to me that you had no idea he was in Cancún."

Caity's dad politely exited the vicinity, along with Hélène, who gave Camille a concerned look. She probably regretted ever meeting Grace. Caity, for her part, hung back but didn't leave, the nosy fucking bitch. (Even as Grace admitted to herself that yes, she would eavesdrop too if she were in that position.)

Tiff paced angrily through the sand as Grace cast around, trying to think of what to say.

"How many times?" Tiff demanded.

"How many times what?"

"How many times have you seen him on this trip, Grace? I know you don't actually go on nighttime walks by yourself on the beach."

"You are here the whole time," Camille said in disbelief, more to herself than Josh.

When Grace still didn't say anything, Tiff plowed ahead, her voice back to a level where it could be heard in several counties. "So what? This was your plan all along? Fuck Josh and come back to us like it never happened? What about Daniel? Did you fuck him the same day, or did you at least wait a day in between?"

Grace gasped. Tiff was right to be angry but that was . . . low.

A deep voice from behind them called jovially, "Who's fucking Daniel the same day?"

The blood drained from Grace's face and her veins turned to ice.

So it *could* get worse.

Daniel walked up to the group, and Grace (powerlessly) watched him take in the scene: Tiff fuming, Camille standing stock-still but somehow disapproving all the same, Josh eyeing Daniel. And Grace? Dead. Or wishing she were.

"Hey," she managed weakly. Her feet were glued to the sand.

"What's going on?" he asked uneasily.

God, he looked delicious. He was in a pink short-sleeve button-down with palm trees printed all over it, his biceps radiating the confidence of a guy who pulled off palm trees as a fashion statement. The streak of joy that shot through her was uncomplicated.

Yes, she was absolutely screwed. There could not have been a worse time for him to appear. But that didn't change the fact that, regardless, she was—for a split second—utterly thrilled to see him.

Before she could realize what was happening, Josh was at Grace's side, his arm around her waist. "How do you know my girlfriend?" he asked defiantly.

What the fuck?

Daniel stiffened, then puffed out his chest. "I'm the one whose name she's been screaming lately. Who the fuck are you?"

Jesus Christ. That wasn't going to make things better.

Grace got her shit together enough to shove off Josh and place herself between him and Daniel, arms outstretched to prevent a fistfight.

"It's not what it looks like," Grace said, hating what a cliché those words were.

"Don't listen to her, Daniel," Tiff shouted, her drunkenness giving way to belligerence. "She's been saying that to all of us tonight."

She wanted to tell Tiff to kindly shut the fuck up for a second. Grace didn't need her making the situation even worse.

She placed herself in front of Daniel with her hands on his chest, as if she could stop him from charging Josh. If Daniel got his hands on Josh, he'd snap him like a fucking twig. She both loved and hated the thought of it. "Can you please just give us a second?" she pleaded.

"You picked Josh!" Tiff screeched, collapsing dramatically onto the sand. "Of course you did! You always pick Josh! You faked an entire fucking vacation just so you could follow him!"

Camille remained standing, simply repeating "Why?" while shaking her head and hands at Grace. "Why? Why do you not tell us?"

"Maybe because you're shitty friends who've been trying to break us up," Josh shot back.

"There's nothing to break up! You already did that!" Tiff yelled. Either she couldn't see that Josh was five feet away and not fifty, or she didn't care.

"Leave my friends out of this," Grace told Josh. He, too, needed to shut the fuck up. He'd already made things worse with that "girlfriend" nonsense—he didn't get to *keep* making it worse.

"Wait a minute, I recognize him," Josh said with a frown, pointing at Daniel. "He's the guy from the photos, isn't he?"

Even though Daniel's stance was relaxed, Grace saw his jaw muscles working. He looked ready to punch someone. "What are you talking about?" Daniel turned to Grace, his voice gruff and short. "What's he talking about?"

"Oh my God, the fucking photos!" Tiff sat on the ground, sand flying as she flailed around. "I *knew* you were being weird about it. No wonder! You didn't want Josh to know about Daniel! I would've thought you fucked him just so you could win back this waste of space!"

Josh turned to Grace, his face unreadable. "You *slept* with him? *This* guy?"

Daniel took a step toward Josh, his eyes narrowing to slits. "And she invited me here, so you can leave now."

"That would be tough to do considering this is a party for *my* work." Josh glared back. "Why don't you ask Grace why she invited you to her boyfriend's work party?"

"She's not his girlfriend!" a voice cried out. They all turned to find Caity on the edge of the conversation, her unexpected addition not totally welcome.

Sure, she'd backed up Grace's side of the story, but why the fuck was she inserting herself in the first place? Still, confirmation was confirmation, no matter where it came from.

"See?" Grace said to Daniel, her voice desperate. "He's not my boyfriend. I had no idea he'd be here tonight."

"But you knew he'd be somewhere nearby!" Tiff added, her sarcastic commentary more and more bitter with each word. "After all, you're the one who planned it! *Let's go to Cancún*," Tiff mimicked, finally making her way back to standing. "*It'll be so fun! My sleazy piece-of-shit ex-boyfriend just so happens to be there!*"

"This is his company party?" Daniel asked.

Grace could see she was losing him.

"It's *our* company party," Caity replied, stepping closer to Josh. "And *Grace* is the one who showed up because she's been stalking him."

That fucking bitch.

Every terrible thought Grace had ever thought about Caity had been completely justified. One might even argue the thoughts hadn't been mean *enough*.

"I'm not stalking him!" Grace cried. "I didn't even know he'd be here!"

Caity shot her a condescending look. "Let's not play games. I know you're still in love with him, but Josh is trying to move on, and you need to let him."

"Who the fuck invited you into this conversation?" Tiff yelled.

"Seriously!" Grace moved to align herself with Tiff. "None of this is your business."

"I'm not saying that to help you," Tiff exclaimed, stepping away from Grace.

"Maybe if Tiffany could stop *screaming* at everyone for five seconds we could all calm down," Josh said.

"Oh, am I making too much of a *scene* for you?" Tiff howled.

Daniel shook his head, irritation in his voice. "Why are we here, Grace?"

It was clear he wanted to give her the benefit of the doubt—for her to give *some* kind of reasonable explanation for what was going on—but she didn't have one. Everything about this situation was a huge fucking viper pit, and she was stuck being Indiana Jones.

"Snakes. Why did it have to be snakes?"

"Looks like she was just killing time with you until I was available," Josh said to Daniel, completely ignoring Caity. "Must be tough finding out you're nothing but a consolation prize."

"The fuck I am." Daniel started toward Josh. "Talk to me like that again and I'll drag you out of here and beat your scrawny ass. I don't give a fuck whose party it is."

"Daniel, don't." Grace knew it was unfair to ask him to stand down, but she just couldn't deal with another aggro attitude right now. Him fighting Josh would just make everything worse.

"Yeah, Daniel. Don't," Josh repeated.

Daniel looked down at Grace incredulously. "Seriously? This guy?"

She grimaced. "It's complicated." There was no way she was going to explain it all in front of Josh and Caity. "Can you just give me a minute, and then we can leave?" she pleaded.

Daniel pulled Grace's hands off him, still agitated. "Why can't you just leave right now?"

He waited only a beat before his expression flattened. "Got it. You want me to just wait here until he's done with you, is that it?"

Ouch.

Grace tried reaching for him again, but Daniel was too quick. "This is . . ." He shook his head. "I don't need this." He turned and stalked off, back the way he came.

"You see how he treats you? How your friends treat you?" Josh asked. "They all think they can tell you what to do."

"Josh, shut up!" Grace yelled, trying to pull herself in every direction to keep everything from falling apart. She wanted so badly to run after Daniel, but there was too much other shit she needed to take care of first.

"Stop telling everyone to shut up," Caity snapped. "You're the one who showed up here without an invitation."

Grace ignored Caity, dropping to her knees in front of Tiff. "I'm so sorry," she begged, tears springing to her eyes. "I wish I could take it all back."

Tiff looked down on her with contempt. "*Do you* though?"

"This is no accident," Camille said with equal scorn. "You lie to us."

"I know!" Grace burst out. "And I felt guilty about it every second of every day!"

"You should," both Tiff and Camille replied.

"Josh, let's go," Caity said, trying to urge him away.

"I'm not leaving until I talk to Grace," Josh said.

"I don't want to talk to you right now!" Grace screamed. She was in the middle of a full-blown crisis. She may have spent the past half a year obsessing over him, but now that it was all standing in front of her, Grace would give up Josh in a heartbeat to keep Tiff and Camille.

"Guys, please," she pleaded. "I wasn't thinking."

"No, you just thought you'd use me for my money. Next time, at least be honest about it." Tiff grabbed Camille's hand, and they walked toward wherever Hélène had fled to. "Enjoy your prize," Tiff called over her shoulder, her voice flat. "You certainly worked hard for it."

The shards from the explosion of her life lodged into Grace's chest as she watched her friends go in one direction and Daniel in the other—even the sun was rushing toward the horizon to get away.

"You didn't really sleep with him, did you?"

Grace looked up, almost dazed, to find Josh still present, still asking the most unreasonable of questions.

"Of course she did, didn't you hear her friends? Didn't you hear *him*?" Caity put in. "Josh, why do you put up with this?"

Grace didn't think she could feel another stab wound, but there it was: a full knife to the chest from her mortal enemy. It surprised Grace more than it should have.

"What about you?" Grace replied to Josh. "Are you going to let your new girlfriend stand there and talk for you all night?"

"We're just *friends*," Caity said with a withering look. "But I'm a friend who *actually* cares about him instead of playing games with his head."

"Caity, can I talk to Grace alone?" Josh asked.

Caity looked offended but complied. She flounced off, with

a final warning before she did. "Stalking's a crime, you know. You're lucky I don't ask my dad to throw you out of here."

"It's a public beach!" Grace hollered after her. Grace wished she'd thrown sand at her.

"Grace, you're making a scene," Josh hissed.

"Your fucking girlfriend is making a scene!"

"For the thousandth time, there is nothing going on between Caity and me!"

"Then why is she out here protecting your honor like a fucking white knight?"

Josh sighed wearily. "Do you have to swear so much? It's impossible to talk to you when you're like this."

Grace almost laughed. It was almost funny.

"Listen," Josh said. "Caity *might* have a tiny bit of a crush on me. But that doesn't mean I have any feelings for her."

"No, you just have her in your bedroom at all hours of the night and travel to foreign countries with her."

"For a job!" Josh exclaimed. "I told you. All of this was just for work."

"But you've known Caity liked you all this time." Grace said it as a statement, but her insides rioted with more questions.

Josh nodded hesitantly. "She was going to help me get a job on set—what was I supposed to say to that?"

Grace blinked in disbelief. She'd really been so disposable that Josh had dropped her for a job. A job he was doing for *free*. All the while leading on another girl. Grace almost felt sorry for Caity.

"So you, what? Used her by pretending to like her back so you could get this job?"

"I never so much as kissed her," Josh insisted. "Unlike you, who was apparently sleeping with other people. I thought we agreed not to do that."

"Monogamy is for couples, Josh. You broke up with me. I don't owe you anything."

That managed to get under Josh's skin. "So, what, do you *like* this guy or something? Someone who talks about you with vulgarity and threatens to beat up other people? Really?"

Josh had zero room to judge, but no, Grace *hadn't* loved some of the things that had come out of Daniel's mouth. She also couldn't blame him for saying them, considering the clusterfuck he walked into.

"I'm not discussing Daniel with you," she said flatly.

"Oh, *Daniel*," Josh muttered back.

Maybe Grace *had* flirted with Daniel at the beginning because of her own nefarious purposes. But she certainly hadn't *used* him the way Josh had with Caity.

God, was she really getting riled up on Caity's behalf? What about how Josh had treated *her*?

"Why did you call me your girlfriend back there?" Grace demanded. "You're the one who kept insisting I *wasn't* your girlfriend, but suddenly there's some other guy and you want to act like we're together?"

"I was just doing it to protect you from that guy."

"So you *didn't* mean it."

Josh hesitated, and Grace swore she could see him consider his options.

"I want you," he said haltingly. "That's not a secret. And I know I don't have the right to ask you for anything, but yeah, I was jealous, okay? I don't like the idea of you with anyone else."

"But you also don't like the idea of me with you."

"I still said it, didn't I?" Josh argued. "I said it even though Caity was standing there and I knew she'd be pissed. I was willing to give all of it up for you. Doesn't that count for something?"

Grace was disgusted. But more than that, she was heartbroken.

She'd really given him the benefit of the doubt all this time. She'd bought into the idea that his offer to set her free was self-sacrificing—done because he cared about her *too* much.

She'd thought she was in love.

"What is it you want, Josh?"

"I just said. I want *you*."

"As what? Someone you can call to come over and fuck whenever it's convenient?"

Josh winced, but Grace had phrased it that way on purpose. After all, strictly speaking, that's what it had been. His feelings didn't "count" (in his words) if they lacked the actions to back them up. Daniel had shown her that.

"I don't like seeing you with other guys, Grace. It makes me crazy. I especially hated seeing you with another guy in person. So if this is the only way I can keep from seeing that again, then I'm in. Let's do this."

"Huh?"

Grace hadn't been expecting that.

"Let's get back together," Josh said. "We've pretty much been together this whole time anyway."

Grace nearly got whiplash from the sudden change in Josh's attitude. But this was what she'd come to Cancún for. Her ridiculous plan—hatched on a hangover and a pile of desperation—to plant herself in his proximity so he'd want her back had worked.

But what if she *wasn't* in proximity?

"Why now?" she asked. "If we've 'pretty much been together' this whole time, why are you suddenly willing to claim it?"

Josh frowned. "I told you. I swear, when I heard that other guy say the two of you had hooked up, I almost lost my mind. I don't even want to *think* of someone else touching you. I want to be the only person who sees your underwear."

As if needing to prove it, Josh stepped closer and gathered Grace's hands in his own. Meanwhile, she was trying to make sense of his words.

Grace was a *thing* to him. A possession that only he could put his hands on, but never played with unless someone else wanted to. If Daniel hadn't come along, Josh would probably have assumed Grace would wait for him forever.

She still loved him. She couldn't shut that off. But she couldn't overlook the misery he put her through when he could have simply snapped his fingers and fixed the issue any time he'd wanted. And now, she couldn't overlook the gap between what Josh provided and what Grace now knew she wanted in her sex life.

"I don't want this," she said, clarity finally coming to her. "I don't want any of this."

"What?"

Grace pulled her hands away from his. "I don't want to get back together."

Now it was Josh's turn to be shocked. "What are you talking about? That's *all* you've wanted. And now I'm telling you you have it. You have me."

He held out his arms, as though he expected Grace to fall into them like she always did. He was home to her.

But Daniel had said home was easily moved.

"I changed my mind," she said simply. "I don't want someone I had to force into a relationship, or who only dates me so I can't date anyone else. I don't want someone who's happy to string me along, knowing how unhappy they're making me. That's not love, Josh."

"How am I the bad guy here?" Josh's voice was raising, causing people at the fringes of their volume bubble to slide another step farther out. "Tell me! I've been up front this entire time. I never promised you anything I couldn't give."

His wording would make lawyers weep with joy. So careful to outline his limitations and restrictions as if he'd one day be called to testify about them.

"I know," she said.

"So how am I the bad guy here?"

Even in this, Josh was worried about his character—that she'd label him as a literal "bad guy" when he'd been so careful not to seem like one. But it didn't matter. Grace knew what a good guy looked like now, and she couldn't imagine ever settling for someone who wasn't.

"You're not the bad guy," Grace reassured him. "If that's what you need to hear, then fine. You're not the bad guy." Grace flung her hands toward him, as if absolving him of his sins. "But you're not the good guy either," she added.

That was about as epic of a line Grace was going to be able to come up with, so on that, she turned and walked away.

CHAPTER TWENTY

"You will ride eternal, shiny and chrome."
—Mad Max: Fury Road (2015)

The sand felt softer, Grace trudging through it with leaden feet to search for her friends. Camille may have been right that Grace and Tiff argued constantly, but it was usually more of a sibling-type bickering. What happened earlier was not that.

Grace had messed up. Royally. Massively. Spectacularly.

And she wasn't sure how to even begin to atone for it.

Grace circled each of the bonfires slowly, searching over heads for a glimpse of Camille's pixie cut. It was harder than she'd expected. Apparently a lot of people on film crews were tall, skinny, and white. And with each person she passed who *wasn't* Camille, Grace's worry grew—maybe they had decided she wasn't worth sticking around for. Like Daniel had.

Not that she could blame any of them.

By the time Grace eventually found the two of them, Tiff was swaying on her feet, a half-empty bottle of tequila clutched in one hand. Relief surged through Grace.

"I found you!" Grace went to throw her arms around each of them before stopping herself at the last second. Fuck. She knew what it was like to be touched by someone she was pissed at—Josh had just done the same thing to her. Like a cheap way of manufacturing intimacy so they wouldn't be as mad at you. Hell, she'd done it earlier. Both Daniel and Tiff had shaken Grace off like she was an insect that had crawled onto them.

Grace settled for clasping her hands behind her, her fingers twining to keep her from trying to do it again.

"Oh, look who has time for us again," Tiff drawled, taking another swig from the bottle like she was an unruly pirate. "Camille, can you ask Grace what she wants? Maybe cab fare to go to Josh's hotel?"

Ouch.

"I thought . . . maybe you left," Grace confessed in a small voice.

"I wanted to. This one wouldn't let me," Tiff said, jerking a thumb toward Camille.

She might have convinced Tiff to stay, but Camille didn't look any less pissed about Grace's lie. Lie*s.*

All of Grace's emotions collided at once—her anger about Josh, hurt about all of it ending, the guilt about all of her lies, and, of course, the copious amounts of alcohol she'd had. Tears welled in her eyes, starting to leak out the corners.

"I'm sorry, okay?" she burst out in a half sob. "I know I'm

a shitty friend. I know what I did was wrong. Can you just yell at me and get it over with?"

She was used to Tiff yelling. It was how they settled most of their arguments. Grace said or did something thoughtless, Tiff blew up—or vice versa—and the whole thing was forgotten by the next day. The cool detachment Tiff had adopted on this trip was unnerving. Like maybe Tiff was over Grace's bullshit and no longer cared enough to get angry.

But it was Camille who spoke first. "You lie to us. You have so many chances to tell. We have conversations about him. But still, you lie."

The hurt on her face dropped Grace to her lowest point yet.

But Camille wasn't done. "You look at your friends, and you lie. For *him*."

Grace's heart broke. Camille was completely right. Grace's lies had all been premeditated—exactly what had hurt her about Josh's lies.

"She lied for money," Tiff corrected. "She couldn't afford to chase him on her own. So she used our offer of a trip to cheer her up to come here and stalk him instead."

Tiff turned her back on Grace, taking another swig of the liquor in her hand.

"I wasn't thinking," Grace said. "I mean, I was, but not clearly." She tried desperately to make her friends understand. "I was just so freaked by seeing him with Caity that night. He canceled on going to the LA Film Festival with me so he could come here, with *her*, and I just . . . I felt like if I didn't do something fast, I would lose him."

"You had already lost him!" Tiff whipped around, yelling at Grace. "He broke up with you!"

Camille steered the two of them farther away from both

the fire and other people. She'd probably never let either of them anywhere near Hélène again after the scene they'd caused.

But the shame of *that* was going to have to wait because Grace could only deal with one thing at a time.

"It didn't *feel* like we'd broken up," Grace protested, knowing even as she said the words how ridiculous they sounded aloud. She swiped at the tears that refused to stop as she tried to explain. "He was still telling me he cared about me. That he wanted to spend time with me. Nothing changed except that we weren't technically together anymore."

Tiff rolled her eyes. "God, Grace. You really are naive."

"Yes! Okay? I'm naive." Grace flung her arms out, begging to be attacked. "I was in love with him. I wanted to believe anything he told me. That's what being in love does to you."

Tiff scoffed again and took another swig. Camille's expression softened into a frown.

"And every time you told me he wasn't worth it, or how much he sucked, or all the ways you wished you could mutilate him, it just made me feel like you thought I was stupid for being in love with him."

Grace swiped at more tears, her second burst of adrenaline wearing off and her emotional reserve quickly fading.

"You *were* stupid for being in love with him!" Tiff cried. "He treated you like fucking trash! He cut you off from your friends and turned you into this . . . this . . . this *field mouse*!"

Grace sniffled. "Why a field mouse?"

"Because it was the first fucking creature I could think of that was timid!"

The tension cracked, their emotions spilling over, and the three of them broke down into laughter, Grace's mingling with her tears.

"But why a *field* mouse specifically?" Grace asked. "As opposed to what? City mouse?"

Tiff was trying to hold back laughing but couldn't. "Shut up. I was mad at you, okay?"

"You're still mad at me," Grace pointed out.

"I know. Camille is too."

In response, Camille grabbed the bottle from Tiff's hands and took a healthy chug of it, spluttering afterward. "This is not like the tequila we drink at the house."

"That's because Tiff only buys bougie shit," Grace said.

"I didn't hear you complaining when I bought your ticket down here so you could go fuck that greasy-haired weasel."

Tiff said it like a joke, but the issue still hung between them. It would be foolish to think it wouldn't.

"I'm sorry," Grace apologized again, this time more somberly. "I really am. You have every right to be mad at me. You both do."

Tiff grabbed the bottle from Camille and thrust it at Grace. "Drink first, talk later. This isn't a conversation I want to have sober."

"You are not sober now," Camille pointed out.

In response, Tiff let out a loud burp. "Well, Hélène left. There's no reason to stick around." She marched up to one of the coolers and grabbed another bottle of something, slapping some bills down in an attempt to pay for the liquor she was taking—at a party none of them had really been invited to. "Now, let's get the fuck out of here before I punch Josh in the balls."

That was the best idea Grace had heard all day.

The three girls wandered along the shoreline with their tequila (the second bottle slightly better than the first) and got properly trashed. Like, raccoons-pawing-through-a-dumpster trashed. The combination of drinking, crying, and the humidity had left Grace a mess, every swipe of her hand under her eyes coming away with fresh smears of black as her mascara practically melted off her.

She really needed to invest in better waterproof mascara.

"*¡Viva la Mexico!*" Tiff shouted, taking a swig of alcohol and lifting a fist into the air.

Camille only just managed to dodge Tiff's flying hand, falling off-balance and into the water. She landed with a small scream, but bounced back up so fast it looked as though she'd been electrocuted.

Grace really had the best friends. Not only were they deeply loyal and mercifully forgiving, but they were also *fun.* She would miss Camille so much if she didn't come back next year. And not only because she kept the peace between Grace and Tiff.

Grace drank from her own bottle and let out a little sniffle. "Camille, it was so nice of you to introduce us to Hélène. I don't know if I said thank you yet, but it was truly one of the coolest moments of my life, and I'm sorry I spoiled it."

"Are you crying *again*?" Camille asked, attempting to wipe wet sand off her hands.

Grace sniffled, still trying to wipe the tears that kept leaking out. "I'm not even sad right now. I can't help it. Alcohol makes me emotional."

"Maybe you are sad and you don't realize," Camille said. "Some say alcohol makes people tell the truth. Maybe this is your truth."

"That I'm secretly sad?" Grace asked.

"She can't be sad—she's finally free of Josh!" Tiff yelled, throwing her arms up to the sky. "If that doesn't make you believe in God, I don't know what will."

Grace gasped. "Was that today?"

Tiff lifted her bottle up and squinted at it in the moonlight. "Based on the amount we've drunk, and that there are three of us with only two bottles, I'd say it was about two hours ago."

Grace gaped at her. "Aren't you supposed to be drunk? You're out here doing math and shit," she slurred. No wonder her legs were so tired.

"Grace, seriously. Seriously," Camille cut in, trying to maintain a somber face as she wrung water out of her shirt. "Seriously. How do you feel about being done with Josh? Are you okay?"

Grace could feel the tears welling back up in her eyes, and she laughed to try to cover it up. "Seriously? I have no idea. But I think? I'll be okay? Probably?"

Camille flashed her a sarcastic thumbs-up. "Very confident. I like it."

Tiff slapped a hand onto Grace's shoulder, half for balance and half for moral support. "I didn't mean to make you feel like shit. I really thought I was helping you get over him."

Grace wrapped an arm around Tiff. "I know you did. But you really did make it worse."

"Really?"

"You made me feel like I had to choose between you," Grace admitted. "And that if I chose him, you'd drop me."

Tiff's eyes widened. "I would never drop you!"

"You drop *everyone*," Grace said. "Anyone or anything that

makes you mad, or you get sick of, or whatever. You just drop it and never look back."

Tiff stopped dead, pulling Grace to a halt too. "That's really what you think?"

Camille continued ahead, but Grace kept talking, "How many hobbies or activities or phases have you been through? I just figured you'd eventually move on from me too."

"That's not fair," Tiff argued. "You can't compare us to something like tennis."

Grace cast her eyes to the ground, unable to look at Tiff when she said the next piece. She was relieved Camille wasn't within earshot. "Haven't you noticed it's always just the two of us? No matter who else we make friends with, it never lasts. And you never miss them."

Tiff opened her mouth to respond but closed it without a word. "I'm just not big on dwelling on the past," she finally said.

Grace shot her a sideways glance. "Says the girl literally obsessed with history."

Tiff blew out a breath. "Shit. Okay, maybe you're right. I *might* have the tendency to cut people off. But you're basically my sister. I'm not going to cut off my family. No matter how pissed I am at you."

It didn't necessarily solve the problem of them not being able to retain friends, but Grace was at least relieved to hear that Tiff wasn't putting her on the chopping block. The two started walking again, hand in hand.

"So are you?" Grace asked hesitantly. "Still pissed?"

"Hell yeah, I am!" But there was a laugh in Tiff's voice. "But I'm also proud of you for finally getting rid of him. Assuming you actually did."

"I did," Grace quickly confirmed.

"I for sure want to hear all the gory details about it later. Just . . . not today. I'm not sure there's enough alcohol for me to even hear his name right now."

Grace nodded. "Fair enough."

The two of them clinked their bottles together in a toast as Camille cried out, "Salut!" from the water, where she was half swimming, half wading in the dark.

"Okay, no more alcohol for her," Grace said.

The two of them kicked along the edge of the water, Grace surprised at how warm it still was, even at night.

"I can't believe it's already our last night here." She sighed. "I wish I hadn't wasted so much of it on Josh."

Grace knew she'd needed that time to finally pull away, but it seemed as though she'd never stop regretting all the foolish things she did for him. If only there had been a way to learn everything she had over the past few days *without* having had sex with him in the meantime. He didn't deserve that last time with her.

"I'm going to regret asking this, but how many times did you see him?" Tiff asked.

"Maybe it's best if we don't share *all* the details," Grace said, thinking of the morning she snuck out after Tiff praised her for being a good friend.

"Don't get me wrong, I'm still mad and I'm going to be for a good long while. But I want to at least know you made it worth it," Tiff reasoned. "Come on, you owe me."

Grace blew out a puff of air. "Fine. Only twice by choice."

Tiff tsked. "Not a great ratio, dollars to face time–wise."

"Sorry for the poor investment, I'll make sure to reimburse you," Grace said sarcastically.

"You could never afford it," Tiff replied airily.

"I'd rather try than have you hold this over my head forever."

"I don't do that!"

Camille cleared her throat, now happily seated in the sand. "You tell me the cost two times while we are here, how much the things I order from the supermarket." She waved two fingers in the air. "Two times," she repeated.

Tiff collapsed next to Camille. "I really talk about money that much?"

Camille nodded.

"It's not *that* much," Grace offered, sitting down too. It felt incredible to get off her feet. "But . . . sometimes it gives off this vibe like you deserve to be in charge of everything because you're the one paying for it."

"Okay . . ." Tiff answered slowly. "But . . . the person paying *should* be in charge."

"Maybe sometimes," Grace said. "But not all the time. Like, you think of the purple house as *your* house because you pay more of the rent. So, when you said Josh couldn't come over anymore, it felt like I literally *couldn't* bring him over, even though it's my place too."

"Fuck." Tiff scrubbed a hand over her face. "I'm sorry. I was just *so mad* at you for letting him treat you like that, you know? I know I'm not the most sincere person, but I love you, and watching you get smaller and smaller for him was so fucking painful. I know it's selfish but I just couldn't deal with it. I couldn't deal with *him*."

Camille's mouth was pressed into a single, disapproving line. "Even the first time I meet Josh, I already know I don't like him. He explain French movies to me."

Grace cringed. "Yeah. He does do that."

Grace was sure that with the passage of time, more of Josh's negative qualities would jump out to her. And her friends would probably be happy to remind her.

"He cannot even pronounce my name," Camille added.

Grace wasn't sure he ever tried all that hard to, to be honest.

"All these red flags," Grace moaned, flopping onto her back without a care for all the sand that would surely now permeate every single crevice in her body. "Did you know it turns out that Josh wasn't at all what I wanted in bed?" She asked the question up to the sky, which was beautifully clear, stars visible over the water.

Grace saw Tiff and Camille exchange glances, barely holding back their giggles.

"I'm shocked. *Shocked*, I tell you!" Tiff exclaimed, causing Camille to fall over laughing.

"This is why you do not marry someone you don't have sex with," Camille posited. "Sex is too important to not know before this."

Grace continued confessing her troubles to the stars. "I know I need to take some personal responsibility for the decision to keep sleeping with Josh, but realizing now that he was subtly pressuring me into it this whole time is just . . . blech." She let a shiver run through her body, shaking her limbs as though they could rid themselves of the memory.

Daniel hadn't pressured her into a damn thing, and yet he was the one she sent away. All because she felt she owed Josh something because of their past.

History really was a bitch.

Camille clapped loudly in approval, lifting both thumbs up this time. "Blech. Perfect summary."

"What about Daniel?" Tiff asked.

"What about him?" Grace replied. "He never wants to see me again."

Tiff looked over at Grace. "Did he say that?"

"Does he have to?"

Tiff sighed. "I really thought for a minute that you guys might even make it past a vacation fling."

"Really?" She was surprised to hear Tiff thought long-term about anybody, even for her friends.

"You two could've had such beautiful brown Asian babies together. Imagine their hair!"

"Yes, because this is the obvious next step," Camille said dryly.

Grace sat up to take another drink before flopping onto her back again. "I at least wanted the chance to sleep with him." Surely she should be allowed to mourn *that* loss.

Tiff picked up a handful of sand and drizzled it over Grace's legs. "You *like* like this boy," she teased.

"I do," Grace admitted sadly. "I know I thought Josh was a nice guy, but I think Daniel is *actually* a nice guy. Like, come on, I've been a hot mess every time he's seen me, but for some reason, he keeps coming back."

Tiff reached over to punch Grace's boob, her drunken aim off, and hit her bicep instead.

"Ow! Stop doing that!" Grace cried, shaking out her arm.

"You're doing it again," Tiff slurred, shaking her finger at Grace. "I like Daniel, but treating you with respect and letting you express normal human emotions is just basic decency. I would hope you like him for more than just that."

"I do! He's also very, very hot."

Tiff shot her a look.

"Okay, okay. I hear you." Grace sighed, laboring to get enough air into her drunken lungs. (Could lungs get drunk?) "I don't mean to go all astrology about it, but I just feel like we have this . . . connection. Like we just click."

"That's called sexual chemistry, babes."

"No, it's more than that. I don't know how to explain it. He makes me comfortable. Like nothing is off-limits, you know?"

"Still sexual chemistry," Tiff sang.

Grace swung an arm out to punch Tiff but missed. "I don't mean sexually. I mean yes, we have plenty of chemistry there too. But I'm talking about more of like . . . a shared experience. I don't have to explain certain things through my specific cultural experience because he already gets it. Oh my God, is this why so many people date exclusively within their own community?"

Tiff gasped. "Alert the Supreme Court—Grace wants to overturn interracial marriage!"

"I hate you."

Tiff laughed, leaning over Grace but toppling onto her. "You love me. Everyone does. Even your boy toy, Daniel, does. He said the actual words. I heard 'em."

"You hear other people when they talk?" Camille said with innocence.

Tiff threw a handful of sand at Camille, who squealed and immediately threw one back, and suddenly Grace was unwillingly stuck in the middle of a sand fight.

"Don't get sand in the tequila!" she cried. Grace clamped a hand over the mouth of her bottle as she tried to curl her body around it like a shell, protecting the precious liquid from the sand fight her friends were engaged in.

"Gah! You got sand in my eye!" Camille cried.

Grace quickly unfurled and rushed over (okay, army crawled at a slightly faster pace) to help, but all she had was her bottle of tequila. She might be drunk, but even she could figure out that pouring alcohol into Camille's eyes was probably a bad idea.

"Do you want me to shine my phone light into your eye?" she asked.

Camille fluttered a hand in front of her face, blinking rapidly. "How will that help?"

"It won't."

"Then why do you offer?"

"It's all I have," Grace said dramatically, flinging herself back into the sand and looking up at the stars again. If this was her last night, she wanted to soak up every moment of it. Even if it was questionable whether she'd remember any of it the next day.

Tequila was an unforgiving bitch too.

She took a few more pulls, staring out into the expanse of space. Grace didn't want to get all existential, but thinking about the universe and how vast it was really helped put her problems in perspective. What was one boy—or two, really—in the grand scheme of things? How much of a difference would her life and her choices make for humankind? Or even the totality of her life?

Well, that was depressing.

"None of this matters," she yelled up at the sky.

"Pipe down," Tiff shot from somewhere behind.

Grace could hear Tiff and Camille whispering back and forth, mixed with giggling. There really wasn't a more accurate description. It was giggling.

"No bullying!" Grace called from her spot on the sand. "You bullies are excluding me!"

"This isn't kindergarten," Tiff called back. "There's no one here to save you."

"If Daniel were here, he'd save me," Grace moped, mostly to herself. He was so good about making sure her friends felt included—folding them into the conversation and pronouncing their goddamn names right. That is, after she reminded him of what those names were.

Grace had liked Josh in spite of her friends. But what if the guy just . . . got along with her friends from the beginning? She wanted someone who would love Tiff and Camille just as fiercely as she did, even when they were gigantic pains in the ass. She didn't want to have to section herself off again, giving only pieces of herself to each person. Grace was done fractioning herself for anything.

Ugh. She was going to have to adopt Caity's "I'm not half of two races, I'm 100 percent of each" mantra, wasn't she?

Tiff's face appeared over hers, the curtain of curly hair hanging down like decorative vines.

"You look like a garden," she told Tiff.

Tiff held out her hands to help Grace up. "I'm flattered. Now let's go get you watered."

"What the fuck does that mean?" Grace laughed, still protecting the open tequila bottle as she staggered up to standing.

"I have no idea," Tiff confessed. "It seemed like a good double entendre when I said it."

"*Entendre*," Camille corrected as she danced around, her wet clothes matted with sand.

"Whatever. My throat doesn't make those sounds," Tiff said dismissively, heading away from the ocean. "Walk this way."

When they reached the street, Grace had to brace herself on her knees. Her drunk lungs were waving a white flag, and her legs felt like they could give out at any moment. "Are we going home now?" she heaved, closing her eyes as she tried to get control of her breathing.

"Something like that," Tiff said. "On y va!"

When Grace opened her eyes, there was a black sedan waiting.

"Holy shit, are you a magician?" she whispered loudly.

"Yes, I took off my cloak, and you missed it," Tiff said dryly. "Exactly how drunk *are* you, Lord of the Ring?"

Camille opened the door to the car but lost her grip on the handle and stumbled backward. The driver took one look at her and shouted "No!" before speeding off. All three girls stood, slack-jawed, staring at their quickly vanishing ride.

"Did he just . . . ?" Tiff couldn't even finish her sentence.

Camille looked down at herself. "Ah, I see."

She looked absolutely disgusting—her body caked in sand, her short hair filthy.

"Another car will be here in five," Tiff said, tapping a few buttons on her phone. "We need to beat the sand off Camille before then."

Camille looked alarmed. "We must what?"

Tiff and Grace drunkenly swatted at Camille, knocking sand off her but also just sort of slapping her as she howled and morphed her body into different shapes.

"I know I complain about you being bossy, but I'm realizing maybe I put up with it because I'm actually a sub," Grace told Tiff. "Like you say 'hit,' I say 'who?'" Grace whacked a chunk of sand from Camille's back and then said in a low voice, "It turns out Daniel can get bossy too, and I am very into it."

"Sand!" Camille was now trying to fend off her attackers, swiping back at them. "You said to clean the sand! Not just hit!"

"Look how well it's working though." Tiff pointed to the circle of sand that had piled up around Camille. Then she and Grace resumed their conversation as though neither of them even heard Camille's complaints. "So, you think you might be into BDSM?"

"Let's not get carried away," Grace said, narrowly missing Camille's leg as it moved out of reach. "I just like when he starts dictating stuff. Like you do. It just makes everything easier, you know?"

Tiff squatted down to reach Camille's ankles, only once having to keep herself from tipping over. "I cannot begin to tell you how weird it is you're comparing me to your *sex life*, but okay. I get it, I think? So . . . thanks?"

Camille jumped away from the two overly enthusiastic rug beaters. "Done! I am clean!"

Grace shook her head vigorously, making herself dizzy. "No, I just meant that if I can trust someone like Daniel to be looking out for me, then I should have trusted you too. You're like my life dom."

Tiff swept Grace into a hug and kissed her temple just as a car pulled up. "You, my darling, could not have dreamt of better timing for that." Releasing her, Tiff opened the back door with all the pomp and circumstance of a royal guard. "Get in, my little sub. I have plans for you."

CHAPTER TWENTY-ONE

"One morning I shot an elephant in my pajamas.
How he got in my pajamas, I don't know."
—Animal Crackers (1930)

Grace took in the sights of Cancún one last time as the car sped toward their beach house. She had her face resting against the window, its coolness offering a measure of comfort. Camille was seated in the middle, which, in hindsight, was a little rude of them since Camille had by far the longest legs. Camille didn't look so hot. She was bent in half, her head between her knees. Tiff, meanwhile, was googling the history of colonialism in Mexico, stopping every few minutes to read a random fact aloud.

Some 17 million Indigenous people are in Mexico, which is 15 percent of its total population.

The Maya people date back to 2600 BCE.

Malinchista, *a popular insult to describe people who like other cultures more than their own, came from the name of the enslaved Indigenous woman who helped Cortés conquer the Aztec Empire.*

Go figure. All the bad shit was pinned on a woman.

Just then, the car hit a pothole in the road, and Camille held up a hand, the other hand firmly clasped over her mouth.

"See? Even Camille is disgusted by Cortés," Tiff quipped.

"Maybe it's just the unsolicited history lesson," Grace said under her breath. "Aren't you supposed to be drunk?"

Camille shook her head, refusing to remove her hand from over her mouth. Instead, she used the other hand to point and wave wildly.

Tiff frowned. "Is this some kind of French mime game? I don't get it."

"Does she want us to open the window?" Grace guessed.

Camille nodded vigorously, right before leaning over and vomiting.

Out of sheer instinct, Tiff held her hands under it, the puke running over the sides of her cupped hands and down her arms as Grace frantically rolled down the window.

But the driver must have noticed their sudden scrambling because he slammed on the brakes and spun around. His eyes fell on Tiff, who offered him the cupped handful of puke as if she were the pope offering a blessing. "Out of the car!" he bellowed.

Grace didn't need to be asked twice. She scrambled out, rushing over to Tiff's side to open the door.

"I'm sorry," Tiff cried as the driver peeled away. "I'll leave you a big tip!" she yelled, finally emptying her hands onto the ground.

Grace looked around; there was nothing to see but a waist-high retaining wall with iron bars over it. "Uh, are we at a jail?"

"If you had to puke, you picked the right time," Tiff said, making a big show of wiping her hands on the grass. "We're here."

"Where is here?" Grace asked.

Camille looked half asleep and more than a little dazed but she stepped away to reveal the sign on the wall. Two words jumped out to Grace: Fútbol Academia.

"Voilà," Camille announced. Or rather, yawned out.

Grace's stomach churned, and she sincerely hoped it was because of the alcohol and not because her friends were possibly setting her up to win the Stalker of the Year award. Not one surprise attack but two? Especially after joking about doing it?

She was feeling secondhand embarrassment for *herself.*

Tiff shot her a look without Grace even voicing the question. "You know why."

Grace immediately started panicking. "I can't see him like this," she said, her hands immediately flying up to fan her overheated face.

"He's seen you drunk before, babes."

"Yeah, but he still liked me then!"

"You should drink some coffee," Camille advised.

"Okay, you are banned from further suggestions," Tiff said, making a show of looking around at the sparse neighborhood. What possibilities might have existed were all closed because it was the middle of the night. "Where the hell do you think we're going to get a coffee right now?"

Camille stretched her arms up into the warm night air like

she was announcing the end of a Broadway show set in the thirties. "This is America, land of possibilities."

Tiff stood up and threw a handful of grass at Camille. "We're in Mexico, you buttered croissant."

Grace giggled at the absurdity of Tiff's insult. "Yeah, Camille, stop being such a quiche."

"You're totally being a baguette."

"Brioche."

"French toast."

"French toast sounds so good right now," Grace moaned, visions of fat, syrupy slices of browned bread filling her head.

Tiff snapped her fingers in front of Grace's face. "Focus, focus. We're here to get your man."

"Oh shit." Somehow Grace had managed to block that out for the past fifteen seconds. They were *all* too drunk to be seen right now. And Grace hadn't had the chance to consult a mirror.

She dashed across the front lawn and back again, kicking off her heels when they proved to be too difficult.

"I know you don't like when I say this, but that's your white half showing." Tiff pointed at Grace's bare feet.

Grace tried to give Tiff a look as she ran by but needed to keep her eyes on the grass so she didn't accidentally trip on a stick or something. That was just what she needed in this moment—a broken ankle. Then Daniel would be forced to carry her home, making him think even worse of her than he already did. Yay!

"Grace, what. The. Fuck. Are you doing?" Camille said, each word pronounced with impressive crispness.

"Sobering up," she panted, as if it were obvious.

"All you're getting is sweaty, babes," Tiff said.

Grace stopped her running (jogging, at best) and hunched over, hands braced on her knees. "Sweat is sexy, right?"

The gate opened just then, saving Grace's friends from having to answer. Lúcio winced slightly at the sight of the three girls but easily smoothed it over with a smile. "Good to see you, ladies," he said, politely giving each of them a hug and kiss on each cheek (while maintaining as much physical distance as humanly possible).

Well, that explained how Grace's friends had arranged this little field trip.

Lúcio led the way with Tiff next to him, Camille right behind them, and Grace trailing as far back as she could without losing sight of them in the dark.

She was almost giddy at the thought of getting to see Daniel but also absolutely sick with terror at the thought of a rejection to her face. Oh God, what if she cried again?

Grace forced herself to focus on the conversation happening ahead of her so her brain couldn't talk her out of this. "Do they also train girls at this academy?" Camille asked. "We have this problem in France. So many boys, so little girls. Almost nowhere to train for only girls."

Lúcio shook his head. "Boys ages eight and up."

"Well, that's bullshit," Grace declared loudly, leading her friends to roundly shush her.

"Sorry, but it is," she added, attempting to lower her voice. "That's just like how there are almost *double* the number of male roles as female roles in movies. And sixty percent of those are for white women! Why should a camp only be open to boys when boys are the ones with all the opportunities already?"

Grace plowed on without waiting for anyone to respond. "And I bet the girls who *do* get to go to camps probably come from money."

Camille frowned, trying her hardest to follow Grace's logic.

Tiff, on the other hand, was fluent in drunk Grace. "I don't love that you're equating people of color with poor people, but I get your point," she said. "And I agree. You should make sure to tell Daniel he's sexist the next time you see him."

A door next to them flung open, and as if she'd conjured him, Daniel appeared. He wore nothing but a pair of black boxer briefs and mussed hair—two details that made Grace imagine him (vividly) in bed. She was fairly certain she'd seen him in this state that first night she'd brought him into the beach house, but standing now in front of her like a carved statue of muscle was something else entirely. Between the tiger that stretched across his chest and shoulder and the nicely sized bulge somewhat lower, Grace had to fight to keep her eyes up somewhere near his face.

Lúcio jokingly clamped a hand over Tiff's eyes while Camille covered her mouth with a gasp. "Oh my Jesus," she whispered, sending all three girls and Lúcio into a fit of laughter.

Daniel blinked a few times, his eyes still squinting as if they'd just woken him up.

"What's this about me being sexist?"

Grace's jaw was on the floor, but she recovered fast enough to say, "I think you meant sexi*est*."

The three girls lapsed back into giggles.

Daniel leaned against the doorframe, his arms folded across his chest, looking unamused. "Is that why you're here?"

Ah shit. Grace should have rehearsed what she wanted to say. Hell, she should have *thought* about what she wanted to say. Damn Tiff and her fun facts.

"Listen, um . . ."

"She's really sorry," Tiff put in.

"Shh! I can do this myself," Grace lied, pushing Tiff behind her to stall for more time.

She began again. "I'm really sorry about earlier. I'd say 'Oh, it's not what it looks like,' but everyone says that, and most of the time it *is* what it looks like, so I'm not going to say that, but I *do* want you to know that I definitely told him off, and I swear I didn't know he was going to be there, and the only reason I talked to him first was so that I could just put it behind me, and I wanted to tell you all that then, but you were mad—which is totally fair—but then you left, and I came here because I wanted to see you and say I'm really sorry."

"I have no idea what she's saying," Camille whispered to Tiff.

"I don't either, and I speak English," Tiff whispered back.

"You're not helping," Grace hissed back at them.

"Just so I have this straight: You came down to Cancún to chase your ex but ended up breaking up with him. Again," Daniel summarized.

Grace cringed. "Yes."

"So you broke up with him because of me?"

"God, no." Grace laughed, before realizing how offensive that sounded. "I just mean, I'm not such a weirdo that I, like, tanked an entire relationship for you. Things were already complicated, and I was dragging my feet on ending it all together. Meeting you helped me figure out why we weren't compatible and that I was holding myself back from moving on. But that doesn't mean I'm, like, expecting anything from you," she rushed to clarify.

"Because I'm just a vacation hookup?"

Grace reached for her ear, twisting it as she gritted out the truth. "Um, kind of? I mean, that's what you were supposed to be at first, but I think we're way past that? Because I know I keep wanting to see you. And you got super macho alpha male back there—which, by the way, was way less hot than I thought it'd be—but is probably not something you'd do over a rando?"

It was bold—showing up out of nowhere and asserting that he had feelings for her. But Grace was in fine form and the more she drank, the less of a filter she had. Oh well. At least she wouldn't be going home with any (more) regrets about things left unsaid.

"She's only slept with two guys before you, so it's not like she's just out there banging everyone," Tiff added, her head peeking out from behind Grace. "Which, just so we're clear, would also be fine because sexual empowerment is totally a thing. But Grace isn't like that so her taking you home was, like, a really big deal."

Grace covered her eyes with her hands, the shoes dangling from one hand now sprouting from her forehead. "Oh my God, can you please stop talking?"

Camille dragged Tiff away, though Grace noticed that they remained within earshot because her friends were nosy and her humiliation was probably excellent entertainment for them. If it were anyone other than her suffering through this, Grace would probably think it was pretty entertaining too.

Grace peeked through her fingers and saw Daniel standing in the same position, his expression unmoved. Maybe she should have left out the part about him going alpha male, but honestly, she was glad she said something. Mostly because it also helped her finally understand that while she liked bossy in the bedroom, she didn't care for it everywhere.

She forced herself to lower her hands. "Um, anyway, that's it, pretty much. Just came to apologize. Since I didn't get to earlier. Sorry for showing up like a stalker," she babbled. Once again, she was simply talking to fill the silence while everyone around her was probably dying of secondhand embarrassment.

Finally, Daniel responded. His face was still impassive, body language giving nothing away. "This acting thing. You any good at it?"

This time, it was Camille who jumped in on her behalf. "Of course she is good," she said, affronted at such an accusation.

Grace, for her part, raised her shoulders up around her ears. "Um, I like to think so?"

Ah, that famous stage confidence.

"So . . . this right here." He drew a circle in the air with his pointer finger. "How do I know this isn't just acting?"

Tiff burst out laughing and was quickly shushed with an elbow to the ribs from Camille. "Sorry," Tiff apologized. "But if you think that was good acting, you're dumber than I thought."

"Jesus, Tiff," Grace exclaimed, her hands coming up to bracket the sides of her face. She didn't want to hide behind her hands anymore for the simple reason that it took away precious seconds of seeing Daniel in his underwear. She wanted to finish licking every single inch of that tattoo. And all the inches that weren't tattooed too.

Tiff flicked her wrist dismissively. "It's fine, athletes don't have to be smart. Why else would they give athletic scholarships for college?"

"Don't listen to her," Grace said. "No one thinks you're . . . unintelligent," she improvised. "Or not smart. Or whatever." She was babbling again. "Just that no, this isn't an act. I really am this much of a mess, and I'm trying to fix it because . . . I like you." If Grace was going to confess, she might as well say all of it.

Daniel nodded slowly, as if processing and agreeing with her arguments one at a time. "Yeah, I didn't really think you were acting. I just wanted to make you grovel for a little bit."

Grace's eyes lit up. "Wait, really?"

Daniel shrugged. "Like you said, I'm not *unintelligent.*" He emphasized the word like it was fancy, and Grace realized one of the things she liked most about him was his lack of pretension.

She flung herself at Daniel, wrapping her arms around him in a hug as her shoes thudded against his back. "Really? You're sure you're not mad at me?"

"We all have exes, Grace. It's not like I didn't know you were still talking to him. You weren't exactly spy level at keeping it a secret."

"Oh. Right." The night they met, he'd seen her texting Josh a picture of herself. She'd also accidentally mentioned Josh right before they were about to hook up.

"Would've been nice to have a heads-up before running into him," he continued. "But if you didn't know he was going to be there, you didn't know. And you're right, I didn't mean to make it worse for you. I just reacted." Daniel shook his head. "Man, I really wish I could've just punched that guy in the face."

"He has a very punchable face," Tiff solemnly agreed.

"I think . . . I missed a lot," Lúcio said.

Tiff wrapped herself around his bare arm, running her fingers through his hair for good measure. "Why don't you take me back to your room, and I can explain it to you."

"Make sure to use small words," Daniel called as the two of them sauntered off. "He's still an athlete."

Realizing she was now left alone with the happy couple,

Camille tapped her foot impatiently, looking around as if someone else might appear. "This is a little awkward, yes?" she asked. "But I have nowhere to go."

"Why don't I get dressed and take you both home?" Daniel offered.

"Or . . . you could *not* get dressed and take us home," Grace said with a theatrical wink. "Wait, no. Take *me* home. Well, you'd have to take Camille too, but not like that. She'd just be riding in the car. Oh wait, that sounds sexual too."

Camille, shaking with laughter behind her, clamped a hand over Grace's mouth. "Maybe you stop talking now."

CHAPTER TWENTY-TWO

"Baby, you are gonna miss that plane."
—Before Sunset (2004)

Grace awoke the next morning face down, buried in pillows. What was it about alcohol that turned her face down at night? Maybe her body was trying to prevent her from choking on puke during the night or something. Though judging by the weariness in her limbs, the alcohol from the previous night had been fully absorbed and absolutely none of it expelled.

She hadn't necessarily *felt* that drunk, though everything after her conversation with Josh was pretty much a blur of laughing and stumbling around. And sand—lots and lots of sand. There was Camille puking in the cab, which she did *not* want to think about at the moment, then showing up at Daniel's. Oh, right, her garbled apology.

Grace groaned. That was not how she'd wanted to spend her precious last minutes with him. And now she'd probably never see him again.

Her heart felt heavy as she shuffled downstairs, hoping to catch the recognizable scent of Camille's mocha brewing in the kitchen. Instead, she spotted Daniel, curled up fast asleep on the couch.

Grace's heart jumped into her throat at the sight of him.

He'd stayed.

His sleeping form was so sweet and peaceful, hands folded beneath his cheek like a literal angel. It was absolutely serial killer–esque, but Grace was tempted to go over and pet him, just so she could run her hands over his smooth skin again and imagine the weight of him on top of her. Both in a sexual *and* nonsexual way.

She felt a pang of regret that he hadn't slept in her bed. But her newly informed conscience reminded her that it was, in fact, a great sign that he hadn't tried to force intimacy while she was drunk. She really could trust he wasn't going to take advantage of her.

Grace sighed wistfully, a little louder than she meant to, and Daniel stirred. Before she could bolt back upstairs and *not* make it seem like she'd been standing over him while he slept, Daniel opened his eyes.

"Hey there," he croaked, his morning voice as sexy as she'd ever heard it. Deeper and rougher, she could almost imagine waking up next to it.

Get a handle on yourself, she mentally scolded.

"Hi," she chirped, wishing she'd taken at least a second

to look in a mirror before coming downstairs. She made a quick swipe under her bottom lashes to fend off possible raccoon eyes from her mascara, but there wasn't much more she could do.

She really needed that waterproof mascara.

"You stayed over this time," she joked.

Ah fuck. That wasn't a great lead-in.

"I was safe from flying feet down here," he replied, pushing himself up to sitting.

Grace desperately wished he weren't wearing a T-shirt. Then maybe she'd feel less self-conscious about the amount of skin on display in the tiny ruffled moon-and-star pj's she had no memory of getting into. She pulled her hair into a messy knot atop her head, ignoring the copious amounts of sand in it and hoping it made her look like slightly less of a disaster. "So . . . last night . . ."

Daniel didn't finish the sentence for her, patiently waiting out the awkwardness.

"I'm really sorry," she apologized again.

"So you've said. A lot."

She grimaced. "Would it help if I said it again?"

"Do you really want to keep talking about your ex?" he asked.

Grace sighed with relief, sinking down onto the coffee table in front of him, their knees almost touching. "No. Definitely not."

"Then let's not."

It was so simple when he said it. Like they were grown-ups who could just apologize or accept an apology and move on. Huh.

"Last night you said you were flying out today," Daniel

said, reaching out and curving his hands around the tops of her knees.

A safe starting point. Yet another thing she liked about Daniel—he always eased his way in. (Cue mental image of Camille saying, "That's what she said!")

Grace studied his facial expressions, hoping he'd offer his feelings on it first. "How do you feel about that?" she asked carefully.

"I wish you weren't," he said, his hands pushing a little further.

She leaned forward. "Because?"

Her stupid, stupid heart. It was fully involved now.

Daniel pressed a soft kiss against her lips, positively chaste compared to the way his hands continued to slide their way up her thighs.

Grace clamped her hands around his wrists, halting their progress. It was pure torture, but she had to know the answer first.

Daniel backed up a few inches, his hands sliding safely back toward her knees, giving her space to ask her question again.

He was giving her space.

Understanding careened into her.

Realizing the many ways he'd respected her was enough to make Grace emotional. But to notice it in real time? To see what it looked like when someone respected your words as much as they claimed to? It didn't matter how many times Josh told Grace that he believed in her because at the end of the day, he showed it didn't matter.

It didn't matter that Josh understood she was hurt by the breakup; he dragged it out anyway. It didn't matter that he believed Grace could make it as an actress; he would never push for Hollywood to become more inclusive if it inconvenienced him. And it didn't matter if she didn't want to have sex; he made her feel like she *had* to.

Daniel repeatedly demonstrated that he understood *and* respected what she said. He had already answered her question, multiple times over.

Grace's heart swelled and *whewwwww*. At this rate, he was going to turn Grace into a full-blown after-school special over him. She needed to get a hold of herself.

She needed to get a hold of *him*. It would probably be her last chance.

Grace slid Daniel's hands back up until they spanned her hips, enjoying the rush of heat they left in their wake. "My flight doesn't leave for hours, and I don't think Tiff is even home yet. So."

He leaned closer, their foreheads resting against each other. "So."

"I don't know if you had plans you need to get to or . . ."

"Oh. I have plans," he said, sending a little shiver through Grace.

She loved how quickly the two of them could transition from sexual to nonsexual and back again. He made *conversation* foreplay.

"I'm not big into surprises," she murmured, her brain running a hundred different scenarios of exactly how she hoped he would surprise her.

"You're going to be big into this one," he murmured back, his voice dropping lower. He kept his lips hovering millimeters from hers, just out of reach. Her pulse was skyrocketing.

"Try me."

"I plan to."

Daniel's lips curled into a smile, and Grace stopped breathing. They held eye contact as Daniel's thumbs skated up and down the crease between her leg and pelvis, his other eight fingers clutching her as if they were his last line of defense.

The tension was too much for her. Grace lurched forward and kissed him. His lips parted, and the moment her tongue touched his, Daniel slid her to the edge of the coffee table with his hands still firmly gripping her hips, his knee parting Grace's legs. Her blood turned molten, and she made a small noise that sounded something very much like a whimper.

But before she could sink herself too far into the kiss, Daniel pulled back.

"Was that it?" Grace managed to ask, the fog of lust swirling around her brain.

"You need a shower."

What the—? Grace tried to pull away from him, but he held firm, an amused smile on his lips.

"Are you offended?" he asked.

"Yes."

Grace knew she probably looked (and smelled) not amazing after the previous night's tequila fest and sand wrestling, but he didn't have to say it so bluntly.

"Don't be. I'm offering."

"Offering a shower?"

"Mm-hm."

He waited patiently for her brain to work it out.

He was offering to give her a shower.

Oh.

She tried to pull them both to standing, but his fingers dug into her hips, keeping her pinned to the coffee table.

"Do you want to hear the rest of it?"

Grace bobbed her head, and Daniel gave her another little smile.

"Good girl."

Holy shit. She was going to combust on the spot.

"Now. I'm going to give you a head start." His voice seemed to caress its way around her body, her consciousness lost in his eyes that never left hers.

"Head start?" she asked faintly.

"I'm going to give you exactly thirty seconds to get in the shower."

"Thirty seconds?!" Grace exclaimed. She wasn't even sure she could get the water hot in thirty seconds.

Daniel raised his eyebrows, and Grace sealed her lips.

"Thirty seconds," he repeated, daring her to challenge it again. When she didn't, he continued. "By the time I get in, you'd better have your temperature set and your position picked because your hands won't be able to adjust anything after that."

Jesus Christ.

He leaned in, teasing another kiss. "Go."

Grace jumped up like she'd been electrocuted, which wasn't far off from how she felt at the moment. She tore up the stairs with the speed of an Olympic sprinter. Somehow Daniel just *knew* what set her off, even as she was still in the process of figuring it out herself.

She stripped her clothes off so fast she caught her hair in a button, ripping it out instead of taking the time to gently detangle it. What was a few strands of hair, anyway? She quickly rinsed her mouth with mouthwash, and by the time she stepped in the shower, Daniel was coming through the door.

Seeing him stalk in with that kind of focus sent a flutter through her stomach. It would never get old, watching him undress. Not just because he looked fantastic naked (and he did), but because the process of him getting undressed was a sport unto itself. He made taking off sweatpants and a T-shirt hot as fuck. She didn't even stop to wonder why the hell someone would be wearing sweatpants in Cancún in the middle of June.

The shower door flung open, and Grace let out a little gasp, as if she'd been caught. Like playing kiss or kill on the playground except kiss was the only option.

"Your hair is still dry," he observed.

Grace absently patted her hair. So it was.

She hadn't been able to do much of anything since she'd gotten in, standing motionless as she anticipated his arrival. And despite the glass shower panels beginning to steam up, goose bumps broke out across her skin as he drew closer.

She couldn't fucking believe she really had another opportunity to be naked with this man.

Without further conversation, he cupped her face and kissed her—the deep, probing, knee-quivering kiss they'd started (but hadn't finished) earlier—before walking them back a step so they were directly under the water coming down from the rain showerhead. Grace squeezed her eyes shut, warm water running over Daniel's hands and down the sides of her face, his body distractingly far away from hers. Every time she tried to move closer, he backed his feet up, keeping them apart everywhere but their mouths.

She pulled away, panting. "Is there a reason you're torturing me?" she asked.

"Yes."

She feigned outrage. "Why? I've been waiting five days for this!"

He smirked. "Have you now?"

"Yes."

He tilted his head as he thought aloud. "Hm. There was yesterday, when you showed up at my place like a little stalker."

"Hey!"

He took a step closer and she backed up, keeping the distance between them. She wasn't about to go diving back into his arms after a little quip like that. Even if it was true.

"And before that, when you traumatized an entire family at Punta Sur," he said.

"That was your idea."

Another step, this time his left hand skimming along her hip bone.

"And two days before *that*, when I got to see all the faces you make when you're coming."

Grace blushed at that one, no easy retort springing to mind.

"And the day before *that*," he said, walking them back another step, "when you tempted me with a very small yellow dress and then left me standing alone on the sidewalk. Which means"—he pressed her up against the glass wall, and she gasped in shock from the cold against her skin—"if you've been waiting five days, that means you wanted this the night you met me."

Damn it. There was that pesky math again.

"I admit nothing," Grace declared. At this point she couldn't remember how she'd felt about Daniel that night, apart from the kiss at the end. *Had* she wanted to sleep with him? That seemed unlikely.

Daniel tsked. "That's too bad."

She was almost afraid to ask, his left arm now fully encircling her waist, the fingers of his right hand drawing lazy circles around her collarbones and down between her breasts, slowly making their way across her abdomen before going lower. "Why?"

"Because now I'll have to draw things out until you admit it."

Grace gasped as two fingers breached her and the heat of Daniel's body pressed against her front.

"You were saying?" he asked, his voice low and his breath on her neck.

Grace tried to form words, but her brain seemed unable to process anything beyond what was happening to her. "How?" she finally managed.

What she meant was, how was it possible he got better each time? How had there even been any room for improvement?

Daniel trailed kisses along the side of her neck and up behind her ear, his left arm wrapped around her waist to keep her from collapsing. "Did I forget to mention I'm right-handed?" he asked, pressing another finger into her as his thumb worked its magic independently. "Last time I used my left."

Grace's knees really did give out at that, her back sagging against the glass. She really hadn't any idea what she'd gotten herself into.

"No, no, no. No going boneless yet," Daniel ordered, dragging her back under the water. "Can you stand at all?"

Dazedly, Grace shook her head. It was all too much. The heat, the steam, and oh yes—the shower too. She somehow felt everything and nothing at the same time, every single nerve in her body fried to within an inch of their lives. It was like being struck with lightning.

Still holding her up by the waist, Daniel reached over and turned the knob to cold. The water changed immediately, spraying the two of them with an icy blast.

Grace shrieked and scrambled out of his hold, her brain now back on full alert. "What was that for?"

"Couldn't have you passing out on me."

"You really are a sadist."

Daniel smiled again, and all Grace could think about was how truly beautiful he was when he smiled. It wasn't practiced or partial. His teeth were mostly straight but not so perfect as to be blinding; his dimple amplifying each smile as it peeked out. Grace was dangerously close to falling head over heels for this guy.

Daniel turned the knob again, this time to warm, and pulled her back under the spray. He kissed her with more force, hands roving over her skin and into her hair like they were on a deadline—which, technically, they were.

She kissed him back with urgency, no need for additional foreplay. She just needed him as fast as possible. Hooking a leg around his waist, she positioned herself with his thigh between her legs to give herself as much friction as possible.

He walked them back to the glass wall, her shriek of protest at the coldness of the tiles swallowed by his mouth. They kissed for what seemed like hours, Grace growing more impatient by the second. The splash of cold water earlier had stopped her on the brink, and she was anxious to get back to it. She pulled at his shoulders and waist, frantically rubbing herself against him, hoping he'd get the message. But to no effect—he continued to pretend like they had all the time in the world.

It wouldn't do.

"Can you get inside me already?" She gasped, pulling her mouth away from his. "I don't have all day."

Daniel chuckled, his voice vibrating against her body and setting her more on edge. "I thought we agreed I was in charge here."

As a response, she reached down and grabbed him, Daniel finally experiencing the breath-stealing intensity of first touch at her hands. "You can be in charge next time," she said. "You're taking too long."

He didn't need the extra encouragement. Pulling a condom out of the shower niche (when had he put that there?), he had it on and was inside of her within seconds.

Maybe it was the buildup of five days of anticipation, but there was no issue with pulling him all the way in in one thrust. No discomfort, no tears. No jokes about how his dick was too big.

Instead, he grabbed the underside of her thigh and lifted the leg a little higher, changing the angle he hit.

"Holy shit," she ground out, letting her head drop against the wall as her eyes rolled back in her head. "I always did want to try this position."

"Glad I could be of service," he replied.

"And can I just say, I'm so happy right now that you're athletic."

"You know what they say about soccer players." When it was clear she did not, in fact, know, he waggled his eyebrows and added, "We can go for ninety minutes."

Grace groaned at the joke, even while recognizing there might be some truth to it. She was definitely reaping the rewards of all his previous hard work. He wound her hair around a fist and tugged gently to bring her head back up. "Eyes on me, remember?"

"You're such a diva." She leaned forward and sank her teeth into his shoulder, relishing the strangled grunt it elicited before he pulled her off by the hair. Her scalp tingled, both from the sensation and from knowing he could simply move her head wherever he wanted.

Giving up control was so fucking hot when she knew the other person could be trusted not to pressure her into anything

"Just trying to make sure you're not thinking of anyone else this time," he said, tugging her head to the side and scraping his teeth lightly against the side of her neck.

Grace was in hell.

But the hell where, like, sinners went after having too much carnal fun.

Good hell.

"Mmm, what was it again?" she asked, striving to keep the moans out of her words. "David? Derek? Damien?"

Daniel tugged her hair harder this time, and Grace couldn't keep the sound from escaping this time when he thrust.

"Damien? Really?" he panted.

Grace felt like a fucking goddess, watching his eyes heat at the prospect of trying to get her to stop taunting and lose control. She could be her full, authentic, smart-ass self and somehow it turned him on. If this was how sex was always supposed to be, she mourned for all the lost years.

Well, she'd mourn later. Right now she had an orgasm to chase.

"I guess you'd better be extra memorable, then," she said with mock regret.

Daniel let go of her hair and smacked her ass, the sound reverberating off the shower walls.

"Holy shit, you *hit* me," Grace exclaimed. She rubbed the spot, the sting of it fading fast.

Daniel went still, biting his lip. "Too much?"

She thought for a moment.

"Surprisingly hot," she decided, reassuring him by wrapping her arms back around his neck and plastering her body against his. Grace was willing to bet there wasn't much Daniel could do right now that she *wouldn't* be turned on by.

He looked more than a little relieved. "I'm so fucking turned on right now," he confessed. "But please. Tell me if I go too far, okay?"

Grace arched an eyebrow. "Have you been holding out on me?"

He settled back into a similarly challenging expression. "I didn't realize there were complaints."

"Oh, there aren't. I just want to know what my options are."

Daniel's smile went wolfish. "Very cute you think you get to choose."

Grace's mind scrambled for a response as her heart rate sped toward cardiac arrest.

It was the most alive she'd ever felt.

Grace pushed off her standing foot, attempting to wrap her other leg around Daniel's middle. But she didn't push off nearly hard enough, nor was she athletic enough to pull off the move on her own. The two of them stumbled instead, Daniel grabbing for the falling leg. He managed to right them, Grace's eyes wide and unblinking.

Days without a workplace incidence: zero.

"This," he said, "is why you don't get choices."

Grace laughed, and he spanked her again, this time on the other side. She dropped her mouth open in mock protest.

Daniel leaned in and lowered his voice, his tone just the tiniest bit threatening. "You keep your mouth open like that and I'm going to find something to fill it with."

True to his word, they went the full ninety minutes. Grace collapsed onto the bed and pulled the sheets over her, certain death was waiting for her around the corner.

Blissful death, but death regardless.

She was going to start calling herself an athlete from now on. She hadn't even known it was possible for sex and sex-adjacent activities to go for that long.

"I think you deserve some kind of trophy," Grace called from the bed to Daniel, who was in the bathroom disposing of the (latest) condom. She didn't know whether to be impressed by his planning or annoyed at his presumption. She settled on profoundly grateful. She had no idea how she was just supposed to say farewell to all of this.

Fuck.

She sat up before tears could accumulate. That was absolutely the worst impression to leave with Daniel. She wanted to be one of those girls he would always get wistful over, like Rose in *Titanic* recounting her one hot encounter with Leo DiCaprio even though it had happened decades ago and she'd married and had kids with someone else.

Or something like that.

Daniel walked out, still naked and so achingly beautiful it made Grace's heart hurt. The man was like a piece of fucking artwork (yes, another pun) he was so perfectly sculpted.

That he had a personality to match it seemed almost unfair.

"I heard something about a trophy?" he asked.

The bastard didn't even sound tired. Meanwhile, Grace was a heartbeat away from googling how to get on the lung transplant list because she still had a hard time catching her breath.

"Your mantel doesn't have enough of those already?" she teased.

He padded toward her, face filled with intent. "I don't know whatever the hell a mantel is, but I'm never going to turn down awards. Especially for whatever it is I did today to earn one," he added as he crawled onto the bed.

"Wait, you don't know what a mantel is?" she asked, trying to keep the conversation on something more lighthearted. Neutral, even.

He stretched out over of her, a grin on his face. "Is it really important for you to explain it to me right now?"

She was safely wrapped in the sheets, but the heat of his body still enveloped her, and whatever she'd thought to say a moment ago was lost. He was so good at that—gently redirecting conversation before she could put up her defenses.

"I do eventually have to leave, you know." There was absolutely zero conviction in her voice.

He nibbled her lower lip. "So you keep saying."

God, if she hadn't already scammed Tiff and Camille once on this trip, Grace wouldn't be above running downstairs and begging them to change their flight so she could have just one more day with Daniel.

How was she supposed to say goodbye to this?

Fortunately, her body waved the white flag first.

"I physically cannot have sex again, or I might die," she said, pushing Daniel off her a fraction. "That's *not* a challenge," she added when Daniel raised an eyebrow.

He rose without complaint, retrieving his clothes while Grace wept inside at the thought she might never get to see those muscles again. This was why people sent nudes, wasn't it?

"Okay, just hand over the trophy and I'll leave," he said with a resigned tone, hand held out expectantly.

Not knowing what else to do, Grace sat up and slapped his palm in a low five. "There it is. Job well done."

He looked down at his hand as if he couldn't believe she had really low-fived him after sex. "I'll be sure to pass this along to my parents. They'll be so proud."

"Tell them to put it on their mantel," she quipped.

"You talk a lot of shit for someone who only speaks one language."

"Excuse me! I took two whole semesters of French in high school."

Daniel raised his eyebrows. "Híjole!"

Grace didn't know what that meant, but it had sounded sarcastic. "You better not be secretly insulting me," she warned.

"Guess there's no way for you to know."

She flopped back with a big sigh. "Great. I'm going to go look up all the things you've said to me and find out you picked me up using a grocery list or something, aren't I?"

Daniel's lips twitched. "Or something."

Grace sat back up, thinking it over. "I mean, shopping for food *is* pretty sexy. You could get at least a dozen women to go home with you with the word 'cheese' alone. Me? I'm a chocolate girl."

Daniel chuckled as he pulled his T-shirt over his head. "You are . . . very different from anyone I've ever met."

"I'm going to pretend that was a compliment."

Unique was good, right? Hot dog hands won an Oscar. Lots of Oscars.

He grinned. "You do that."

"Well," Grace ventured, deciding to risk a return compliment without the undercurrent of flirty banter, "you're also very different from anyone I've ever met."

Daniel looked into her eyes, and she clutched the sheet a little tighter around her chest for safety. It was silly, considering all the angles at which he'd seen her naked by now. But his teasing look had disappeared, replaced with something more serious, and it scared her. Everything up to now had been genuine, but lighthearted.

She held her breath and forced herself to hold his gaze while the air around them grew steadily thicker.

"I guess we're a couple of one-of-a-kind people," he finally said.

"Then it's good we met each other," she replied.

They stared for a few more moments, Daniel caving first. "Let's get you packed up," he said, looking around the room at the mess Grace had left.

Clothes were strewn pretty much everywhere, jewelry scattered on every surface, and towels heaped on the floors.

"You live like a little pig," he commented, scooping up the towels and taking them into the bathroom.

"Hey!"

"I'm just saying. I know guys can be gross, but living with girls has taught me they are much grosser." He held up the towels as evidence, walking back to the bathroom to hang them up properly. "Who just drops a wet towel on the floor?"

"In my defense, I was a little distracted at the time." Grace took the opportunity while he was in the bathroom to throw on a bra and underwear.

He reappeared, an eyebrow cocked. "Only a *little* distracted?"

Grace snorted. "There you go, fishing for compliments again."

"Come on," he coaxed. "Tell me I'm pretty."

"You're prettier with your shirt off."

A wide grin spread across Daniel's face as he tugged off his T-shirt in one smooth motion. "Like this?"

"I think you're just looking for an excuse to walk around half naked," Grace said, grabbing the shirt out of his hands. "I approve."

She wanted to bury her face in the soft material, soaking up his scent, but settled for a more discreet (and far less creepy) sniff.

It didn't go unnoticed.

"You want some time alone with that shirt?" he asked.

Surprisingly, Grace wasn't as embarrassed about getting caught as she thought she would be. "Call it a souvenir," she said, turning around to her suitcase with the shirt still in hand.

"You're really going to steal my shirt?"

Grace gave him an appraising look. "I'm doing you *and* the female population of Cancún—okay, and I guess probably some of the male population too—a favor. Trust me."

Daniel shook his head with a chuckle. "I really don't know what it is that makes girls want to steal guy's clothes, but if you want to keep it, it's yours. For now," he added.

Grace smiled at the victory. "Cute you think you're ever getting this back."

It wasn't a hoodie, but she could use it as a sleeping shirt after she'd exhausted all the Daniel scent from it.

He enveloped her in a big hug, Grace's hands trapped between their bodies, still clutching the shirt. "Don't lose it. The next time I run into you, I'm going to expect it back," he said with a kiss on her forehead.

Grace rested her head against his chest, wringing every last possible second out of it. She kept her hands on the shirt instead of hugging him back. Because if she did, she wasn't sure she'd be able to let go of him.

But this was vacation. And it was over.

"Thank you," she said. Not just for the shirt, but for everything he'd given her this week. Time. Effort. Fun. A hell of a life lesson on dating.

And a lot of orgasms.

He hugged her tighter and pressed another kiss to her forehead. "Anytime."

By the time Grace and Daniel finally made it downstairs, Tiff was back. Hers and Camille's luggage was already neatly lined up next to the door while the two of them sat on the couch with their morning mochas.

"Well, *hello* there." Tiff grinned, Camille stifling a laugh behind her mug.

"Hello," Grace said cautiously. "Have a good night last night?"

"Not as good as your morning, apparently," Tiff quipped.

"The walls here are very thin," Camille added with a pointed sip.

Grace's face burned with embarrassment as she buried it in Daniel's shoulder, wishing they could somehow bypass her friends on their way to the door. Daniel, for his part, laughed and wrapped an arm around her.

"Nice to see you again, Daniel," Tiff said, raising her mug in a toast to him. "Thanks for *coming*."

Camille let out a noticeable snort, and even Grace let out a small groan, the terrible pun so awful she forgot she was ignoring them.

"I hate you," she said to Tiff, who only toasted her back in response.

"The car will be here in fifteen, so you'd better go pack," she told Grace. "I would've helped but I thought you might want some privacy."

"Which, according to you, we didn't have anyway," Grace replied.

Being able to discuss her sex life in explicit detail was one thing; having her friends actually hear her sex noises in real time was quite another.

Tiff shrugged. "At least now I approve of Daniel more than I already did."

Camille nodded vigorously, lifting her hands and applauding. "Yes, yes. We approve. Good job, Daniel."

Grace swore she could feel his ego inflating next to her, his stride breaking into a bit more of a strut as he grinned at them. She'd roll her eyes except that he really did deserve the accolades. Like she'd said in the room, it was trophy-worthy.

When they reached the door, Daniel turned to her one last time. "So."

An inside joke. They had an inside joke.

She smiled. "So."

He wrapped both arms around her, her friends more than likely pretending they weren't watching, and Grace told herself to memorize the feeling of this exact moment.

"Have a safe flight," Daniel said, giving Grace a kiss and releasing her.

"It's been real," she replied.

Grace shut the door behind him, not wanting to watch Daniel leave. This was how she'd remember him. This was how she'd remember this week.

CHAPTER TWENTY-THREE

"Swoon. I'll catch you."
— The English Patient (1996)

The mood on the way home was markedly different from the flight on the way there, all of the girls happy and toasting with champagne in their seats. Or as Camille was quick to point out, *sparkling wine*, because "champagne only comes from the Champagne region of France."

"In case I didn't say it properly before," Grace said to Tiff, "thank you for this trip. I know I didn't deserve it, but I'm really lucky to have friends as forgiving as you two."

"You'd do the same for me, babes," Tiff replied. "I mean, on a lower-scale budget, but I'll bet you could throw me one hell of a movie night. You know, in our living room. With movies from the subscription services I pay for."

All three of them laughed, Grace giving Tiff a playful punch in the boob.

"Ow! That really *does* hurt! Why do you let me do that?" Tiff pressed her arm across her chest, her other hand holding it for reinforcement.

Grace rolled her eyes. "Yes, *we're* the problem in this situation."

Tiff laughed and downed the rest of her champagne. "Okay, fine. I'll stop. Or I'll at least try to stop."

Grace's phone buzzed, and with passengers still boarding, she pulled it out to check.

Daniel: you make it on the plane ok?

Grace: are you asking if i can still walk? bc the answer is yes

Daniel: damn ok I see you're throwing down more challenges

Grace: was the challenge to make me NOT be able to walk

Daniel: you did accuse me of being a sadist

Daniel: I had to google what that was btw

Grace: how old did you say you were

Grace: i didn't realize i was supposed to card you

Daniel: [joints creaking]

Daniel: [tells you you look fat then offers you food]

Grace: um

Daniel: IT WAS A JOKE

Daniel: you don't have aunties that do this to you ???

Daniel: please say you do

Grace: relax i got the joke

Grace: but i like making you sweat

Daniel: I know you do you little freak

Grace: stop sexting me you're going to get me arrested by the faa

Daniel: you'd look hot in cuffs

"What is Daniel sexting you?" Tiff asked.

Grace looked up in alarm. "What?"

Tiff shot a look that answered Grace's unasked question. "Babes. Your face is fifty shades of red, and you look like you're ready to hump your phone."

Grace tucked it away with a guilty swallow. She didn't want to repeat the mistake of prioritizing a boy over her friends.

"So what are we talking about?" she asked, picking up her champagne flute and choosing to ignore Tiff's teasing accusation.

"Lúcio," Camille answered with a dainty sip of her drink. She was back to being tidy, perfect French Camille.

This was exactly what Grace needed right now—a reverse interrogation.

"I never did get to hear all the dirty details," Grace said, using Tiff's own words against her. "I think I only made it as far as 'he's not circumcised.'"

Tiff waved a hand. "It was good but nothing worth keeping in touch for. I definitely wasn't making the same noises you were."

Grace flushed again at the reminder. "Like I said. I didn't know you guys could hear."

Though even if she had, Grace wasn't sure she would have been *able* to hold back.

"I'm not shaming you!" Tiff insisted. "Be free, come loud. That's my motto."

"I have never once heard you say that before."

Tiff lifted her chin so her gold septum piercing was on full display. "I'm like Serena. I'm evolving."

Grace's lips couldn't help turning up at the corners. "You and Serena Williams. The two of you have a lot in common?" she teased.

Tiff counted off the similarities on her fingers. "She has curly hair, I have curly hair. She's rich, I *want* to be rich."

"Honestly, it's a wonder the two of you aren't best friends yet with a connection like that," Grace said with a straight face.

Tiff sighed. "I'm never going to be able to mix with celebs by flying commercial."

Camille gave her a sympathetic shake of the head as she surveyed the rest of the first-class seats. "Ah yes, true problems."

"Not sure private planes fit into your eco-friendly kick," Grace said.

"Sustainable wellness," Tiff clarified. "And flying on a private jet would definitely sustain my mental wellness."

Wanting more money was truly the one thing that united just about everyone. Even the rich never felt rich enough. In the Bay, they didn't even think of themselves as rich. When billionaires lived nearby, a mere six figures was looked at as struggling. But Grace wasn't about to point that out while sitting in a first-class seat Tiff's money paid for.

Grace's phone buzzed again, and she instinctively reached for it. Before checking the message, she looked to Tiff and Camille.

Tiff rolled her eyes. "Just go. We'll get you when they shut down the Wi-Fi."

Grace eagerly opened her messages.

Daniel: did you get arrested?

Grace: acab baby

Daniel: i'm having to google again

Grace: put down the phone before you hurt yourself

Daniel: shouldn't you be taking off soon?

Grace: i can't they're holding the plane until i get off the phone with you

Daniel: really?

Grace: no

Passengers continued filing into the plane, Grace not paying them any attention.

She didn't want the conversation with Daniel to end. But she also needed something to keep it going.

Grace: did i hurt your feelings

Daniel: i once had a coach who screamed so close to your face that he'd get spit on you and you couldn't make a face or he'd yell more

Grace: yes but was he insulting you

Daniel: yes

Grace: i don't understand sports at all

Daniel: happy to explain

Grace: you'll have to keep me awake while you do it

Three dots appeared and disappeared several times, Daniel clearly struggling with how to respond. She liked that she could throw him off-balance.

Finally, a response.

Daniel: i'm done here the first week of August

Daniel: how do you feel about me making a stopover in SF on my way home?

"Oh my God." Grace hadn't meant to say it aloud, but it slipped out.

"What?" Tiff demanded.

"He . . . mentioned coming to the Bay Area in August?" Grace tried to make it sound nonchalant, like her heart wasn't turning cartwheels in her chest.

Both Tiff and Camille gasped, Tiff recovering first. "I knew it!" she crowed. "I *told* you he'd make it past a vacation fling!"

Camille gave a coy smile. "Maybe Tiffany is a romantic in her heart."

"If it's possible to fuck your way to love, maybe," Tiff replied. "I guess we'll find out."

Grace was too busy panicking to comprehend that Tiff had just hinged her entire view of romance on the outcome of Grace and Daniel's relationship. "That's like six weeks from now. That's a long time, right? Or is it short?"

How the hell was she going to survive waiting six weeks? This was why people didn't do long-distance relationships.

Camille cleared her throat for their attention, her plastic flute already raised. "A toast," she declared.

"We already did toasts," Tiff said.

"Another toast," Camille insisted. She waited for her friends to pick up their glasses before resuming. "I called my parents this morning. While you two are *busy*," she added with a stern look at each of them.

Grace blew her a kiss. Tiff flipped her off.

Camille took a fortifying breath before announcing, "I will be back in the fall."

Grace and Tiff both squealed loudly before remembering they were on a plane. The poor flight attendant working first class was looking at a rough six-hour flight if they kept this up.

"Next time," Camille continued, her finger signaling she

wasn't finished yet. "I choose the destination. No more little boys for me; I am not a nanny."

Grace and Tiff laughed, palpably relieved they wouldn't saying goodbye to their friend just yet. "Fair." Grace nodded. "Totally fair."

Grace: camille is coming back in the fall

Daniel: congrats

Grace: also she demands reparations for always leaving her with andres

Daniel: poor kid, he had such high hopes

Grace: how old was he really

Daniel: tell her i'll make it up to her

Grace: THAT'S NOT AN ANSWER

Daniel: i'll make it up to you too

Daniel: when I see you in August

Grace: i'll get the trophies ready

ACKNOWLEDGMENTS

It's hard to overstate the impact MTV had on my generation. I imagine it's something like how the previous generation felt about the '60s—you just had to be there. I probably spent more hours watching music videos and *TRL* in just my high school years than I spent writing this book. So getting to publish under that brand feels like some kind of life achievement I never knew I wanted.

Thank you so much to my agent, Kiki Nguyen, for knowing exactly the types of stories I like to write, and for being brave enough to tell me when a joke is bad. And Christian Trimmer, my editor, who is more than an editor and who entrusted me with this messy wasian story. Thanks to the entire teams at MTV Books and Atria, particularly Melanie Iglesias, Elizabeth Hitti, Adam Benepe, Zakiya Jamal, Holly Rice, Kaitlyn Vella, and anyone else I may have forgotten. Also Jes

Vu and the team at CAPE, as well as Matthew Dekneef, who generously took the time to explain the ʻokina to me.

A shout-out to the Hallmark Channel and their year-round romantic programming, which I steadily consumed to remind myself that not every boy I write can be trash. But if I could make an appeal directly to the executives, it's to let Paul Campbell and Kimberley Sustad write more of your movies, because those two do not miss. (Also, can I get a job in casting? Because I have thoughts.)

Thank you to all my friends and groups that light up my day: the naggy shrews, 99 dead, and bridging the gap. But thanks especially to my bestie, Naz Kutub, who talks me through my breakfast every morning but never stays for lunch. I never get tired of seeing your face.

Thank you to Noe Valley Bakery for their delicious red velvet cake that I dangle in front of myself as an incentive to finish whichever stage of writing I'm at—you have been worth every penny. I am finally learning to celebrate progress, no matter how small.

My family is incredibly understanding about my having to work manic hours sometimes (especially now that they know there's cake at every deadline!), and I thank them for any extra sleep they let me have. The creative brain needs rest.

Lastly, thank you to all of the readers. I'm humbled and grateful you chose to spend any of your precious moments on earth reading my words. I hope each of you have people in your lives who love you as you are and appreciate your worth. May you all find friends who will bankroll a trip to a foreign country on a moment's notice. If you do, please introduce them to me.

ABOUT THE AUTHOR

Anna Gracia was born and raised in Minnesota, where she survived on Dairy Queen Blizzards and the joy of fall colors—neither of which exist in San Francisco, where she now lives. She is the author of the YA novels *The Misdirection of Fault Lines* and the highly acclaimed *Boys I Know*, which was both an American Booksellers Association Indies Introduce and Indie Next pick, as well as the adult novel *The Breakup Vacation*. Her books have been featured in the *New York Times*, *Paste*, *Seventeen*, and more. You can find her advocating for public schools or at Anna-Gracia.com.